HIVERTON

Aster
Victorious

LIZ HURLEY

By Liz Hurley

The Hiverton Sisters Series

Dear Diary (novella)
A New Life for Arianna Byrne
High Heels in the Highlands
Cornish Dreams at Cockleshell Cottage
From Ireland with Love
Aster Victorious

Writing as Anna Penrose
The Golden Mystery Series

The Body in the Wall
Dead Winter Bones
Death at Castle Wolf

DEDICATION

Dear Reader,
This one's for you! Thank you for your patience.

First published 2024 by Mudlark's Press

ISBN 9781913628161

http://www.mudlarkspress.com/

Chapter One

Aster Byrne looked across the darkened space, illuminated by strobe lights and phone screens, and glowered. She was staring into the abyss and the worst of it was she had volunteered. She had attended university with the soon-to-be bride and had been genuinely surprised when she received an invitation to the hen party. Olivia had even sent Aster a private note begging she attend.

Her curiosity had been piqued. She and Olivia hadn't been close, but when she had hinted at low attendance numbers, Aster had felt an unusual spurt of sympathy for the girl she hardly knew. How desperate must her situation be to be relying on Aster, of all people, to come out to a nightclub for a hen party?

A man was walking through the crowd towards her. She had clocked him watching her and had been about to move away when a group of girls blocked her way as they headed for the bar. They were all giggling and calling back and forth to each other, and Aster fervently prayed that he was heading for them. He was wearing all the latest gear and good looking enough, but none of that appealed to Aster.

'Alright?' He towered over her, one arm leaning on the wall above her head, and leant down to talk to her. He was so close that Aster could see the threads in his buttons. 'You're out late on a school night?'

Aster had been planning to ignore him and make her exit, ducking under his arm, but now she stared up at him in astonishment.

'Do you think I'm underage? And you're trying to pick me up?'

He stepped back quickly, hearing the hostility in her voice.

'Chill. Just saying you looked young. I mean, with being short and all.'

'Like a schoolgirl? Should I have worn make-up? Is it the freckles? Or the brown hair? Do you like it plain like this? Does it make me look more innocent? Do you like children?'

'No. God, no.' He was stammering, and Aster continued to stare at him coldly. Now that he had retreated, she had to shout to make herself heard.

'Shall we call the bouncers over to check my ID?'

She may have shouted louder than was necessary. Even under the flashing lights, Aster could see him pale as he glanced over his shoulder. Then, calling her a name, he moved away and headed onto the dancefloor. Aster watched him leave and took a photo as he turned away. You never knew when it would be useful. Paedos weren't all dirty old men.

Looking around, she wondered how much longer she could stay. Whistles was exactly the sort of place she avoided like the plague. She had never been before, but its reputation raced ahead of it. Wannabe socialites rubbing shoulders with the well-heeled and well-oiled. It was a melting pot of alcohol, avarice and ambition.

After being introduced as 'Lady Aster' to the large gaggle of girls, she quickly realised the reason for her invitation. Olivia was trophy gathering and wanted to show off that she socialised with the nobility. Some of the girls had made silly noises and one went so far as to ask if she knew the royal family. Aster stared at the girl until she fell silent. Then, glaring at Olivia, she headed to the bar and grabbed a bottle of water. The idea of being nobility was a ridiculous, outdated concept. Hell, she hadn't even known she had a title until she was eighteen, when the death of a family branch meant that her eldest sister inherited the Hiverton Estate. If anything, the title was as much an embarrassment as it was a boon. She only used it when she needed something.

She had been tempted to leave the party then and there, but she was the one at fault for falling for Olivia's sob story. Clearly, she wasn't short of friends, just decency. Aster was cross with herself for not reading the situation properly. As a punishment, she made a bargain with herself: she would have to endure an hour before leaving. This was a mistake she wouldn't make twice.

She checked her phone. Time seemed to have slowed down. Despite having already been here for an eternity, only thirty minutes had actually elapsed. As the DJ asked if everyone was having a good time, Aster made her way back to the bar. She lived within walking distance of the venue, so she'd walk home. It wasn't even late and the streets in Mayfair were about as safe as you could get in London. Besides, anyone attacking Aster was in for a dreadful surprise. As the youngest of five sisters, she could scrap with the best of them. As a child, her father was concerned that her small stature put her at a disadvantage and taught her and all her sisters how to fight properly. She was ten when he died, so she turned to the lads on the street who would all spar with her. Initially, they were reluctant to lay hands on such a small girl. Soon it became a badge of honour to be able to knock her down.

Squeezing past a crowd all jumping to the beat, Aster made it to the bar. Next to her was a tall girl with waist-length blonde hair, a killer figure and wearing a Gucci jacket. She was clearly going to get served first. Turning, she smiled down at Aster and shouted over the music.

'It's mayhem in here tonight.'

Aster surprised herself by smiling back. The girl reminded her of Paddy, one of her sisters. Paddy used to be a catwalk model, but she was also the warmest of people and was forever starting up conversations with random strangers. They each stepped forwards as the man in front of them got served and left a space at the bar. In an attempt to balance a tray of drinks in his hands, he carefully manoeuvred past them, smiling at the tall girl as he passed her. In turn, she made a quip about what a job he had. He didn't notice Aster.

She checked her phone. Incredibly, only two minutes had passed. The girl next to her asked for a Cosmo and Aster smiled. It was even Paddy's favourite drink, so when the barman asked for her drink, she ordered the same. Further down the bar, a loud roar lifted over the sound of the music. A bunch of lads had clearly had too much to drink already. From the look of them, Aster figured they were up for the weekend, a school reunion, or just taking a break from shooting everything in the countryside. Hal, Paddy's husband, had probably been much the same at their age, but she suspected Seb, her oldest sister's husband, had probably not been such an eejit. She liked both men. They took care of her sisters and doted on their children, and that was enough for Aster. But of the two, Hal was certainly the more boisterous. There was another shout as one of the lads attempted a game of skittles on the actual bar. There was a shout of protest as a champagne bottle shot down the bar, spraying everyone as it sped past. Aster quickly snatched the two glasses of Cosmo in front of her and lifted them out of the way.

'Boys are such idiots,' said the taller girl. Aster nodded, holding the drinks aloft. 'Which one's mine?' The two girls looked at the identical cocktails.

Aster apologised. 'I didn't really pay attention.'

'Not to worry, I haven't taken a sip yet. Lucky you had such fast reflexes.'

Aster shrugged and smiled quietly as she handed the girl one of the glasses.

Thanking her, the girl made her way from the bar and Aster watched her leave as others also turned and watched her walk by. Some creepy dude who had been waiting at the bar now slunk off after her. He hadn't even ordered. Whistles was clearly attracting all the creeps that night. Maybe there was a special on, creeps half price. Sighing, Aster took a sip of her drink and then headed off in search of a quiet spot. She would enjoy her drink, watch people, and then get the hell out of here. She was in the middle of a collection of Orwell's essays and couldn't think of anywhere she'd rather be right now than at home, considering the dichotomy between those who knew how to grab power and those who didn't. Wealth helped, so did birth, but ultimately some people were born to lead and others to follow. And some were stuck in a stupid nightclub because they felt sorry for an acquaintance.

Across the dancefloor she could see Olivia frantically waving at her to come and join them, so Aster turned and walked in the opposite direction until she found a quiet section on the way to the upper dancefloor. This seemed to be a perfect dead zone between the speakers from the two dancefloors. She leant against the wall and took another sip. She wished she'd brought her book, but the pockets in her stupid dress weren't deep enough for anything other than a few fortune cookies.

From where she was standing, she could only see a few booths and a corner of the dancefloor. People were heading back and forth and she enjoyed guessing everyone's backstory. Girls' night out, office party, first club of the evening. One girl was traipsing along behind a group of friends and Aster spotted a fellow sufferer.

'Ah, you've found my favourite spot,' said a voice from beside her. Turning round, she saw a large man standing by the wall. He dwarfed her, even as he leant against the wall, people walking past couldn't take their eyes off him.

He had a classically handsome face with chiselled features - high cheekbones, a strong jawline, an aquiline nose. His dark hair was just the right amount of artfully tousled. Intense blue eyes swept the room, framed by thick brows.

He wore an impeccably tailored suit that showed off his muscular physique to full advantage. Broad shoulders and muscular arms strained the expensive fabric of his jacket. His white dress shirt was opened at the neck, giving an air of a man at rest.

She blinked up at him.

'Your spot?' Thirsty, she took a larger sip this time.

He smiled down at her. It was like the sun emerging on an overcast day - warm, radiant, melting hearts with devastating efficacy. His deep voice had a sultry timbre that sent shivers down her spine when he spoke.

'It's the quietest place in the club. Some sort of dead zone.'

Aster nodded, unsure of herself.

'I do think that if they are going to charge us so much to enter their torture den, the least they could do would be to lay on a reading room.'

Aster giggled. He smiled down at her and continued.

'It's not too much to ask. Surely?'

Aster took another sip, then grinned up at him. 'A bookshelf, at the very least.'

'Well, it would be a start. What books would you consider essential?'

Aster paused, sharing favourite books felt like an uninvited intimacy. But that was silly.

'Banks. Xu. Austen. Cicero.' She watched as his eyebrows raised in surprise and was pleased that he nodded along. At least he seemed to know the authors she was mentioning. 'Although that's not the books they'll have on their shelves.'

'It's not?'

'Of course it's not. Look at this place. Go on.' Aster stumbled and leant against him, giggling as she apologised and took another sip, surprised that her glass was empty. She shook her head and felt a bit swimmy. What had she been talking about? 'The bookshelf!' she shouted. 'What books would they have?'

He looked down at her and Aster wondered why he was frowning.

'Come on, you can think of something. What about *How to Make a Killing in Crypto*? *Verbier: A Photographic Retrospective.*'

'*You Are Enough. Avoid Toxic Relationships.*'

Aster laughed loudly and slapped him on his arm, marvelling at the size of his muscles.

'Those are exactly the sort of books they'd have on their shelves.'

Across the way, she could see the tall girl from the bar shouting at the creep that had followed her, and she was pleased to see the sisterhood fighting loud and proud. She lifted her glass in salute and shouted out to her.

'You tell him, sister!'

She leant back against the wall and was alarmed to discover it was moving. Throwing out a hand, she grabbed at her companion to steady herself.

'Sorry. Think that drink was stronger than I realised?'

She screwed her eyes up, then blinked rapidly. She felt really weird.

'Are you okay?'

She looked up at the man standing beside her, who seemed to sway. Her skin was flushed and she pulled at the sleeves of her blouse, trying to roll them up.

'Do you want to step outside?'

Aster shook her head. That sounded like a bad idea. She wanted to sober up. That was it, she'd go to the loo and splash some water on her face.

'Come on. Let's get some fresh air.'

'Okay.'

Taking her hand, she followed him out of the club. Her hand looked tiny wrapped up in his and she stumbled as she missed a step. Before she fell, he had wrapped his arm around her waist. Leaning against him, she stumbled out into the night air. She was aware of the warmth of his arm against her waist. Her sheer blouse was offering little protection in the cold air, her heart beating in her ears, and she had a sense of having been too long at sea and unable to stand on dry land.

She tried to focus and call a cab. Why was she outside? There was a man standing beside her, although she couldn't remember where he had come from. Was he her driver? Remembering that she lived nearby, she stepped off the kerb and was once again whisked up into his arms. He was speaking to her, but her head lolled loosely and she couldn't frame a reply.

Edward Montclair closed the door and softly made his way back to the kitchen. He hadn't been planning on an early night anyway, but he hadn't envisaged staying up all night to safeguard a complete stranger. Hell, he didn't even know her name. He should have called the police, taken her to hospital, found her friends, but for some reason that he hadn't fully processed, he'd brought her home.

From the moment he had spotted her in the nightclub, she had intrigued him. She was looking so angry, like a small storm cloud moving around the club. Amongst all the butterflies, she was bringing the rain and he was intrigued. She seemed fed up with the crowd of gigglers she'd arrived with and had quickly peeled away from them. He'd watched as she weaved through groups of strangers and laughed when she "accidentally" knocked over a pint, causing a creep to jump back in alarm from a single girl trying to avoid his attentions. She had walked across the dancefloor, not bumping into anyone and made a few rounds of the club, yawning now and then. Almost no one approached her, but on one occasion a man had started to come near. Edward could only see the man's face and it was a picture, he had looked so confident as he swaggered towards her and then his face froze and he swerved left. She didn't stop and he chuckled as she headed towards the bar.

There was something about her that stood out and he found himself watching her as she headed over to the only quiet spot that he had found in the whole club. From their first conversation as she joked with him about installing a library, he knew he was going to spend the rest of the evening chatting with her, swapping favourite authors, favourite books. That is if she didn't chew him up and spit him out like she had everyone else in here.

But within a couple of sentences, he watched her disappear in front of his eyes and knew she'd been drugged. For a moment he stared, paralysed in horror, and then became so angry. That such a free spirit should have been targeted for harm. His fists clenched and then he threw his arm around her and supported her out of the club. And now here she was, drugged and unconscious in his drawing room.

He picked up the phone and waited for it to be answered.

'John, it's Edward Montclair – Yes, I know what time it is. There's someone spiking drinks in Whistles. Get on the phone and alert your bar staff and bouncers – I don't care who you're entertaining. Do it now.'

If he could have slammed the phone down, he would have. Instead, he opened his laptop and started work. It was daytime in India, he'd be able to follow a few leads. It was an ill wind that blew no good, but as the hours passed, he found himself constantly distracted by the girl in his front room. When she woke up, he would do everything she needed. He would take her home. He would see that she was safe, and then he would track down the man that had done this to her and annihilate him.

Chapter Two

Aster became aware of lying on a sofa. It was daylight outside and the light was shining in around the edge of a pair of large, heavy curtains. She didn't know where she was and rolled over in confusion. By the side of the sofa was a pint of water, a blister packet of painkillers, and a bucket.

Groaning, she leant over for the ibuprofen. Her head was splitting, and she was desperate for some water. The last thing she remembered was chatting to a mountain of a man about books. What had happened after that? She was under a blanket. Pushing it back, she saw with relief she was still wearing all her clothes, even her shoes. Sitting up, she waited for the nausea to subside. Her only memory was of her first drink, causing her to flush with shame. Had she been drugged? How could she have been so stupid? She groaned. Everyone knew the dangers of drinks being spiked, but Aster had never thought to have fallen prey to such a despicable practice. Not her. Not clever, suspicious, cautious Aster.

There was a knock on the living room door and she froze. Where was she? There was a window behind her. If she stayed quiet, she would slip out that way when the person at the door went away.

The door edged open and the man from the night before peered around. When he saw she was sitting up, he smiled. Aster grabbed at the blanket and pulled it up to her chin.

'You're okay. I think someone spiked your drink last night.' He took a step into the room but stayed by the door.

Aster just stared at him.

'I thought it would be best just to get you to a place of safety.'

Aster remained silent. He was huge, and she was terrified that she wouldn't be able to fight him off. She looked around the room. At the end of the sofa was a brass candlestick. At least she had a weapon.

'Here, I made you a tape to reassure you.'

He inched into the room and placed a memory stick on a low padded footstool.

'It's internal security footage. I thought it would help you see nothing happened to you last night.'

Could she grab the stick and then get to the window before he could? She shook her head. She wanted to look behind her, at her potential escape route, but she wasn't taking her eyes off him, no matter how nicely he smiled.

'Look, I'm going to make you some breakfast.' His voice was soft and slow, like he was talking to a cornered animal. 'You follow the sounds of the radio when you're ready. I've already been out to get some croissants and the coffee is brewing.'

He walked slowly back out of the room and left the door wide open. Aster waited until she could hear the radio in the distance and, throwing the blanket off, she grabbed the memory stick. The sudden movement made her feel queasy and spinning sharply, she threw up into the bucket and then paused, panting. Taking another gulp of water and another two painkillers, she edged towards the door.

As she peered out into the corridor, she could hear a deep baritone voice singing along to the Spice Girls, of all things. Across the hallway was a waxed wooden door with a white painted frame. The corridor boasted a nicely furnished interior, complete with a wide rug that ran along the length of the parquet floor and led directly to a front door. Looking in the direction of the music, a flight of stairs headed to the floor above and the hallway continued towards the back of the house. She could make out another turning in the staircase down to a lower floor. Creeping away from the singing, she edged towards the door. Turning the handle as carefully as she could, she swung it open into the blinding sunlight.

She blinked and put her hand up to her eyes, trying to shield them from the light, and then just as quietly pulled the door shut behind her. She was at the top of a small flight of steps with two neat bay trees in black pots at the bottom. It was a quiet residential street with large town houses opposite her and parked cars along either side of the street. Holding on to the wrought-iron banister, she climbed down the steps and ran along the pavement as fast as possible until she ran out of breath and paused. Bent over her hands on her knees as she wheezed in the city air. Her bag was still slung across her body. She placed the memory stick in it and pulled out her phone. That would tell her where she was, but her frustration and panic mounted as she stared at a dead screen. She couldn't stop though. She needed to get as far away as she could. She couldn't risk him coming after her. She needed to be safe. She needed to think. Panicking, she tried to jog, but the pain in her head intensified and she stumbled back to an unsteady walk. She tried her phone again, desperate for some clues as to where she was.

'Excuse me!'

Aster looked up quickly and squinted at an elderly woman dressed in a Chanel two-piece suit, walking some sort of yapping rug on a lead.

'I'm sorry,' stammered Aster, 'I'm lost, can you-'

'You're drunk, is what you are. Get away or I'll call the police. This is a respectable neighbourhood.'

Aster swore at her in language that she hoped seriously lowered the tone and lurched away from the woman. A delivery driver across the road shouted at her, laughing at the exchange. She limped across the road, shrieking in alarm as a cyclist swerved to avoid her and treated her to some of his own Anglo-Saxon.

'You alright, love?' asked the driver, who had jogged over to guide her across the road. She shook his arm off in alarm and tried to walk away from him. Why had she thought he could help? She couldn't trust anyone, just needed to get home. The daylight was killing her eyes and she tried to walk, sheltering her face in the palms of her hand squinting out, trying to see anything familiar.

'Hello?'

Aster turned quickly, her brain swinging and crashing in her skull as she saw the delivery driver had followed her.

'Can I help? You don't look so good.'

'I'm lost. I want to go home.' Even in her befuddled state she knew how pathetic she sounded.

'Where do you live?'

Aster shook her head, not trusting herself to speak.

'What about the area? No need to give me your actual address. Or I can call the police for you if you want?'

She looked at him properly now. He was in his forties, going bald but artfully combing his hair in an attempt to delay the inevitable shave. The zip on his brown jacket pulled tightly across his belly and he was smiling kindly at her, concern evident in his expression.

'I live near Hyde Park Corner tube station.' She didn't, but she knew her way home from there.

He smiled and nodded.

'Well, that's okay then, you don't have far to go.' As he gave her directions, she could feel his words literally tumble out of her mind. All she could remember was to take the first right.

'I can drive you?'

'No!' Alarmed by his offer, Aster turned swiftly, trying not to panic. She stumbled again, nauseous from the sudden flare of pain in her head, and she hurried off down the road and turned right. Looking over her shoulder to make sure he wasn't following her, or indeed the man in whose house she had woken. Eventually, she spotted some familiar landmarks and finally her familiar family townhouse stood proudly in the street, waiting to welcome her home.

Foix Place was a four-bedroomed terraced town house arranged over four floors in the heart of Mayfair. Her sister, Nicky, kept urging that the family sell it, but so far, the rest of the girls had resisted, and at the moment, it acted as Aster's UK residence. Running up the steps, she put the key in the lock and then, twisting, fell into the house. Slamming the door behind her, she slid the security chain and the deadbolt and then ran to the loo where she threw up again and then, pushing herself into the corner of the bathroom, hugged her knees and began to shake.

Chapter Three

Aster's neck twinged. She'd been sitting on the marble floor for hours. Struggling to stand up, she kicked off her shoes and limped to the kitchen. The window looked out over the garden but the light was still hurting her eyes. So she drew the curtains, switched the kettle on and fired up her laptop sitting on the kitchen table.

As she waited for her apps to load, she made a coffee and was appalled to see her hand was shaking. She hadn't taken her jacket off yet as she couldn't get warm and wrapped her hands around the mug. Taking a deep breath, she looked at the screen of her laptop and took courage from her screen saver.

It was a picture of her sisters at Ariana's wedding. They were all laughing into the camera. Even she was. She and Clem had made bunny ears behind Paddy and Nick's heads and Ari was in the middle of the five of them, her huge white gown creating a lake of tulle. Aster only ever had this screen saver set for home log-ons. If she was in a public space, her laptop showed a basic Microsoft wallpaper. Her obsession with privacy was almost pathological, and it extended to her family. She never gave interviews, had no social media presence beyond her various fake accounts, and unlike some of her sisters, never featured in lifestyle magazines. Despite always being in control, this morning she had woken up in a stranger's house having been drugged.

She had no doubt now that that was what had happened, but she went online to check the symptoms. Lapses of time, confusion, poor memory of the previous night, light aversion, feeling hideously hungover. Well, she had all of that. It was time to see what had happened next. Plugging in the USB stick, she hit play and held her coffee cup to her chest as her evening played out in front of her.

The first scene was of the familiar hallway and the front door opening that she had just escaped from. Aster watched as the stranger almost had to carry her over the threshold as she swayed and stumbled against him. She was fully clothed, her buttons were correctly fastened, her handbag was slung over her chest and her strappy sandals were both in place, although she seemed to be having trouble standing up in them. As horrible as it was to see herself like this, it was her expression that made Aster feel sick. She was looking at a zombie. Her face was lifeless, her mouth was slack and her eyes kept rolling back.

The second time she stumbled, the man paused and picked her up and carried her down the hallway. She had absolutely no memory of this. She watched as the screen flickered and he was now heading down the corridor, through a kitchen, and then he opened a door. The man put Aster on the ground and gently pushed her forward. Aster couldn't see what she did next, but he closed the door and was speaking to her through it. A few seconds later, he spoke again, and she walked out.

Aster was mortified to see that whilst she had clearly managed to go to the loo, she hadn't pulled her skirt all the way down, but at least she had covered her knickers.

Retching, she hit the pause button and took a swig of coffee. Then ran to the kitchen sink and threw up again.

Pouring a glass of milk, she returned to the laptop and breathing deeply, hit play.

She was still incapable of walking properly and once more he picked her up and she followed the security footage as he returned through the kitchen and headed back along the hallway, pushing open a door with his foot. She watched as her limp body was being carried through the house by a complete stranger and shuddered in disgust as she watched her head loll backwards, her arms swinging loosely below her body. The video now flickered to show them entering the room. Aster's head was tipped back, her eyes closed. Flicking a switch, the room was fully illuminated and he walked over to a familiar sofa and laid her down, then walked out.

Aster stared at the screen as nothing happened for a few minutes. She was just lying there, not even moving. Occasionally her eyes would slowly open, then close again. The man re-entered the room. Over one arm was a blanket and in the other hand, he carried a bucket. Placing the bucket on the floor near her head, he returned with a pint of water and some tablets and put them on the floor as well. He then covered her in the blanket. He turned on a sidelight, switched off the main light, then left, closing the door behind him.

She sat and watched the video on fast forward until she watched herself wake up. He had not returned once, and Aster sobbed in relief. She watched as he entered the room, spoke to her, then left. The recording ended as she was still sitting in the room staring at the door.

She stared at the screen and was about to play the footage again when her phone rang with Ari's ring-tone. Her sister was currently on a family holiday in New Zealand. She was desperate not to answer the call, but it was the middle of the night. Nighttime calls were always bad news.

She tapped on her phone. Thousands of miles away, her call connected.

'What's wrong?'

Aster almost sagged in relief when she heard her sister chuckle softly.

'Nothing. But Hector has been throwing up all night and I've given up trying to sleep, so I thought I'd call and say hi. Hi.'

'Have you taken him to the doctors? The hospital. Could it be food poisoning?'

Aster had already opened up her browser and was checking the CDC site for known health issues.

'He's fine. Too many ice creams and chocolate.'

'You're sure?'

'Of course I'm sure. I know what happens to children whose eyes are bigger than their tummies. Trust me, no need to start investigating.'

She laughed again. Everyone knew Aster was the first to spot a problem and then to solve it. Aster tried to laugh and found her voice broke. Her panic about the children blended into the past few hours and she felt her emotions swiftly unravelling.

'Aster. Are you okay?'

'Yes', said Aster in a very small voice.

'What's wrong?'

'Bad day.' She hitched a breath.

'Aster. You're crying!'

Ari's alarm was clear and Aster hurried to reassure her sister, but couldn't find the right words.

'I'm coming home.'

'No,' moaned Aster. 'I'm fine. Honest. I've just had a shock. I'll be fine soon. By the time you got back, I'd be okay.'

As she spoke, she calmed down. She knew her sister would probably try to fly home from the other side of the world and Aster would not be responsible for spoiling their holiday.

'Tell me what's happened and I'll be the judge.'

And so Aster told her big sister everything that she could remember and felt like a kid all over again.

'He taped you!' Ariana's screech could probably be heard without the need of a transatlantic line.

'Honestly. It's not as creepy as it sounds. He obviously has some inbuilt security system. I think he showed me the footage to try to reassure me. I mean, it's as unnerving as hell, but I think it was done in good faith.'

'In good faith? Aster, are you insane?'

Ari broke off and Aster could hear her muttering to Seb in the background.

'I've spoken to Seb. We're packing up now.'

'No. Don't do that. I'm fine.'

'Listen to yourself. You just said that the man who drugged you was acting in good faith.'

Aster tried to catch up with what Ari was saying, and the penny dropped.

'I don't think it was him. That doesn't make sense.'

'Psychopaths don't.'

'Yes, they do actually, but think about it. What was his goal? And why give me the footage? Honestly, I think he was just a good Samaritan.'

'Aster, someone drugged you. You're not thinking clearly.'

'Call it a gut instinct. I genuinely don't think he was involved.'

She thought back to him in the club. He'd been friendly and chatting about books. She remembered his smile was quite endearing, as though he wasn't aware of how good looking he was. But then, of course, she was under the influence.

'You've gone quiet. Look, I don't care. I'm coming home.'

Aster groaned. This was not what she wanted.

'Tell you what. I'll call Clem.'

There was silence on the other end of the phone.

'You will?'

'Yes. If you promise not to cancel your holiday.'

After a few more words, Aster asked to speak to Seb. Her brother-in-law was a lovely man and worshipped the ground that Ari walked on, but he was also level-headed and wouldn't be as emotionally involved as his wife.

'Aster. We are on our way.'

Aster ground her teeth.

'Stop it. Seb, seriously, I'm okay. A bit freaked out, but nothing happened. Honestly. I'm fine. I'm going to call Clemmie and I'll see you next week when you're back for the board meeting.'

Having finally reassured them there was no need to drop everything, she hung up and made a coffee. There was no point in calling Clem. She was in the middle of a collection and wouldn't answer her phone or pick up e-mails or messages until she was happy with the new designs. Instead, Aster hit play on the footage again.

Somebody had just made the mistake of his life, and Aster was about to destroy him.

Chapter Four

A few hours later, Aster cricked her neck. What she had thought might be difficult was easy, and where she expected to breeze through was proving impossible.

Her first concern was to investigate her stranger. Ari was convinced his behaviour was deeply suspicious, but Aster didn't feel the same and wanted to know more about him. Her first option had been to look at the metadata on the video clip and was surprised to see it was clean of all IP markers. Without those, she had no way to hack into his system. Had he scrubbed the files deliberately, or was that part of his security measures? Either way, it was a red flag. Next, she re-examined the tape for clues. It was a decent size house with a staircase leading up and down. This was a private residence somewhere in Mayfair and hadn't been split into flats. The owner was clearly loaded. She looked back at the footage from the room she had slept in and saw various paintings on the wall. Looking closely at one, it looked familiar and she took a screen grab and googled it. A few minutes later, she whistled to herself. Either her rescuer had an inbuilt security system for a collection of pretty prints, or that was a genuine Monet on his wall.

She wasn't sure if this was a red flag or not. People with that sort of wealth thought they were untouchable. Above the law. Well, they might be, but they weren't beyond Aster's version of justice.

Putting her search into him aside for a moment, she tackled the nightclub instead. She had expected this to be tricky, but after only a few minutes she found the club's router, and after that it was child's play. They hadn't even changed the password from the factory settings. And once she was behind the firewall, she headed straight for the security footage.

Watching herself move around the club was less disconcerting than before. So far, she was behaving exactly as she should. She watched as she bought a bottle of water from the bar. No one was near her and she could remember breaking the seal to the bottle. So the bottle was out of the running. She kept scrolling until she saw herself heading towards the bar. The barman handed her her drink, and she put it on the counter. There was some confusion as a champagne bottle careered across the top of the bar, sending drinks flying. For a second, Aster missed it. A hand flashed out of shot. She rewound and this time ignored the champagne bottle hurtling towards the drinks. Instead, she kept her eyes solely focused on her glass and almost missed the hand again, because it didn't spike her glass. It spiked the glass to her left. The drink the girl standing next to her had ordered. Aster watched as the disembodied hand quickly covered the glass. A few seconds later, her own hands shot forwards to lift both glasses, and then she handed the girl her own glass and Aster walked away with the spiked glass.

She hadn't been the intended victim. Aster sighed in relief. At least that made sense.

Now she could get to work. Aster picked another camera angle and this time saw her assailant clearly. It was the creep who had followed the other girl from the bar. She watched as he hovered around her for a while and then tried to approach her, causing her to change from polite dismissal to eventually shouting at him to leave her alone. Across the floor, Aster saw herself waving and shouting. She didn't bother to zoom in. Instead, she returned her attention to the man in question. After half an hour, she had screen grabs of his face, a full body shot and also a close up of his mobile phone screen with his Facebook account on full display.

An hour later, she knew his name, his home address, and his place of work. She sat back, and for the first time that day, she smiled. Somebody's life was about to become very miserable.

Pricking her ears, she heard the front door click and had an instant rush of panic. Had he found her? Had he somehow tracked her down? Her fear was instantly replaced by a familiar voice shouting at her to undo the chains and deadbolts.

Jumping up, she flew to the front door, undoing all the locks, and threw open the door to see her gorgeous sister staring down at her.

'Paddy!'

Rushing forward, she hugged Paddy tightly until her sister tapped her on the shoulder.

'If I could have just a small breath?'

Instantly, Aster stepped back and felt awkward. She never hugged her sisters, but right then she could have squeezed the very air out of Paddy's lungs. Paddy lived in Cornwall, what was she doing here? As she watched, Paddy turned and waved down to a waiting Range Rover. Hal leant out of the window, gave Aster a quick salute, and then drove off.

Stepping inside quickly, Paddy followed Aster and put a small overnight bag on the floor and then looked her up and down, tears welling up in her eyes.

'You haven't even changed.'

Aster looked at her clothes and realised that Paddy was right. She was still in the clothes she had been wearing to the club. In the search for the truth, she had got carried away. Now that Paddy was here, she had to stop and the events caught up with her again.

'Do you want to go to the police? Report the crime? What can I do?'

Aster paused. 'I don't. I…' She stuttered to a halt. Now that one of her sisters was standing in front of her, she felt a wave of emotions flooding through her again and she was struggling to stay in control. She wanted to tell Paddy she was fine but was terrified that if she spoke, she'd burst into tears and that was not going to happen. She had just got in control of the situation and now her stupid emotions were going to ruin everything.

'Okay. Physically, are you okay?' asked Paddy, her face full of worry. 'You can just nod if you prefer.'

Aster nodded as Paddy continued to stare at her and then rolled into action.

'Here's the plan. I'm going to run you a bath and you're going to get changed into your pjs. Then I'm going to cook us supper. Chicken, rice and peas. And then we'll have chocolate mousse and hot chocolates. Okay?'

Chicken, rice and peas had been their childhood staple when they were ill and had proved remarkably effective against hangovers as well.

Aster smiled and gave a small laugh.

'You don't need to mother me.'

Paddy shrugged her coat off.

'Are you still standing there? Go get your jammies.'

With a laugh, the two girls ran upstairs as Paddy headed for the main bathroom. Aster headed into her bedroom and changed. From the bathroom, Paddy shouted that the bath was running and to keep an eye on it. Then she headed downstairs, telling her to take as long as she liked.

Aster headed into the bathroom and grinned as she looked at all the face masks, body scrubs and moisturisers that Paddy had lined up. Shaking her head, she slipped into the bath and began to relax.

Half an hour later, Paddy shouted that the food was almost ready. Aster wrapped herself in a big floor-length fluffy dressing gown and headed back downstairs.

Looking her up and down, Paddy nodded in approval and handed her a hot chocolate laden with whipped cream, a flake and marshmallows. The joys of having a pantry stocked for children as well as adults meant there was always a quick treat on standby.

'Now,' said Paddy, 'I know you don't want to talk about it, but if I'm going to stop Ari from getting on the next flight home can you please tell me something? I've already spoken to her and she's beside herself. We all are.'

Aster headed over to the squishy sofa and tucked her feet up and snuggled down before polishing off the flake.

'I didn't know she was going to call you?'

'She was worried when you mentioned calling Clem. We all know that Clem's working, she'll never answer her phone.

So when you said that, Ari panicked and thought you had really lost it. So she called me.'

'Do I look like I lost it?'

'Not at all. I told her you probably said that just to get her off the phone.'

Aster gave a small wince and a smile.

'Maybe. So if you didn't think I was losing it, why did you come up?'

Paddy glared at her.

'Why do you think? Jesus, Aster, you've been assaulted. Wild horses wouldn't have kept me in Cornwall. I told Hal what had happened. He called the babysitter. I packed a bag and we drove straight up here. He's staying with friends tonight, by the way. Felt you'd prefer that.'

'I like Hal!' protested Aster quickly.

'No one's saying you don't. He just felt that you deserved a bit of privacy, but I tell you what Aster, he was all for packing his guns. This guy who recorded you is lucky not to be looking like a colander.'

Aster shook her head and asked Paddy to pass over her laptop whilst she drank her chocolate. The warm milky sweetness was hitting the spot and she was pleased to notice that internally she was calming down.

Chapter Five

'Look here,' Aster pulled up the footage of the nightclub and handed the laptop to Paddy, who sat down next to her. 'This is the security footage from the nightclub. I've re-sequenced it to show who was responsible and how he did it.'

As she drank her chocolate, she watched the video and was pleased that she could watch it now without shaking. She had seen it so many times that she was beginning to detach. Paddy, on the other hand, was suffering.

'You've taken the wrong glass!'

She turned and looked at Aster, her face full of horror.

'Lucky her, hey?'

Aster had watched this girl a hundred times. One simple twist of fate and now she felt tied to a stranger who didn't even know what she had escaped.

Paddy grabbed Aster's hand and gave it a squeeze as Aster hit pause.

'Do you think he was targeting her directly?'

'No. I think he was just hoping to get lucky. When you watch the tape, you can see that he approaches her later but she dismisses him. They don't appear to know each other at all.'

Paddy shook her head. 'I hate this world.'

'No you don't,' said Aster. 'I rely on you to be the one that always sees the good in the world. Don't change now.'

'Well I hate him, whoever he is.'

'That's fine. I do as well. Now, the next section is pretty hard to watch. Or at least it was for me. But I'm showing you this to show that the man who took me home behaved honourably.'

She hit play again and now Aster could be seen leaning against the wall in the nightclub and the stranger come over and chat to her. As Aster stumbled, Paddy gasped and gripped Aster's hand.

'You look drunk!'

'Until that point, I had one bottle of water and a few sips of my cocktail.'

Aster drank little and rarely got drunk. Losing control was an anathema to her and yet here she was swaying in a nightclub in front of a total stranger.

'Oh God,' moaned Paddy as Aster walked off behind the tall man, her small frame trailing in his wake as she swayed and stumbled until he stopped and put his arm around her. 'Aster. I can't-' Tears were rolling down her face.

'It's okay. Remember, nothing happened.'

'But look at you.' Paddy's voice was broken with further tears. 'Look how vulnerable you are. Can you be certain he didn't do anything?'

'Okay. Watch the next video, but just look at my clothes.'

She tapped on the keyboard and brought up the second video, showing Aster being carried into a hallway by the same stranger.

'I don't have any footage between leaving the club and arriving at his house. But see, everything is still in place.'

Paddy was silent for a while, and Aster watched as she struggled to formulate a question. Guessing what she was trying to ask, she stepped in.

'Paddy, I haven't had sex in months. I have no soreness. Nothing. I genuinely don't think he took advantage of me.'

'But what about during the night?'

'Watch.'

Aster hit play, and Paddy watched her sister stagger and fall. She watched as he sent her to the loo and then tucked her in for the night. By the time the video showed Aster creeping out the front door, Paddy was furiously wiping tears off her face, and then hugged Aster as tightly as Aster had hugged her earlier.

'My turn to breathe,' joked Aster through her sobs.

'I'm so sorry. That was horrible to watch.'

'Yep.'

'I have to tell Ari you weren't assaulted.'

Aster gave a short laugh. 'Not crying like that, you won't. Wait until after supper.' She closed the laptop and turned to look at Paddy. 'Food?'

Taking a deep breath, Aster watched as her sister gathered herself and sprang up and plated up their food. Rather than plating it elegantly, Paddy chopped the chicken into small chunks and stirred it into the rice and peas. Ladling two scoops in a bowl, she topped it with salt and butter and passed one bowl to Aster and the two of them sat at the table breathing in the comforting smells. They ate in silence as Aster wolfed her food down. The food and the hot chocolate were hitting the spot and some of the jitters in her body were calming down as she stuffed herself with carbs.

'Chocolate mousse?'

Aster laughed in delight. 'I swear to God. I have no idea how you pulled it all together. There's no cream in the house.'

'I know! Your fridge is woefully understocked. How do you cook anything?'

'I don't. I get it delivered. The joys of being single.'

Paddy rolled her eyes, but went to the fridge and came back with two bowls of a dark unctuous mousse. Aster dug her spoon in and sighed in delight as the rich sweetness filled her mouth.

'Oh my God, Paddy, you are the best!'

Aster would never speak against her mother's culinary skills. The truth was, she barely remembered them, but Paddy was in a league of her own, and Aster waved her spoon in Paddy's direction.

'This is sublime.'

Paddy grinned.

'Not too shabby, is it? It's a rare treat for me as Hal has banned it from the house. He says he'll turn into a whale. So, it's for high days and holidays only.'

'I could eat that all day long.'

'Well then, you'll be pleased to know there's still half a mixing bowl in the fridge.'

With a sigh, Paddy pushed her bowl away. Giving her spoon a final lick, she cleared her throat.

'Now what?'

Aster looked blankly at her sister.

'Don't give me that,' said Paddy sternly. 'What do you plan to do about it?'

'Nothing,' lied Aster.

Paddy stared at her.

Aster relented. 'Nothing that I want any of the family involved in.'

'You're not going to go to the police?'

'No. What will they do?'

'They can arrest him?'

Aster scoffed. 'I have other plans.'

'Aster-'

'No, Paddy. This is something I have to do myself. Don't worry, it won't affect the family.' Since Ari's inheritance and the sisters' rise into the public eye, Aster had learnt to be more circumspect. 'But you can help me with something?'

Paddy leant forwards.

'Anything.'

'I want to find that man,' she said, pointing to the screen at the man who had rescued her. 'Or at least find his house. Would you walk with me tomorrow and see if we can retrace my steps? I can't remember much from this morning, but something might jog my memory.'

Once Paddy had agreed, Aster headed for bed. She spoke to Ari again and had no doubt that Paddy and Ari would talk again once she had gone to bed, but for now she was reassured that Ari wouldn't fly home early.

It had been a dreadful day, but had ended well. Paddy always raised her spirits, and now she had a plan of attack.

Chapter Six

'Does nothing ring a bell?' asked Paddy.

Aster looked around the Mayfair street and shook her head. She and Paddy had been walking around for over an hour. The soft spring air was warm enough but still required a coat, and the two women were feeling the cold seep in.

'No, it's a blank,' Aster could feel the frustration building. This gap in her memory was intolerable, and it was slowly dawning on her it would never come back. A UPS van was heading towards them and parked up drawing alongside a row of already parked cars. Delivering here must be a nightmare, thought Aster absentmindedly and was surprised when the driver hopped out of the van and headed straight towards her.

'Hello again. Did you get home alright?'

Aster stared at him in confusion and Paddy jumped in.

'Have you seen my sister before?'

'Yesterday morning. She was lost and looked pretty upset.'

Aster continued to stare at him. This wasn't the man who spiked her drink and it wasn't the man who took her home. Who was he?

'I don't remember you.'

'Well,' he scratched his hair, embarrassed, 'you were quite – confused.'

'Where was I?'

'Belmond Street. That's just a few streets over. When I saw you, you'd been shouting at an old woman and then nearly got run over by a bike. Not the sort of thing you'd forget. Unless…' He scratched his head again. 'I did suggest calling the police?'

He looked at the two sisters and Aster quickly changed the subject.

'I reckon I just drank too much. That was all.'

The driver looked at her closely and shrugged.

'If you say so. But you're alright now?'

'I am. Can you tell us how to get to Belmond Street?'

Thanking the driver, the girls walked off as Paddy slipped her arm through Aster's.

'Well now we have a lead,' said Paddy brightly.

'I don't remember him at all. Or swearing at some woman.'

'What about the bike?'

'Nothing. Only don't mention the bike thing to Nick. You know how she gets about pedestrians stepping off pavements.'

'I promise. Now look,' the girls entered Belmond Street. 'Does any of this look familiar?'

'Jesus, Paddy. I just told you I can't even remember talking to that man, why would I remember the bloody street?' Paddy was about to reply, then left her words unspoken in a big sigh.

'Cup of tea? That place looks nice.' Across the street was a pretty little café with decorative bowers of flowers around the windows and door. A milk churn was propping up a blackboard with the day's specials on it and a bike with a wicker basket was propped up on the other side of the entrance. Normally, this close to home they wouldn't have bothered, but Paddy wanted to make sure Aster was comfortable being in a public space with strangers.

Aster nodded her head. 'Let's grab an inside table, though. It's too cold to sit outside no matter how toasty those heaters are.'

The sisters made their way into the café and ordered a pot of tea to share but nothing to eat. Paddy had nipped out early and bought enough provisions for a full English, which Aster devoured.

'It's so pretty around here,' said Paddy. 'I forget how lovely London can be. I do love Cornwall, but honestly, the lack of mud is such a relief.'

She poured Aster a cup of tea and then poured herself one as she carried on chatting. 'Did you see all those pretty planters along that street? With the small bay trees? I think I'm going to buy a pair for Hiverton House. What do you think? Would you mind?'

Aster rolled her eyes. She was trying to regain her memory and Paddy was window dressing. 'Whatever.'

Aster drank her tea in a sullen silence, then pushed her chair back.

'This is a waste of time. I'm going home.'

She was nearly home when Paddy caught her up, having had to queue to pay for their tea.

'Aster, I'm sorry. I was just trying to distract you. Take your mind off everything.'

Aster whirled round and shouted at her sister. 'I don't want to take my mind off everything. I want my bloody mind focusing on everything.' She balled her fists up in fury. 'I want to remember.'

An older couple were walking along the pavement on the other side of the road and looked at Aster shouting at Paddy.

'What?' spat out Aster across the street. 'Do you want an autograph?'

'Aster! Apologise right now!'

Aster stared at her sister in astonishment.

'I'm not kidding. Right now.'

For a second, Aster held her ground and then ran across the road and spoke quickly to the couple before walking home on the other side of the street. As she looked over her shoulder, Paddy trailed miserably after her.

Slamming the front door behind her, all her energy dissipated in the slam. She was halfway up the stairs when she stopped. What was she going to do? Run to her bedroom? Slam that door as well? Paddy had just spoken to her like she was a child. Well, maybe she shouldn't behave like one. She slumped down onto the step and started to breathe deeply. A moment later, the front door opened and closed and Paddy called out.

'Aster? I'm sorry.'

Paddy rubbed her eyes.

'No, I'm sorry.' She watched as her sister ran up the staircase, her coat undone and her hair dishevelled. Aster hadn't noticed when they were shouting in the street, but Paddy must have had to sprint out of the café to catch up with her.

'You look a mess.'

Paddy tucked her hair behind her ear and laughed.

'You should see me back home. I spend most of my days looking like a scarecrow.' She took a deep breath. 'Look, I'm sorry about back there. I was just talking nonsense to try to entertain you.'

'I know you were, and I appreciate it. Honestly, I do. It's just…'

'It's just when you have something on your mind, you don't want to be distracted until it's resolved.'

'Exactly.'

'So, then. How do you plan to resolve this?'

Aster sat up straighter. 'I'm going to do as you suggest.'

Paddy tilted her head in surprise. 'You are?'

'Yes, I'm going to report this to the police and I'm also going back to the club, report it to them as well. See if I can get them to look at the tapes.'

Paddy breathed out a sigh of relief.

'I think that's a good idea. Where shall we go first?'

Now Aster took Paddy's hand and squeezed it.

'We aren't doing anything. I need to do this by myself.'

Paddy frowned, but Aster ploughed on. 'Look, I know you love me. I know you want to help, but you know me. I want to do this by myself. It's just how I am.'

'But-'

'I'm fine and this will take days. You need to get home to your gorgeous children.' Paddy was about to protest again, but Aster knew she was already missing the little ones. 'I shall call you every hour. I will even switch on my phone's locator.'

'You will?!'

'I will. I'll be fine, honestly. You've helped me through the worst of it. Now I need to get on with it myself.'

The two girls sat in silence for a while and then Aster saw Paddy breathe out deeply and knew she had won.

'Very well. I'll call Hal to get me. And you promise you aren't going to go after him. try to get revenge?'

Aster shrugged. 'I guess I'll just go to the police.' She laughed at such an unlikely concept. Aster always fixed problems herself, but if it made Paddy happy, then she would do it. Plus, it might help prove her point. That victims have no justice in the legal system. 'And then I'll see you at Hiverton.'

Paddy looked momentarily confused.

'Easter,' prompted Aster.

'Of course. Do you think Clemmie will make it?'

'I think if she doesn't,' said Aster, grinning. 'Ari will storm up to Scotland and drag her out of her castle by her hair.'

Both girls laughed, remembering some of their childhood scraps. They were rare, but occasionally Ari and Clem would tear the world apart when they fought. After their parents died, they never fought again, but they continued to disagree from time to time.

'Besides, she has to give her report at the board meeting.'

Paddy shook her head. God, her reports made Nicky weep. She mimicked her sister's voice: 'I'm a genius. Who cares what it costs?' Aster was laughing openly now. Paddy was a brilliant mimic. Now Paddy did Nicky: 'God dammit Clem, we're running a business!'

Both girls were howling with laughter as Paddy continued in her sisters' voices until Aster waved her arm in defeat.

'Enough!' she wheezed through her laughter. Then, slapping her thighs decisively, she stood up. 'Time for me to go.'

Hugging her sister goodbye, and assuring her for the umpteenth time that she would be alright, she headed out the front door smiling.

Two hours later, she strode briskly back to the house, her face set in a scowl. Her first call had been to the club. During the daytime clubs are very different places, and Aster stepped over hoover cables as the cleaners moved around the brightly lit rooms. Asking for the manager, she was directed to an upstairs office. The manager was defensive and when she asked him to review the security footage, he said that wasn't possible. When pressed, he cited GPDR legislation and that only a warrant could get him to share this information.

Her next port of call was the police. Things deteriorated when the male police officer asked if she had any evidence. She mentioned that there would be video footage at the club, as she didn't want to explain how she had hacked their system. He dismissed her suggestion and pointed out that she should have had a blood test for any drugs in her system. He then asked if she might have had too much to drink. At this point, Aster asked for a female police officer. When none was available, she was told that she was being taken seriously. Her accusation would be written up but as she hadn't been assaulted, had no blood test, or any eyewitnesses, and refused a rape test, there wasn't anything else to do.

'You could look at the tapes,' said Aster in complete frustration.

Eventually she headed home and called out as she walked through the door, but she could already tell that Paddy had left. The house felt empty. Aster headed into the kitchen and switched the radio on. Opening the fridge in search of the leftover chocolate mousse, she stared in amazement.

Paddy had fully stocked it with ready meals from the local deli, bags of salad and berries, some bottles of wine, a big juicy steak, and a second bowl full of chocolate mousse. In front of the bowl was a little note reminding Aster to eat.

Sticking her finger in the mousse, she took a lick and then headed off to get changed and got to work.

Two hours later, Aster sat motionless in front of her computer screen, the harsh glow illuminating her furrowed brow. Marcus Barrie's life was laid bare before her - a thirty-two-year-old telemarketing salesman with a business degree, living in a flat share north of the city. No long-term relationships. Rarely visited his hometown of Leicester. The usual pattern emerged: strong, unsavoury opinions scattered across various online forums.

Her fingers hovered over the keyboard, poised to unleash digital retribution as she had done countless times before. But something held her back. Aster shook her head, trying to clear the fog that seemed to have settled over her usually razor-sharp mind.

'This should be simple,' she muttered, pushing away from the desk and beginning to pace. Her steps echoed in the empty house, a rhythm that usually helped her think. But tonight, it only emphasised the hollowness she felt inside.

She returned to the computer, staring at the damning evidence - the video of Barrie spiking her drink. It should have filled her with righteous anger, fuelled her desire for justice. Instead, she felt... disconnected.

She had promised Paddy that she wouldn't take revenge, but she was so tempted. But what was the point? He hadn't actually hurt her and the other girl had escaped.

With a deep sigh, Aster composed an e-mail. She attached the video and warned Barrie never to try that again, or she'd take the evidence to the police. Her finger hesitated over the 'Send' button for a long moment before finally pressing it.

As she closed her laptop, Aster expected to feel a sense of accomplishment, or at least relief. But the unease lingered. She wandered to the window, gazing out at the London night. Her mind drifting to the stranger who had come to her rescue. The gap in her memory gnawed at her. If only she knew his name. That was what was unsettling her, why she still felt unresolved.

Aster nodded to herself, clinging to this explanation. It had to be the reason for her hesitation, her lack of focus. Nothing about this felt right, but then she had never been the focus of a crime. Maybe this was just how it felt. Clearly, she just needed to be able to thank her good Samaritan, and then she'd be back to her old self.

As she headed to bed, Aster's thoughts continued to circle around the mysterious rescuer. She tossed and turned, her dreams a confusing mix of faceless strangers and dimly lit nightclubs. In her sleep, she reached out, trying to grasp a shadow that always remained just beyond her fingertips.

Chapter Seven

The smell of magnolias lightened the heavy air as Aster walked towards the convent. It was Maundy Thursday and Aster had some alms to drop off.

She hadn't been sleeping well for the past few nights and was certain that her mysterious rescuer was the source of her disquiet. She had heard nothing from Barrie but she had been monitoring the video feeds of several of his haunts and was gratified to see that he hadn't shown up at any of them. As an added bonus, the venue in which she had been spiked had suddenly closed down. It appeared to be the result of a licensing issue, but they had ceased trading immediately. As far as Aster was concerned, it couldn't happen to more deserving people. For a moment she wondered why she hadn't engineered that herself and then shook her head. She had done all she could. She couldn't risk dragging the family name into the fray. Nodding to herself that that was the reason, she yawned and then turned down the street towards the Sisters of the Divine Mercy Convent & Chapel.

When she was a kid, she had read about the Queens of England handing out money to the needy on Maundy Thursday. Never one to be cowed by tradition, Aster decided she would do the same. When she was little, she used to pinch chocolate bars and bags of sweets from Woolies and then post them through letter-boxes of people on the street that she knew were having a hard time, but only those that had helped her family. Her charity was very judgemental and built on stolen goods. Nowadays, she had enough money that she didn't need to pinch sweets from the local shops, but she rarely had the time to post money through letter-boxes. Instead, she often gave the money to people she thought could properly distribute it. And one of those organisations was the Sisters of the Divine Mercy.

She turned off the main street and down an even smaller one that ended at a large brick building and a painted blue door. The sign on the wall declared the convent and Aster opened the door. This little chapel was open to the public, but few visited due to its tucked away nature and attached convent, assuming it was a closed order.

Aster pushed through the door and into the familiar little hallway. To the left-hand side was another blue door with the words 'convent' and 'closed' beneath it. To the right, the corridor trailed away with a little wooden sign saying, 'to the chapel'. Whilst she didn't believe in God, she had been raised a Catholic by two Catholic parents, and found it was very hard to escape the symbolism and culture of her upbringing. In fact, she didn't try very hard; she rather embraced it. She had been fairly certain from a very young age that no such mythical character lived on high but she adored all of the rituals: the smoke of the incense, the silence of the cathedrals, the routines of the year, the occasions where family would come together and celebrate, in particular, Easter, which was just around the corner. She was particularly looking forward to rejoining all her sisters up in their ancestral home.

But before she headed off to Norfolk, she had a few tasks to do first. Pushing the door open into the chapel, she saw that it was, as usual, empty, or at least almost empty. At the far end of the chapel, she could see Sister Bernard cleaning the wax from the candle spills. Clearing her throat so as not to alarm the nun, Aster coughed loudly.

Sister Bernard was as small as she was wide and had been blessed with a quite prestigious beard, which Aster found almost revolutionary in her disregard for perceived feminine beauty. Coming forward, the nun threw her arms out wide, and then seemed to catch herself and stopped a metre or two back from Aster. Aster was not one for hugs and was grateful that she had remembered.

'What a sight for sore eyes you are! But you look tired, my dear. Are you ailing?'

'Not sleeping too well recently, but I'm sure it will pass.'

The nun peered at her critically and then decided to change tack.

'And what brings you here on Maundy Thursday?'

'I've come to bring a gift,' Aster began, pleased to change the subject, and reached into her bag to pull out an envelope of cash. Her eyes drifted around the empty chapel as she spoke, lingering on the faded blue and gold accents left over from its more opulent past. Though humble now, this place still held meaning.

A flicker of memories surfaced in her mind of her own childhood, receiving charity. These nuns devoted their whole lives to serving others less fortunate, despite their own leaky roof and crumbling walls. Such selflessness deserved support.

Shifting her gaze back to Sister Bernard, Aster went on. 'I would rather you have the money to continue helping your projects than give it to some large nameless charity.' The personal touch mattered when distributing aid. Cold bureaucracy helped no one. The sisters supported several UK initiatives as well as a school in India.

'You could, of course, use the money to patch your own roof. Is it still leaking?' Aster gestured upwards with the envelope, a thin smile breaking through her composure at the long-running roof debate between them. Though they saw charity quite differently, she respected the sisters' convictions, even if they allowed this beautiful old chapel to slowly deteriorate.

The leaky roof on the chapel had been a longstanding bone of contention for the nuns. They didn't have the money to repair it themselves, or at least they did, but they sent nearly all of their money overseas. She felt that this attitude was noble, and that was a waste of time. Without taking care of yourselves first, how could you help others? And allowing the convent to deteriorate seemed a foolhardy step to Aster.

'Tell me, how are your lovely sisters and their children?' asked Sister Bernard, keen to distract Aster from her regular admonishment. 'Are the little ones looking forward to Easter?'

Aster smiled and nodded. She had no desire, even with somebody as special as Sister Bernard, to discuss the family. A smile could do, and she looked to change the subject.

Her eyes were drawn to a large patch of bare wall, where an old oil painting used to hang.

'Are you having the painting cleaned?'

The painting in question had been a very large oil painting, in a heavy gilt frame. It depicted a sorrowful Mary cradling Jesus after the crucifixion. Despite the decades of accumulated chapel grime, Mary's robes had flowed around her, illuminated by a heavenly glow, whilst Jesus lay pale and limp in her arms. Even with the years of candle smoke and dust dulling the colours, the poignant grief and piety had shone through. Aster was convinced some old master had rendered it centuries prior.

'Yes, our Easter blessing! A gentleman was in here a month ago. Saw our painting and was so taken with it, he asked if he could buy it.'

Aster's face dropped in astonishment.

'He made a very generous offer.'

'I should hope so.'

'He offered us five thousand pounds, and we were thrilled to accept.'

Aster was horrified. Five thousand pounds for an oil painting that size seemed a bargain in anyone's money, but if it was an old master — and who could tell under the centuries of candles, smoke, dust, and wax — had somebody just walked out the convent with an absolute steal?

As Aster worried they had been scammed, Sister Bernard moved across to the other tray of candles and continued with her enthusiastic story.

'Then on top of that blessing, with all the good weather the builders were able to fit us in as a favour, and now we are as dry as Sister Julia's roast chicken on Sundays. For the first time in years we are looking forward to the rain.' She laughed loudly and beamed at Aster. 'Can you imagine it? No more buckets.'

Aster wanted to join in the nun's enthusiasm but she felt a fury simmering within.

'Tell me, do you know the man? Is he one of your parishioners?'

'Not really, he's much like yourself. He comes in here from time to time, but he doesn't say much. But that's okay. However one finds a way to God is enough for us.'

Aster knew that was a slightly pointed comment at herself, but she let it go. Today wasn't the day for a theological discourse, no matter how much she enjoyed them. Now she was worried that the nuns had been ripped off and had lost out on the priceless treasure.

Aster left the chapel, deep in thought.

Pulling up the photos on her phone until she found an image of the painting in the chapel, she then rang Clemmie in an attempt to track down Otto. Her phone rang and rang, causing Aster to frown. She was either out of signal range or still up to her eyeballs in her collection. She had three days until Easter Sunday and the board meeting on Monday. If she missed either, Nick and Ari would both be furious. Ari because she missed a family gathering, Nick because she missed the annual board meeting. In fairness there were four meetings a year, but Clem's business was a major driver in the company. Her design studio had established the Hiverton rebirth, although Nick was careful to make sure it wasn't the sole income stream. Relying on Clemmie was not just unfair, it was also unwise.

Ari, however, would be less easy to mollify. Family was everything and she adored the few times a year everyone was together.

Christmas was increasingly difficult as partners' families also wanted to see their sons and grandchildren. Aster had less concern for their needs, but Ari said everyone's wants had to be taken into consideration.

Aster crossed at the zebra crossing and into the leafy Mayfair streets. She had wanted to speak to Clem first but now she called Otto direct. When Aster had been introduced to Otto, she had only known her as her Grandfather's mistress but within one conversation she found a kindred spirit. Otto had a very secretive past which included being a master forger, escaping from Italian mobsters and evading the long arm of Interpol. She had a sharp mind and kept herself to herself. Pulling her into the family had been one of Ari's best steps. Besides which, it was safer for the family's reputation to have her within the fold.

'Hello, it's me.'

'Evidently.'

Sometimes Otto could come across as prickly, but Aster grinned to herself. She liked someone who didn't waste time on pleasantries or small talk.

'I have a picture I want you to look at. I think it's particularly fine. Can you suggest an artist? It's roughly four by five foot. Sending now.'

Aster hit send and waited for a reply.

'Received. Any other images?'

'No.'

'Will call later.'

'Wait!' shouted Aster into the phone.

Otto was about to hang up but now listened in silence.

'I need to know about it as quickly as possible.'

There was a deep exhalation of breath at the other end and then Aster could hear Otto mumble to someone in the background. No doubt Louis was currently rolling his eyes. For decades Louis had pursued this international art thief and forger across Europe. It was only once he retired that the two of them were able to fall in love. Otto returned to the phone.

'It would help if I had another image.'

'I'll see what I can find. Will I see you on Sunday?'

'Of course. Who am I to refuse a royal command?'

'Otto!' said Aster sharply. The old woman wasn't strictly family, but Ari viewed her as such. Aster was very fond of Otto, but no one got to dismiss Ari.

'Keep your hair on, I'm not criticising her. My fingers are aching this morning and I'm feeling grouchy. Louis and I will be driving up tomorrow. Please ensure the weather remains fine.'

With that, Otto ended the call and Aster frowned. Normally conversations with Otto were fast and fun. Today Otto sounded properly fed up and Aster made a note to call Ari and make sure Otto and Louis had the stable cottage. It had a lovely patio amongst the gardens but more importantly, no stairs. If her fingers were hurting, her hip would be killing her. She'd also recommend that Ari whack the heating up. Otto was increasingly spending time in the south of France rather than Scotland and Aster suspected the heat was as much a factor as her gorgeous Frenchman.

Popping back into the house, she pulled a weekend bag together. With both Otto and Louis on the case, she was confident that she would soon have some answers about the painting. For the first time in days she was relieved that she had a new puzzle to focus on. Recently she had taken to driving up and down the lanes trying to jog her memory but nothing was working. At least now she felt she could move on.

Chapter Eight

The sun was shining and the countryside was basking in it.

Ariana Hiverton, Countess of Hiverton, sank into a feather-filled sofa and raised a glass of champagne to her sisters.

'Happy Easter!'

Her sisters, all similarly leaning back on armchairs and sofas, raised their glasses in return.

'I'm never going to move again,' exclaimed Nick, who was already regretting her second helping of lamb. 'Paddy, that trifle was the last straw.'

Paddy languidly threw a cushion at her but it failed to make it even halfway across the room.

Seb, Hal and Gabe were entertaining the children out on the lawn. Otto and Louis had gone for a nap and Mary was out in the garden watching the children play.

'Granny's pretty wonderful, isn't she?' said Nick fondly, causing Clemmie to raise an eye.

'What makes you say that?'

'Because she's giving us this time together.'

'I think she just enjoys watching her great grandchildren,' said Clem, shrugging.

'No,' said Aster. 'She's giving this to us.'

'Well, I'm grateful that she is,' said Ari. 'I don't get enough time with just you four.'

Paddy raised her glass in a lazy salute. For so long, it had been the five of them against the world and now they had husbands, partners, and children and even a grandmother. And as for Otto, as far as the girls were concerned, they had reframed her into the role of eccentric aunt.

Ari drew a breath and then let it out again.

'So, Aster. How are you doing?'

Clem had been about to take a sip of champagne but the glass paused mid-air. Nick put her magazine down and Paddy held her breath. No one looked at Aster, who was busy glaring at her eldest sister.

'I'm fine.'

'You can ditch that tone, I'm concerned.'

Aster stood up. 'I told you I'm fine. Shall I call the children in?'

Eager to break the tension, Paddy pulled on Aster's sleeve and tugged her to sit back down. 'So, what's everyone getting Granny for her birthday?'

As the other sisters pounced on the change of conversation, Aster gave a sigh of relief. She loved her sister's concern, but she still wasn't ready to talk about it. The vulnerability left her too raw. If she could talk to her rescuer, she felt certain it would help her. If only so that she could retrace her steps, even if she might never remember them. She knew memories could be re-written. If she walked that route enough times, she may be able to kid herself that, for that part at least, she wasn't out of control. She shuddered and then looked around the room quickly. Ari, Clem and Paddy were locked in a debate about a photo album or a holiday but Nick was watching her. For a second, she just stared at Aster then nodded and smiled and joined in the conversation suggesting that they all go outside to get some group photos. They could then get them added to an album or turned into a large canvas.

As the girls headed out of the patio doors, Nick linked her arm through Aster's.

'Did you find the identity of the other man? The one that helped. I have a few contacts with access to facial recognition databases.'

Aster shook her head. 'So do I. But I don't want strangers involved.'

'Plus you don't want anyone else to know about him until you do?'

Aster sighed in relief. People waffled on about safe spaces, but it wasn't down to spaces. It was down to people and her four sisters were hers.

'Exactly.'

'Okay. If you ever get a name and want any help, let me know. In the meantime, let's go get pretty for the camera. Remember not to stand anywhere near Paddy!'

The two sisters walked out into the sunlight. Aster was still laughing at Nick's comment. Paddy might be the model in the family, but her twin sister wasn't exactly a walrus herself. Aster grabbed Leo and Will, deciding that the days were running out when she would be taller than them and needed photographic evidence. However, she hadn't been five minutes in the garden when Ari came over and shooed the boys away.

'Aster, we need to talk. Paddy told me the police aren't pursuing the case.'

'That's right.'

'And you're okay with that?'

Aster glared at Ari. 'Of course I'm not okay with that. Why the hell would I be?'

'So what are you going to do?'

'Do? Nothing. I'm going to do nothing. Like I told Paddy, I sent him an e-mail warning him off. I've been checking Whistles' security cameras and he hasn't been back. So that will have to do.'

Ari looked at her little sister, her brow furrowed and Aster felt her stomach clutch. That she should be a figure of sympathy weakened her and weakened the family. Aster was the problem solver, not the one that others worried about.

'But that doesn't sound like you.'

'Oh for Christ's sake, Ari. Let it go. I'm fine. The situation is fine. Everything is just fucking fine, okay!'

Ari's jaw dropped in astonishment as Aster stormed back into the house.

As the sisters played with the children, their husbands and partner looked on.

'How did we get so lucky?' said Seb, smiling at the group. Hal shook his head.

'Rory didn't,' said Hal.

Seb shrugged his shoulders, 'Clem's a fool.'

'Planning on telling her that?' asked Hal with a raised eyebrow.

Seb choked on his beer and shook his head, laughing.

'Thought not,' continued Hal, grinning. 'Mind you, I wouldn't either. I like Rory, he was perfect for her, but it turns out he has a stubborn streak a mile long.'

'Can you blame him? He's probably had enough.'

'I know Clem can be a nightmare, but she's a total marshmallow underneath the prickles,' said Seb, quick to defend his difficult sister-in-law. 'I wouldn't rule Rory out of the picture just yet. Clem refuses to have him mentioned in her presence.'

'Sounds to me like a done deal,' muttered Gabe.

'I'm with Seb,' said Hal, 'that sort of refusal suggests strong emotions are still at play.'

'I don't see it.'

'That's because you married an angel. How she puts up with you, I have no idea.'

'Shall I tell your wife that you are calling another woman an angel?'

'Letta? She'd be the first to agree with me. In fact, woe betide anyone that casts shade on her twin.'

'They all protect each other, don't they?'

'In their own way.'

The men fell silent as they contemplated the most protective sister of all, who was currently engaged in an intense conversation with Ari.

'Oh dear,' said Seb, 'that doesn't look good.'

The men watched as the two sisters had a brief exchange of words and then Aster appeared to lose her temper and turned back towards the house, leaving a dumbfounded Ari staring after her.

'Oh, hell.'

'Problem?' said Gabe. 'The girls bicker all the time. You should hear Letta and Clem on the phone sometimes.'

'Not the same at all,' said Hal, and Seb shook his head in agreement.

'I've known this lot the longest and whilst I wouldn't claim to understand Aster, I can promise that hell would freeze over before she lost her temper with Ari. She almost views her as a saint. In Aster's eyes, she can do no wrong.'

'Well from what I just saw, Satan must be shivering right now.'

'Agreed,' said Hal. 'Do you think this is to do with the spiking incident? Paddy told me that she thought it was resolved.'

Seb watched Ari and Paddy deep in conversation and shook his head. 'I think that's what they all hoped, but from Aster's behaviour just now, I think it's a long way from resolved.'

'Do you think there's anything we can do to help her?' asked Hal quietly.

'Ari told me not to interfere.'

'Letta said the same.'

'As did Paddy, but I ignored her.'

The other two men turned to look at him.

'And?'

'Well, Aster can't track down the man that took her home, and that's been bugging her.'

'Understandable. I've never seen a more self-controlled girl and you've all met Letta.'

'What have you found?' said Seb.

'Not much if I'm honest but I went to uni with the owner of the nightclub. We haven't stayed in touch much, he's based in the Peak District, but I've dropped him a line to see if I can get a private viewing of the security footage.'

'I looked into the owner,' said Gabe thoughtfully. 'It's part of a chain. And the owners are a brewery? Does your friend own the brewery?'

Hal shook his head. 'He owns the property. Not the nightclub.'

'Oh, right. Well, do you think a landlord could get eyes on those security tapes?'

'Worth a try.'

Seb nodded. 'Still. I'd tread carefully. So far no one knows Aster's involvement in this whole ordeal. If you reveal that, all hell will break out and I doubt Paddy will be able to protect you.'

'I suspect she'd be the first to slaughter me. Don't worry. I'll tread carefully. He hasn't even replied yet. It may come to nothing. But dammit, I really like Aster. It slays me that this happened to her.'

'We all feel the same,' said Gabe. 'It was her intervention that saved Letta from prison.'

'Do you think she'll ever forgive you?' laughed Hal. 'Fancy being sent to spy on Nick and then getting the wrong person.'

'I thank my lucky stars daily. I just want to repay the debt and help Aster.' The three men watched as she re-emerged and began playing with her nephews as if nothing had happened. 'I mean, look at her, she's tiny.'

'You're mistaking that for weakness,' said Seb. 'And where Aster is concerned, that is a major mistake.'

'So are you just doing nothing?'

'I dropped her a line.'

'What? Condolences?' asked Hal, aghast.

'Of course not. I told her when she needed help, I would do anything she needed.'

'We all will, but Aster tends to skate close to the legal edge.'

Hal snorted.

'I suspect she skates right over the edge. Letta says she is a walking liability.'

'Boys!' Mary's voice shouted across the lawn. 'Come and get your photos taken.'

'Time to oblige,' laughed Seb.

As they walked across the lawn, Aster got to her feet, brushed her legs down and stepped to the side of the group and away from the husbands. She remained smiling, but now she had reverted to her normal watchfulness. Seb caught her eyes and smiled. She smiled back warmly. He knew she trusted him and it always made him proud that he had impressed the youngest of the Hiverton sisters.

After the photos were taken, Otto and Louis appeared as if by a prearranged signal. Otto never appeared in any of the family photos. This was widely agreed to be a good idea. The statute of limitations had probably passed on all her previous activities, but it was wisest not to draw undue attention. When she had unwittingly appeared in a magazine feature on Clem, it had nearly been the undoing of the Hivertons' reputation.

Aster made her way across to where they were sitting and kissed both of them on the cheeks. She knew she had stepped over the line with Ari and was trying to put the incident out of her mind. At least Otto wouldn't waste time asking how she was. She had a better relationship with Otto than Mary. They had more in common and Aster still struggled to reconcile the fact that Mary had failed to track down her son, Aster's father. She fully understood the explanation and she didn't doubt Mary's sincerity. It was just that she failed. And Aster's Da had grown up unloved. Aster found that very hard to forgive.

Now she sat down and Louis rose to his feet.

'Let me get you a drink whilst the pair of you scheme. The less I know the better.'

'Silly man,' scoffed Otto. 'We don't scheme.'

'That's right,' said Aster, her youthful face mirroring Otto's lined expression. 'We plan.'

Louis rolled his eyes as the two women smiled at each other and he made his way over to chat to Hal. Aster watched him leave, then turned to Otto.

'Well?'

Otto shrugged. 'Well nothing. The photo you sent wasn't much to go on, was it?'

'I enhanced it.'

'All the better to see the dirt with. That picture was in a dreadful condition.'

Aster drummed her fingers on the wrought-iron table.

'It's not like you to fail.'

'Indeed.'

They fell into silence as Louis returned with a glass and stared at the two women.

'Have you told her what you have uncovered?'

Aster looked up at him. 'She has not. She said she failed.'

'I did not.'

Aster reviewed the conversation and inclined her head in a small nod of acknowledgement.

'Indeed.'

Louis handed Aster her glass and then quickly departed.

'I'm sorry. I've been out of sorts. What have you found?'

Otto leant over and patted her hand briefly and then sat back in her chair.

'No need to apologise. I was trying to be dramatic.'

'You have discovered the artist?'

Otto shook her head quickly as the birds sang in the warmth of the afternoon sun. On the other side of the lawn, the children were playing British Bulldog with their parents.

'I haven't, but from the photo I would agree with your assessment that it was possibly painted by a master. But the dirt is so intense, it could also be someone working in the style of one of the masters.'

Aster frowned and tipped her head back, looking up at the sky.

'I was afraid of that. Looks like the nuns have been hoodwinked.' She looked across at Otto, who was sipping her wine. 'Louis said you had uncovered something?'

'Yes. It's going to auction in a few weeks.'

'What!'

Aster pulled her phone out of her pocket and tapped in the website as Otto gave her the details.

'Got it.' Aster looked at the small screen, but it was clearly the same painting. 'Sold without provenance or attribution. Guide price, fifty thousand pounds.' Aster whistled. 'That's one hell of a guide price for something with no track record. What gives?'

'It suggests the auction house likes the painting and is hoping to draw attention to the fact that it might be a sleeper.'

'At that price!'

'If it is an old master, fifty grand is a steal.' Otto looked at Aster and raised an eyebrow. 'What are you going to do?'

'I'm going to get that painting back to the nuns.'

'But they sold it willingly. You won't get far with a stolen goods defence.'

'I don't intend to. Will you still be in England when the auction is on?'

Otto grinned. 'We had been planning on a few days in New York, but I think I can persuade Louis to postpone. What do you have in mind?'

'Nothing yet. But I will do. Let's talk.'

Chapter Nine

The following morning, the sisters gathered in the dining room. Each woman was surrounded by piles of folders and laptops in varying degrees. Clem had samples of fabrics and an artist's portfolio folder with sheets of loose papers spilling out. Glimpses of sketches promised another exciting collection. Nick had two laptops, Paddy had a pink iMac, Ari was almost swamped by folders and portfolios. Aster had a phone.

Partners and children were occupied elsewhere. Tomorrow they would decamp to London for the official board meeting, but today it was just the sisters thrashing things out.

'Okay,' began Ari. 'Let's start at the top. The charity is running smoothly. I'll give a more detailed account tomorrow, but I think I would like to spend another year at our current pace, make sure everything is actually running smoothly then increase our reach. Thoughts?'

All eyes turned to the twins. Nick held the purse strings and Paddy had been responsible for setting up the Cornish retreat in the family house at Tregiskey.

'Sounds smart to me,' said Paddy, smiling. 'Michelle will give a complete brief in tomorrow's meeting but I can say it is truly wonderful watching people come for a week and properly relax. Aster, your idea of employing a counsellor was inspired.'

Aster shrugged. She'd had another bad night's sleep compounded by her behaviour yesterday. Ari hadn't said another word, but she knew she had behaved unforgivably and was desperate to apologise. The problem was she couldn't think of a way to do it that didn't bring up the whole spiking incident again. For now, though, she would focus on contributing to the meeting and putting her personal issues to one side. 'People seem to want to talk. Especially when they're struggling.'

The idea of sharing her innermost concerns with a stranger was anathema to her, but she was partial to a spot of confession. Growing up, she had quickly cottoned on to the fact that she could tell the priest anything and he couldn't blab about it to anyone. Since then, she made a habit to offload her concerns whenever she passed a church. She knew it wasn't what the Catholic Church had in mind when they established the sacrament of confession, but she had always adapted any situation to suit her needs. It would never occur to her to talk to someone who could then rat her out or judge her. She could barely talk to her sisters, but a priest was fine.

'Well, it's going down a dream,' said Paddy. 'For some people, all they needed was a sympathetic ear. For others, we've been able to set them up with ongoing counselling when they get back home.'

'So long as the counsellors aren't stringing things out,' muttered Aster. Talking was fine, but there was no need to go on.

'They're not,' said Nick. 'We only hire counsellors with the most professional of attitudes. That said, Ari, I think the idea of consolidating this year is a good idea. The inner-city schemes are running well, as is the Cornish one. The Indian division is still getting settled and I don't want to rush that one along.'

'We've been damned lucky with the new government trade tariffs,' said Ari, looking at the figures.

'Well, I would normally say it's not luck if you plan for it, but yes, that was unexpected.'

'Hal says Jones has a bad reputation for being a bully in his private circles,' said Paddy, passing on her husband's wisdom. Not only was Hal well connected, he was also an awful gossip and loved to get the lowdown wherever he went.

'He may well be,' continued Nick, 'but if the Foreign Secretary wants to start making beneficial trades deals between the Commonwealth countries and we happen to have a business in India, then three cheers for Anthony Jones, I say. The business is really beginning to flourish. Clem, have you got more to say on that?'

Aster watched Clem's face pinch and felt her suspicions confirmed. She was not the right person to be involved in this scheme, but Nick had been determined to ignore Aster's warning, saying that Clem was more than capable of monitoring the venture.

'It seems to be okay. Like I said, I am busy with my own job. Although these knock-off fabrics aren't helping.'

'What knock-off fabrics?' asked Ari. 'You haven't mentioned them before?'

'I have. Look, I've brought some samples.'

Ari frowned, but before she could respond, Clem leant down and pulled out several lengths of muslin from her bag. Tossing them across the table, the sisters pulled various samples towards themselves.

'The ones with the red felt marker pen are not from our supply.'

Aster pulled them close towards her and compared the two samples.

'Are you sure?'

'Of course I'm bloody sure. I bought them, didn't I?'

'But they look identical?'

'They aren't, trust me.'

'Hang on,' said Ari, cutting Clem and Aster off. 'I thought we were the only manufacturers. Surely we have complete control over the supply line. Nick?'

Nick nodded, confirming Ari's statement as Aster continued to study the two fabrics.

'So, what's happened?' asked Aster, still comparing the two.

Two years ago, Ari had found a seed archive in the attics. They were for various plants that the family's fabric business was based on. Flax, cotton, linen. She had been listing all the seeds to Clem when she had mentioned *Gossypium arboreum var. neglecta*, written out in beautiful copperplate and Clem screamed down the phone. This was the seed that grew a particular cotton responsible for the fabled and apparently extinct Dhaka muslin of the nineteenth century. It only grew in northern India and Bangladesh and was responsible for the world's finest muslin. However, it was so fine that it undercut the British muslin market and the East India Company suppressed trade until the Bengali industry suffered and collapsed. Even worse, the plant fell out of production and was lost to the mists of time. Subsequent attempts to revive the plant had failed as no seeds had ever been saved. Until Ariana found them in the family archives.

'We don't own the patent on the seeds,' said Nick sourly. 'Now that the plant has been reintroduced, anyone can grow the seeds and raise a harvest.'

'But we paid for the workers to harvest the crop and the spinners to turn it into fabric?'

'Yes, we own several hectares. But we gifted the seeds to the people of the region.' There was some muttering and Ari laughed. 'There's no use you grumbling at me, Nick. You know it was the right decision. We are reintroducing a top-quality product into the world. The region can take pride in their reclaimed industry. And we support moving the region out of poverty.'

It was their new charitable enterprise that Ari was really proud of. So far, they had built a school and a new doctor's surgery beyond the small factory and had launched the fabric to critical acclaim.

'I think it would have been reasonable to ask for exclusivity.'

'Nick. We've been over this. They're our seeds and our technology that created the plants, but it's their climate and landscape that grow the cotton. Plus we have got a two-year head start on any other producer.'

Ideally Ari had wanted to base the business in Bangladesh by the Meghna River, where the plant had originally grown, but Nick said the red tape was killing her and felt that financially it would be better to try India first. If the crop failed, then she would try Bangladesh again. However, they had chosen a location close to the border and the plant had flourished and the business was literally blooming.

'Except we clearly haven't,' said Clem as she waved the piece of fabric with the red marker on it. 'This is every bit as good as ours.'

Ari sighed. 'Well, that's disappointing, obviously.'

'No, it's worse than that. We wholesale this fabric to only one stockist at seven hundred pounds a yard. I bought these on the open market for one hundred pounds a yard.'

'Bloody hell,' swore Nick. 'Who the hell is selling it at that price?'

'Several companies. I bought from a few different companies, assuming they were trading on the name but delivering an inferior product. But it's clearly the same product.'

'Clem, you should have raised this sooner,' said Ari in alarm.

'I told you, I did.'

'You didn't. I'd have remembered something this bad. We won't be able to sell the fabric at our price, and if we can't do that, we'll struggle to support the village through profits alone. We'll have to tap into our own reserves.'

'That's not in the budget.'

'Because that's what matters,' needled Clem.

'Yes, it is what matters,' continued Nick. 'My forecasts are all carefully regulated. If we have to take money to support the Indian enterprise, I may need to make adjustments elsewhere.'

'Well, sell the bloody London house then. Aster can live somewhere else.'

Aster had been quietly listening to her sisters spit back and forth. Unsurprisingly, Paddy had been quiet throughout. She loathed arguments and hated to be dragged onto one side or the other. As Aster watched, Paddy had been furiously doodling on her jotter and now almost a full side was covered. If she turned the page over, Aster knew Nick would lose it with Clem. It was time to intervene.

'Clem, have you looked into the sellers of this fabric?'

'Hardly, I do have deadlines-'

'Of course,' said Aster, cutting her off quickly. 'How about I look into this? I'll see who these sellers are, find out their distribution lines. See if our product has been stolen along the way. If I have no success in the UK, I'll fly out to India.' She looked around the room. 'How does that sound?' Aster was keen to offer a tangible solution and one that put her squarely back in charge of helping the family business, not distracting from it.

Nick and Clem were still glowering, Paddy was smiling and Ari blew out a sigh of relief.

'That sounds like a good plan, thanks. Okay, moving on. Estate management. Paddy, how's the new road working out?'

'Like a dream. Can we officially thank Mary in tomorrow's meeting? She was fabulous at keeping planning and paperwork on track. It's only been a month, but already the one-way system is working like a dream.'

'And the upper carpark?'

'Too soon to tell, but so far so good. People seem to be dropping off and then heading up to the top to park and walk down the hill.'

'And the impact to the villagers?' asked Ari.

'Some grumbles that it's going to spoil the village, but mostly positive.'

'Grumbling because?'

'Because I think Dave really only knows how to grumble.'

As the meeting went on, the tension seemed to dissipate. Clem once more mentioned selling the London townhouse. As Paddy prepared to turn her sheet over to start on a fresh set of doodles, Aster jumped in again.

'Coffee?'

Chapter Ten

In a rush of agreement, the girls leapt up and headed to the coffee maker that had been brought into the dining room for today's meeting.

Nick placed a coffee cup in front of Ari, then moved to her seat and sat down, placing her cup to her right. Clem was sitting opposite and visibly flinched.

'No coffee in my workspace.'

Nick raised her eyebrow and sipped her coffee in silence. Then, placing it back on the table, she shrugged her shoulders.

'This isn't your workspace. Shall we carry on?'

Ari sighed and pulled a notepad towards her, but Clem was on a roll.

'I have sketches and fabrics here. If your coffee spills, it will damage them.'

'So move them.'

There was a stillness in the air, only broken by Ari sighing loudly.

'I don't think-'

'It's okay, Ari, we know what Nick thinks of my work.'

'Do we? Do we really?' snapped Nick. 'Paddy, what do I think of Clem's work?'

'You think she's a genius. And you are, Clem, everyone knows how talented-'

'Aster, what do I think of Clem's work?'

Aster stared at her and then pointedly picked up her phone and started to scroll.

'I'm not getting involved in this.'

'Taking the coward's way out?' sneered Clem.

'No, you blistering bag of cow dung. I'm just not listening to you go on again about what a tortured artist you are. Your collection is no doubt a triumph again, but in the meantime, you are making everyone else's life hell. No wonder Rory left.'

Paddy had been furiously doodling on the second side of paper and Nick slammed her hands on the table, but at Aster's words the room splintered into violent silence.

Clem stared silently at Aster, her eyes sparking in fury. Without missing a beat, she snatched at her portfolio. Ripping it open, she flung the collection of loose leaf drawing across the table at Aster.

'Maybe I am cow dung, because what I've designed is a pile of shit.'

She shouted at Aster as she jumped to her feet. Nick leapt backwards, grabbing at her coffee cup, and watched in horror as some of it splashed on Clem's precious designs.

'Jesus, Clem,' roared Ari. 'What did you do that for?'

'Because it's shit. The whole collection. Nick should pour the rest of her coffee over it.' She screamed once and then collapsed back into her chair, sobbing loudly.

Paddy ran around to the table and hugged her whilst Ari nipped out to get some tissues and a bottle of wine. Aster looked across at Nick and rolled her eyes. She pulled one of the images towards her. It was a sketch of a long gown with frills or ruffles to the side. It looked fine to Aster.

Ari came back into the room with some glasses of wine. Dickie followed with a platter of quiches and salads and left quickly. Aster didn't blame her and wondered if she needed a hand in the kitchen. Instead, she sliced the quiche whilst Nick filled the glasses and Ari handed a still sobbing Clem a tissue.

'These look wonderful. Really, you are so talented.'

'I agree,' said Nick quickly. 'Here, have a glass to celebrate. These are incredible.'

Clem rubbed her face and taking the glass placed it on the table.

'I'm sorry I overreacted.' She looked at her sisters as the silence stretched out. 'This is when you all rush to tell me I wasn't overreacting.' As they continued to look at her, she chuckled weakly. 'Fair enough. But honestly, this collection is dreadful. Paddy, what do you think?'

Clem's voice was almost neutral as she pulled some of the sketches towards her and Paddy stood up and started flicking through them. Bundling them all up, Paddy returned to her chair and studied every single sketch. Clem watched in silence and Aster tucked into her quiche. Nick and Ari had also returned to their seats and were watching Paddy. She was the only one who really understood the industry and properly appreciated Clem's talents. Eventually, she put the last sheet down and looked at Clem.

'They're not shit.'

'See?' said Ari in relief.

'But they're not your best work, either.'

Aster closed her eyes and swallowed quickly. Nick knocked back her glass of wine. And Ari stared at Paddy in horror.

'Paddy, I think-'

'No, Ari. Let Paddy speak,' said Clem quietly.

'I think these designs are good enough for a ready-to-wear line. Hell, they're even suitable for a runway collection. But not by you, Clem.'

Clem smiled at her sister and raised her glass. 'Thank you, I thought I was going insane. Everyone has been telling me this collection was excellent, but it's not. It's missing something.'

'It's missing you, Clem,' said Paddy softly. 'You've had two jaw-dropping collections back-to-back, I think you've choked and got in your own way.'

'What if I've simply run out of ideas?' she said in a small voice. 'What if all I've done was all I had?'

Paddy snorted. 'Like Ari will stop suddenly being able to organise everything, Nick will somehow fail to spot trends in the market, Aster will stop dispensing justice. And I'll stop being drop-dead gorgeous?'

Clem laughed and Paddy ploughed on as the other girls watched.

'You haven't lost anything, but your creative well is exhausted. You need a break from doing anything work wise.'

'And who will make the money if I fail?'

'We all will,' said Nick softly. 'Let me send you some figures about what all the different arms of our business are doing. You are no longer the principal earner. You don't need to create for money anymore. Do what Paddy says, take a break.'

Clem blinked back the tears gathering on her lower lashes. 'But I want to pull my weight. The castle is such a bloody money drain, but I don't want you to sell it. I love it there.'

Ari cleared her throat.

'No one is selling the castle. We're doing fine for money, Clem. If you need to stop working for a whole year, then knock yourself out. Go travelling. Find inspiration. Relax. Put this collection to bed.'

Clem looked hopeful. 'But then I've let you down.'

'Continue to oversee the fabrics franchise if you want.'

As Clem shuddered, Ari hurried on. Clem had always been averse to what she called the tea towels line, as stocked in only the finest establishments. 'Well, if not that, play with the American guests, give them the full Highland experience.' Clem shuddered again. 'Spend some time in the V&A archives. Or go white water rafting in Borneo. Whatever. But be happy, Clem. We really do have enough money that none of us should be burnt out.'

'And I'll sort out this muslin issue,' said Aster quickly. 'This was your brainchild, I'll fix it for you.'

Clem sagged in relief.

'Would you? I wanted to make my new collection in it, but what's the point if every Tom, Dick or Harry has it?'

As the tension left the room Ari sipped from her glass and then put it down.

'I think that's enough for today. We'll take up some of these things tomorrow. Clem, whatever you decide to do, we'll support you, okay?'

As the other girls agreed, Aster narrowed her eyes and thought about how she would get to the bottom of the muslin issue. Now she had two challenges. The old master and the muslin. She had resolved the spiking issue, she just wished her sisters would let it go. She smiled briefly as she considered her fresh challenges and helped herself to another slice of quiche. The painting was a good deed for the nuns, but the muslin was serious. Someone was threatening her family and that was not going to work out well for them.

Chapter Eleven

Tuesday brought rain and set the tone for the week ahead. The board meeting had gone well. Paddy in her role as head of marketing and publicity agreed to change the narrative regarding Clem's collection, which would now take a break as the business was branching out into a ready-to-wear line that anyone could afford. Plus each outfit had a corresponding pattern for those who enjoyed making their own outfits.

Aster had enjoyed watching Clem and Paddy get really energised by that idea and after that, the rest of the meeting went smoothly. The Hiverton Estate was looking forward to another successful year with Ari at the wheel. Now, pleased that her sisters were okay, she moved on to her own projects.

Aster adjusted her pale blue burqa as she stepped out of the cab, ensuring her face and body were completely covered. The anonymity it provided was essential; she needed to remain unnoticed and unrecorded. She didn't know what she was going to do about the nuns' painting, but she didn't want to leave any trace of her involvement until she was decided. At the moment, she hadn't ruled out stealing the painting, selling it on the black-market and giving the money to the nuns. It was monstrous that they should be denied its true worth. However, that was an extreme option and felt clumsy. She was certain she could think of something else.

The imposing facade of the auction house loomed before her. The air was thick with the scent of spring blooms from nearby flower beds. The fragrance reminded her of

Hiverton. She took a moment to ground herself and then strode into the auction house, entering the bustling interior.

Moving through the crowd with a fluid grace, her presence drew minimal attention. Her attire was quite normal amongst the more exclusive shops and auction houses of London. She knew she wasn't the only westerner to take advantage of this opportunity. Hell, she knew some men who also took the chance to move unobserved, but she found her shorter height helped to reduce attention. For good measure she was wearing jewel-encrusted rings and several gold bangles. She would not be challenged and whilst a few heads may turn her way, there was nothing with which they could later identify her.

The hum of conversation and the clinking of glasses surrounded her, a blend of excitement and business as usual. Aster scanned the room, her eyes landing on the reception desk where a poised woman in her mid-forties was efficiently handling inquiries. Approaching with a confident stride, Aster put on her most charming smile beneath the veil. Even if they couldn't see it, people heard a smile.

'Good afternoon,' she began, her voice slightly muffled, 'I'm interested in viewing the latest collection. Is there a catalogue?'

The woman's eyes flickered with professional interest, though her curiosity was clear. 'Of course, ma'am. The preview room is just down the corridor on your left. If you need any assistance, please don't hesitate to ask.'

She handed Aster a catalogue, quickly calculated the worth on Aster's fingers and smiled more fulsomely. Aster nodded her thanks and followed the indicated path. As she entered the preview room, the atmosphere shifted. The space was quieter, more reverent, with art enthusiasts and potential buyers studying the pieces on display. She moved slowly, her gaze sweeping over the various artworks, until she spotted the painting from the convent and swore.

The painting, whilst still dirty and hard to assess, had now been properly lit. Hanging in a room of other fine works of art from the fifteenth to seventeenth centuries, it not only held its own but invited closer inspection.

It hung prominently on the far wall, and as Aster approached it, her brain started racing. Even in its poor condition, she could see that this painting would sell at well beyond its asking price.

A voice interrupted her thoughts. 'Beautiful, isn't it?'

Aster turned to see a man standing beside her. She froze, her heart skipping a beat. It was him — the man who had rescued her in the nightclub. His tall, broad figure and sharp eyes were unmistakable. He was studying the painting with the same intensity he had shown her that night.

For a moment she was speechless, staring up at him. She had a thousand questions to ask. He held the answers to one of the worst nights in her life, and yet she was here incognito.

'Excuse me,' he said, mistaking the reason for her silence. His voice rumbled gently and he was about to move away when she spoke quickly.

'Yes, it is,' she replied, masking her agitation with a composed tone. 'Do you know much about its history?'

For a moment he stared down at her and tilted his head, studying her carefully. Despite her head covering, she felt he was looking straight through the fabric. There was no way he could recognise her and yet something about his appraisal of her suggested he was trying to place her. She coughed and looked down, trying to break the moment.

Apologising, he nodded and stared at the painting instead. 'Not really, but I think it could be something very special. Quite the find.'

'Remarkable,' Aster said, her mind racing. She was torn between the urge to speak to him and the need to maintain her disguise. 'I'm fascinated by the stories behind such pieces. Do you know who brought it here?'

The man gave her a curious look. 'Are you looking to buy?'

'An admirer, mostly,' she responded smoothly. 'And a bit of a history buff.'

He smiled. 'Aren't we all? The painting was delivered by a private collector. I'm afraid I can't divulge more than that.'

Aster nodded, maintaining her composed exterior. 'Of course, I understand. Thank you for the information.'

As she turned to leave, he looked down at her again.

'Forgive my rudeness, but have we met? You seem familiar.'

Falling into character, Aster kept quiet. With a shake of the head, she moved quickly away. From the other side of the room, she began to control her breathing and focused on the other people in the room. She was here to study the painting, not the man, but her eyes kept being drawn to him. Currently he was talking to someone she had recently looked up. Anthony Jones, Minister for Foreign Affairs. Since Nick's dig she had made a quick study of him and at least now recognised him. The two men seemed to be well acquainted and were clearly discussing the painting. Well, they could look all they like, thought Aster. Neither of them would be going home with it. From time to time, her stranger would look over in her direction. Thankfully in her robes he couldn't see that she was also studying him.

As he returned his attention to the MP, Aster felt a stir in the room. A moment later, a small woman entered the room followed by two large men. The woman was dressed in a figure hugging red bodycon dress and a fur bomber jacket. The two men behind her towered over her tiny frame and both had visible earpieces. The law of averages suggested that both men, despite UK law, were carrying concealed weapons. Aster had no idea who the woman was, but clearly the rest of the room did. Anthony Jones walked over to greet the woman. Were politicians ever off duty? Her stranger was about to walk away, but stopped as Jones turned back and invited him to join them.

This was Aster's moment to escape. She had no wish to stay in a room where people were carrying guns, especially if she wasn't. The odds weren't in her favour. She had learnt all she was going to. Her painting was attracting too much attention; she would have to come up with something spectacular to ensure the nuns got their painting back. Relieved that her stranger hadn't noticed her withdrawal, she rushed over to the reception desk. It was alarming that he recognised her from only her voice and she felt exposed.

Her thoughts kept returning to the nightclub. He held the key to what had happened that night. Her heart was pounding and she was struggling to keep her breath steady.

She needed to talk to him, but revealing herself now could ruin later plans for the painting.

Spotting a young assistant arranging brochures, she approached with purposeful strides. 'Excuse me,' she said, lowering her voice to a conspiratorial whisper. 'I'm interested in that painting. Is there anyone here who might know a bit more about its provenance?'

The assistant looked up, slightly startled, but quickly recovering. Aster knew she was pushing her luck, women in burqas normally travelled in groups and weren't quite so forthright. If only she hadn't bumped into her rescuer, he was throwing her off her game. Now the assistant spoke quickly, avoiding eye contact.

'You might want to speak with Mr Adams. He's one of our senior appraisers and knows the ins and outs of most of the pieces here.'

Aster smiled beneath her veil. 'Perfect. Where can I find him?'

'His office is on the second floor. I can take you there.'

Deciding that would be a step too far for her character, she shook her head.

'Could you give me his e-mail?'

She was feeling panicky. Her plan was disintegrating and she wanted to retreat to the safety of her home. This sense of anxiety was unknown to her and she was a heartbeat from bolting. Memories of waking up in a strange sitting room and having no access to her memories were overwhelming her and she knew if she stayed any longer, she could make a mistake.

As the assistant handed her a card with the appraiser's contact details on it, she watched as her stranger walked into the corridor, and her heart pounded again. He looked her way, nodded and ascended a grand staircase. Maybe he worked here? Maybe he was Mr Adams? She almost panicked, thinking the assistant might call him over. In a state of total alarm, she grabbed the card and fled outdoors.

Stepping out of the auction house and into the bustling street, Aster took a deep breath and tried to regain a sense of balance. She needed to find a way to talk to the man from the nightclub without blowing her cover. He held the key to what happened that night, and she couldn't afford to let him slip away again. Her first move was to kill two birds with one stone. She would phone Mr Adams now. She would recognise her rescuer instantly from his voice. If it was him, she had a lead. If it wasn't him, she could ask Mr Adams about the painting.

Pulling her phone out of a pocket, she slipped it under her head covering and tried to dial. Her shaking fingers barely hit the right keys and she shook her hands before trying again. A moment later, an affected older voice answered the phone.

'Mr Adams?'

'Speaking.'

Aster immediately discounted him as the man she had just spoken to.

'Good afternoon,' she began, her voice shaking. 'I'm very interested in Lot Eighty-Seven, currently on display. I was hoping you could tell me more about its provenance.'

She heard a creak and assumed the man was leaning back in his chair. 'Yes, that piece has garnered quite a bit of interest. It was brought in by a private collector, someone who wishes to remain anonymous. The painting itself is certainly promising.'

As he spoke, Aster felt herself calm down as she took a few deep breaths and focused on the matter at hand.

'Do you know where the collector acquired it?' Aster pressed gently.

'It was previously in the care of a religious establishment for many decades. Unfortunately, they had no details as to how it came to be in their possession.'

'Which religious settlement?'

'I'm afraid that information is not publicly available.' Mr Adams replied. 'The collector is quite private and only provided the necessary details for consignment. He did say that he would be happy to share the details with the purchaser.'

Aster nodded, her mind working through the information. 'And the collector, do they often consign pieces here?'

Mr Adams hesitated for a moment before responding. 'They've worked with us before, but they value their privacy. I'm afraid I can't share more than that.'

'Of course,' Aster said, masking her frustration. 'I appreciate your time and information. May I ask, given the poor provenance and lack of attribution, don't you think the guide price is rather high?'

There was an indulgent chuckle at the other end of the line.

'Not at all. If anything, it could be argued that the price is too low, given the clear artistry at work.'

'How long has it been in his possession?' Aster didn't want to get the appraiser's back up, but she was trying to see how far the auction house would go to protect their reputation and that of their client.

'That is private information.'

'Do you understand my concern? Has it been checked on the Art Loss Register?'

The chair creaked again and Aster sensed the call was about to end.

'Of course it has. Whilst we value the probity of our client, we nevertheless check all our items through the ALR. In twenty years we have never had a single sale lot withdrawn or repudiated. Now, I'm afraid I do need to get on. Good day.'

Aster muttered a quick reply and closed the call. She had no further leads on the man who bought the painting from the nuns, but following on from something Mr Adams had just said, she had an idea of how to get the painting back. Unwittingly, he had just revealed a weakness and Aster was prepared to exploit it.

Walking on, she spotted a small alley and ducked down it. Checking no one had followed her, she whipped off her burqa and shoved it into the bag she was carrying underneath. Removing her rings and bangles, she also carefully stowed them in the bag and then walked out of the alley at the other end. Just another Londoner, converse trainers, jeans and a hoodie, her hair swinging loosely underneath a baseball cap that she had pulled out of the bag and firmly pulled down over her forehead. She was about to turn back and walk towards the auction house in the hope of bumping into her rescuer when her phone pinged and she saw she had a text from Nick. Smiling, she tapped it open, then scowled as she read the message.

'What progress on the Dhaka fabric?'

She tapped a quick response telling Nick she was still gathering intel and then started work. In truth, she had done some preliminary research into the current stockists of the cheaper fabric, but in her obsession with the painting and her stranger, she had become momentarily sidetracked. Deciding that she needed to put her own desires on the back bench for a little longer, she headed home.

As she reached Foix Place, she bounded up the steps whistling to herself. She had a bunch of riddles to solve and couldn't be happier. It was time to put her tall, dark and silly-handsome stranger from her mind and get down to important matters. And now she knew how to find him, she could relax and possibly sleep well again.

Chapter Twelve

Ten minutes later, Paddy phoned. Aster rolled her eyes and pushed away from her keyboard.

'Hello, you. What's up?'

Aster could hear children's music in the background and could imagine Paddy had grabbed a quick break whilst Eleanor and Alice were being entertained.

'Really! You're always the same. What's up. No time to just chat, see how life is going.'

Aster laughed.

'Has the sun started to rise in the west, Pads? You know I don't do phone chats.' She smiled, making sure there was no sting in her words, but she had work to do and no inclination to natter.

'I was just thinking of you.'

'Funny that, Nick texted me a few minutes back about counterfeit cloth.'

'Typical Nick, always working. You and her are hewn from the same rock.'

'You're not exactly a slouch yourself.'

'Have you ever wondered why that is?'

Aster said she hadn't, introspection wasn't something that she had much time for.

'I think it's because we watched Clem and Ari sacrificing everything and busting a gut every day to keep us together. I think it taught us to try to live up to them or repay them.'

Aster thought about it and could see no fault with the theory. Although she chaffed at the lack of free will.

'I think I would have always been driven, even if Mum and Da hadn't died.'

'Maybe,' suggested Paddy, 'but look, I didn't phone to talk about them. I phoned to see how you are?'

'I'm fine.'

'Yes, of course you are. That's what you said at Easter, when you practically ripped Ari's head off. You'd be fine if your leg was hanging off. But I still thought I'd check. Because I can't stop thinking about it, and I keep thinking about all those other girls.'

'What other girls?'

'The ones before you, the ones after you.'

'No. I sent him a message telling him to stop, or I'd expose him.'

Paddy didn't reply.

'Hello, are you there?'

'Yes, I'm-' She paused, feeling uncomfortable. Had she missed something?

'What is it?'

'It's just this isn't like you,' said Paddy slowly. 'You told him not to do it again and you left it at that? Am I missing something? Are the police involved?'

'Like they cared.'

'No, but you do. You hate seeing crimes go unpunished. Especially against the vulnerable.'

'But you told me to leave it. To let the police handle it. When they didn't, I sent that piece of scum a warning e-mail. You said that was a good move.'

Now Aster fell silent. She had threatened him and he had stopped. And then she had blocked the incident out of her mind. Every time she thought of waking up alone and unaware she panicked and blocked the incident. Thinking of the man who had saved her, she freaked out. She had spent her time studying old masters and then had rushed up to Norfolk for Easter and the family meeting.

'Aster?'

'Yes?'

'Are you okay? Only, I know I said the e-mail was a good idea. But honestly, I thought you'd do more.'

'Like what?' A thousand scenarios ran through her mind, each more violent than the last.

'I don't know. It's just this sort of passivity doesn't feel like you. Plus, you're looking tired and you lost your temper with Ari and I wondered. Are you actually handling things?'

'I-' Aster coughed and cleared her throat. 'I'm fine. At least,' she paused before rushing on. 'I think I've been avoiding the issue.'

'Oh darling. That's completely understandable. What happened was-'

'What happened was nothing. To me, at least. But you are right. It happened to others as well and in trying to block this out I forgot that.' She took a deep breath. 'Right. I have work to do.'

'Would you like me to-'

'No. Genuinely, I am fine. Thank you. If it helps, that's down to you. I was hiding and that's not me.'

'But Aster…'

'No. Stop it. I know you mean well, but you've done enough, you've woken me up.'

'But-'

Aster laughed. 'Patricia Byrne, will you stop going on? I love you. How about I phone you for the next few days? Will that reassure you?'

'Oh, yes. But if you fail to call even once, I'm on my way up. Is that clear?'

'Yes, Mum. Now go, I can hear the children squabbling.'

Sitting back down at her desk, Aster took a deep breath and gathered evidence. How could she have ignored all those other girls? In her desperation to bury this moment in her life, she had forgotten the real victims of Marcus Barrie. Good God, no wonder she hadn't been sleeping. Her subconscious must have been screaming at her for weeks.

Her fingers flew across the keyboard as she cross-referenced names, addresses, and club locations. She mapped out all the late-night bars and clubs within a five-mile radius of Barrie's known address, highlighting those with CCTV circuits she could tap into and those with records she could access. She built a timeline, compiling reports of drugged victims and matching them to nights and venues.

In the past three months alone, Barrie had drugged and walked out the door with at least ten women. Each victim's account painted a chillingly similar picture: a night out with friends, a few drinks, and then darkness. The pattern was clear — Friday and Saturday nights, never the same venue two nights in a row. Though the sample size was too small to be definitive, it was obvious he was well-versed in his methods.

Aster's concentration was absolute, her focus unbroken even as the hours ticked by. Her neck and back grew stiff from sitting in the same position, her head pounded, and her eyes felt gritty from staring at the screen. She barely noticed the time slipping away until a glance at the clock showed it was four a.m. Stretching her neck, she rubbed her temples and tried to ease the growing tension.

Getting up, she stretched, feeling her muscles protest from the long hours of inactivity. Aster yawned, the exhaustion hitting her in waves. Two hours ago, she had been running on empty; now she was running on fumes. She swore she would rest for just a few minutes, heading towards the sofa.

The sunlight poured in through the living room window and Aster blinked in dismay. For half a second, she had the familiar grip of panic that she had woken up somewhere strange. She could still remember the cold sweat, the disorientation, and the sheer terror of those moments. The fear had lingered, an undercurrent to her daily life, and she had spent all her energy in suppressing those memories.

Giving her head a shake, she went to pour a coffee and swore as she remembered she was out. Tapping in a quick delivery request, she went upstairs for a shower and then headed back downstairs. On her printer were the faces of ten women. Each image was before she was drugged and robbed of even her own natural expression. Here they were smiling, laughing, chatting to friends, dancing. Aster had no wish to look at them after they had been drugged. Like herself, they all wore the same slack face she was all too familiar with.

These ten women needed an answer to what had happened to them. And who knew how many others?

Heading back to the keyboard, she hunted them down across social media profiles and found the same story again and again. Gregarious girls went from posting regularly to a sudden absence of posts. She dug into employment records and found patterns of sickness, verbal warnings, poor performance. Students failed to complete assignments; one girl dropped out altogether. Aster couldn't access police or medical records, but she hadn't found any positive proof that any of them had reported the attack.

Over the course of the day, she had got to know the girls and had a sense of which girls might have tried to take things further. Finally, choosing one girl, she decided to go and talk to her before she took any further action against Barrie. She already had a plan in mind, but enacting it could involve placing people who were already traumatised into the public eye, and she didn't wish to inflict any further harm.

As her coffee arrived, she all but snatched the pods from the delivery driver and five minutes later sighed in relief as she got her caffeine hit. As she sat back, she looked at those ten faces and wondered how many others were out there that she hadn't found. The ones before her. Paddy's words suddenly flashed across her mind. *The ones before you, the ones after you.* Would a man this relentless have really stopped? She had spent the following week checking the security footage of the club she had been at, but now she knew he was hunting in lots of venues.

Aster jumped up and almost stabbed at the keyboard, her fingers furiously racing as she widened her search to dates after she had sent him her warning. She expanded her surveillance to the other clubs and venues in a ten-mile radius of his home.

Two hours later, she spotted him. He was in a nightclub, nine miles from his home. He walked up to the bar and then Aster watched in horror as he leant against the bar and ordered a drink. As he waved his hand to summon the barkeeper's attention, she saw the familiar movement of his left hand dropping something into a drink of a girl walking away from the bar. As gooseflesh crept over Aster's skin, she watched as half an hour later he and the girl walked out of the club.

He hadn't stopped.

Aster leapt up, howling, and flung her coffee across the room. As it smashed against the wall, she broke down into huge wracking sobs. The realisation hit her like a physical blow, driving the air from her lungs.

She moaned as the weight of her decision crashed down upon her. She had assumed that a simple threat from the mighty Aster would be enough. Now, because of her hesitation, her desire to put the whole thing behind her, more victims had fallen into his trap.

Aster's hands clenched into fists, her nails digging crescents into her palms. The pain was a welcome distraction from the tsunami of guilt threatening to drown her. She had failed. She, who prided herself on always being one step ahead, on protecting others, had allowed this predator to continue his hunt.

Her tears gave way to a cold, hard rage as she flung herself back into her seat. The time for half-measures was over.

'Hey.'

'You rang!' said Paddy, smiling.

'You said you'd come up to London if I didn't. I believed you.'

'Well, that's a start. And how are you? Getting anywhere with the fabric?'

'I've put that on hold. I need your advice and I don't want you to talk to the others. Can you do that?'

'Nick?' The twins had no secrets, but Aster hoped that if she stressed the situation Paddy may keep this to herself.

'None of them. I want your opinion.'

'You want my opinion?' She could hear the astonishment in Paddy's voice. 'Scratch that, you want anyone's opinion?'

'Paddy, I'm serious.'

'Okay. I'm listening.'

Aster explained what she had discovered over the past twenty-four hours.

'I thought I'd stopped him. Oh God. That's not it. I hoped I'd stopped him. I didn't follow up because I didn't want to face what had happened to me.'

'Oh, Aster. I wish I was with you.'

'Me too. I've been such an idiot, I've behaved like a kid, but I have a plan.'

As Aster spelt it out, Paddy listened on in silence.

'What do you think?'

'I like it. But I think you're right. You need to speak to the girls and warn them.'

'What if they say no?'

'You can't help that. He has to be stopped. At least you are giving them a warning and maybe you can delete their footage. Are you able to do that?'

'I am, but what about the other girls who I haven't traced?'

'That's down to them and the police.'

'And you really think this is okay?'

'Aster, if you had suggested castrating him with a rusty blade and then shoving his balls down his throat until he choked to death, I would still think it was a good plan.'

Since becoming a mother, Paddy had become fierce. Aster laughed weakly.

'Well, if plan A doesn't work, I'll consider that as a back-up. Now, I'll call you again tomorrow. Do not come to London.'

'I won't, I'd only get in your way and you have work to do. If the others chase you for a fabric update, let me know. I'll keep them off your back.'

'I appreciate that.'

'But I think there's something else you have to do.'

'Yes?'

'You need to find the man that took you home. You're giving those girls closure, but you need it as well.'

'He didn't hurt me.'

'I know. I saw that. But it's a time when you had no control. That must be eating you up. Find him, get some answers.'

Hanging up, Aster grabbed her coat and headed outdoors. She had not been hurt, others had, they were her priority, but she needed to step carefully. She had made the mistake of moving too slowly, she would not compound it by moving too quickly.

Whilst she moved things into place, she would work on the Hiverton muslin issue and with the approaching auction she could also focus on that. By the time she got back to the house she had three plans in place and by the following morning she had her first night's peaceful sleep since the nightclub.

Chapter Thirteen

It was mid-morning and Aster was on the road driving north to Birmingham. The traffic was busy and she was zipping along in her Mini Cooper. She had a list of three separate suppliers, none of whom had replied to her phone calls or answered her e-mails beyond providing her with a price list. Digging deeper, she was concerned when she couldn't find any proper company records about them and digging even further, she was surprised to find that the Department of Trade and Industry hadn't raised any red flags about these companies. Incompetent, red tape bureaucracy or something else? Aster was inclined to go with institutional cock-ups. In her experience, people were mostly useless.

Eventually she peeled off the M40 and headed into the city. Weaving between the buses and lorries, Aster headed to her first address.

As Aster navigated the tangle of busy city streets, her mind was churning. These fabric suppliers were proving irritatingly elusive. Despite her best efforts to make contact and arrange a proper visit, they seemed determined to keep her at arm's length. It didn't sit right. If their business was above board, what reason could they have to stonewall her so thoroughly? They weren't prepared to send samples and they didn't have showrooms. The only option was to purchase online, but Aster wasn't a fan of playing by someone else's rulebook.

The address she pulled up to was nondescript, just another industrial unit amidst a sprawl of similar buildings. No signage, no indication of the business within. Aster's instincts screamed that something was off. She sat for a long moment, eyeing the shuttered windows and deserted car park. Not exactly the welcoming storefront of a legitimate textile wholesaler.

With a sigh, Aster climbed out of her Mini and approached the grimy metal door, rapping sharply. No response. She tried again, the hollow clanging loud in the eerie quiet. Nothing. Looking around there appeared to be no signs of life from any of the other units. Heading back to the car, she jumped in and drove around to the back of the large unit. Sure enough, there was a simple back door and no prying eyes. Parking beside a disused skip and a pile of tyres, Aster got out and tried the back door. This too was locked, but only by a simple padlock. Grinning to herself she returned to the car. Dipping down to the puddle by her tyres, she scooped up a handful of thick mud and smeared her front and back licence plates, then leant into the car, removing a small velvet pouch from the glove compartment.

Whilst her fellow students had taken a gap year after their degree to build elephant shelters or mend school toilets, Aster had headed to Asia and learnt the fine art of breaking and entering, sleight of hand and the subtle art of misdirection. Rather than rescuing elephants, no doubt a noble endeavour, Aster mastered wealth redistribution. She quickly learnt who had too much and was reluctant to even share a smile let alone any of their obscene wealth. She'd quickly relieve them of their burden and share it with those slum dwellers who slept on earthen floors, eating one meal a day if they were lucky. Hobbling on twisted limbs, sharing their fire with Aster, and helping her with their language, Aster had spent months feeling happier than she had in years.

She had travelled to Birmingham and wasn't going to turn back now without answers. Glancing around to ensure she was unobserved, she made swift work of the rudimentary lock. The door swung open with a rusty groan as she stepped through the dirt and plastic wrappers that had accumulated at the back of the warehouse.

Inside, the cavernous space was dark and musty. Aster fumbled along the wall until she found a light switch. Fluorescent tubes flickered and hummed to life, revealing towering metal shelves stacked with boxes and bolts of fabric. The air was thick with the smell of mothballs and stale dust.

Wrinkling her nose, Aster ventured deeper into the warehouse. She ran her fingers over the stacked textiles, marvelling at the uncanny similarity to the Hiverton muslin. To the untrained eye, they would be indistinguishable. Pulling out her phone, she snapped a few quick photos of the stock, the shelving, the general layout. She walked along the aisle looking at other items. Clothes from Dior, bags from Balenciaga. Everywhere she looked was the sort of items that people paid very good money for. This was either stolen or counterfeit. She took more photos for Clem to look at. Her sharp-eyed sister would be able to tell her quickly if these were the genuine article or not, but Aster felt certain that Chanel didn't keep their inventory stored in quite such disreputable premises.

She was so engrossed in her investigation, she almost didn't hear the crunch of tyres on gravel outside. Aster sprinted towards the back door as the front door banged open and she ducked behind a pallet of large packing boxes. Crouched behind the crates, her heart pounded as heavy footsteps entered the warehouse.

'How many more times do I have to tell him to turn the bloody lights out?' muttered a man furiously.

Aster held her breath, her mind racing. She was cornered, and if she was caught trespassing, it would put the whole investigation at risk. Not to mention that Ari would be furious. She needed a distraction, and fast.

Thinking quickly, she waited until the man's back was turned, then grabbing a pair of scissors off the nearest shelf, she hurled them as far as she could towards the other side of the warehouse. They landed with a clatter, and the footsteps immediately headed in that direction.

'Who's there?' shouted the gruff voice.

Seizing her chance, Aster bolted for the back door, keeping low and silent. She slipped out into the wan sunlight, easing the door closed behind her with the barest click. And then she ran, not stopping until she reached her Mini. Throwing herself into the car, she grabbed a balaclava from the glove compartment and dragged it over her head before gunning the engine. Screaming into reverse, she threw the little car into a three-point turn as she screeched around the front of the warehouse.

Out of the corner of her eye, she saw the front door flung open as a heavy-set man with a crooked nose ran out, shouting curses at her.

Only when she was out of the industrial estate did Aster allow herself to breathe and then laughed to herself. Removing her hood, she joined the flow of traffic and soon pulled into the car park, where she hid amongst the cars and cleaned off her licence plates. That had been too close. She couldn't afford any slip ups going forward. But her close call had only affirmed her suspicions - these suppliers were definitely hiding something. And she was more determined than ever to uncover what it was.

Consulting her list, Aster plugged the next address into her GPS, which turned out to be a nondescript retail shop, not even fabrics. She frowned at the generic 'For Lease' sign in the window. This was supposed to be the headquarters of a major textile distributor. It looked more like a shell company, an empty facade with nothing behind it.

Aster's suspicions only deepened as she pulled up to the third and final supplier on her list. Another unremarkable storefront, this time a shabby charity shop with a few sad mannequins in the grimy window. She sat in her car, tapping her fingers on the steering wheel as she surveyed the street. Three different addresses, three different businesses, but the same aura of neglect and subterfuge.

Frustrated and in need of a moment to collect her thoughts, Aster pulled into a nearby roadside café. The cheerful jingle of the bell above the door was a stark contrast to the eerie silence of the abandoned storefronts. Aster slid into a worn vinyl booth and ordered a cup of tea, hoping the familiar ritual would help clear her head.

But when the steaming mug arrived, Aster hesitated. She toyed with the handle, turning the cup around and around, but couldn't bring herself to take a sip. Her mind was too busy spinning with the implications of what she'd uncovered.

Three supposed fabric suppliers, all nothing more than empty fronts. Two had no stock, no staff, no sign of the thriving business their sales figures suggested. One was a warehouse full of hooky goods. It was a web of misdirection and deceit. Aster's instincts were screaming that something was very, very wrong. This was no mere case of textile smuggling or copyright infringement. The scale of the deception, the elaborate lengths taken to conceal the true source of the fabric - it all pointed to a far more sinister game.

But what? And more importantly, who was the puppet master pulling the strings? Aster had a sinking feeling that the answers to those questions would prove more dangerous than she'd bargained for. She needed more information, but the usual channels of investigation seemed woefully inadequate in the face of such a sophisticated operation. Aster was going to have to get creative, to think outside the box if she wanted to unravel this mystery.

As she sat, lost in thought, Aster's gaze fell on her still-full mug of tea. A sudden realisation hit her like a punch to the gut. She hadn't taken a single sip, not because she was too preoccupied, but because some part of her was afraid. Afraid of being drugged, of losing control, of waking up confused and vulnerable like she had that night at the club.

Aster felt a flush of anger and shame. She'd always prided herself on her strength, her resilience. But now, a simple cup of tea in a roadside café was enough to make her hands tremble. She hated this new weakness, this chink in her armour.

Abruptly, Aster pushed the mug away and slid out of the booth. She couldn't sit here wallowing in self-pity. She had work to do, and letting her fear control her would not get it done.

As she strode out of the café and back to her car, Aster silently berated herself. She needed to get a grip, to push past this irrational paranoia. She'd always been resourceful, and she'd never yet met a challenge she couldn't tackle head-on.

But even as she revved the engine and pulled back onto the road, Aster couldn't quite shake the lingering unease. The incident at the club had left scars, invisible but deep. And as much as she hated to admit it, they were affecting her more than she'd realised.

Aster gripped the steering wheel tighter, jaw clenched with determination. She would deal with her own demons along the way. She had to. There was too much at stake to let her personal baggage slow her down.

But as the miles ticked by and the city gave way to open countryside, Aster couldn't escape the feeling that she had taken on too much. She had thought that the fabrics issue was going to be quickly resolved, but what she had seen suggested that this was the tip of a larger issue. On top of that, she had made a promise to herself to get the nuns' oil painting back and she really needed to deal with Marcus Barrie no matter how much she wanted to avoid it.

Biting down on her concerns, she placed a call to Nick and was gratified when she was answered immediately.

'What's up?'

'I need to go out to India. This situation is worse than I thought.'

'Tell me more.'

As Aster explained what she had discovered, Nick listened in silence.

'And what do you think you can do in India?'

'Ask questions. Get a sense for where the problem lies. At this stage, all I want is more intel and I don't think I'm going to find it online. I think we need to go to the source and see what they say at the coalface, so to speak.'

'Very well, when do you want to leave?'

'Can I have a week? I have some other things going on that I need to be here for.'

'Do I need to know what they are?'

'No.'

There was a pause and then Nick sighed. 'Very well. Let me know when you want to travel and I'll put things in place for you.'

Hanging up, Aster smiled to herself; she enjoyed dealing with Nick. She always cut straight to the chase and now Aster rang her other favourite phone companion.

'Yes?'

'Hello, Otto.' Otto's abruptness always made Aster want to waffle just to wind her up. She loved the fact that Otto was even more abrupt than she was.

'Stop playing with chit-chat. What do you want?'

Grinning to herself, Aster applied herself to the matter at hand. When she had spoken to Mr Adams in the auction house, he had said that the house had a twenty-year unblemished reputation. That could only mean one thing.

Something major had happened twenty years ago. Aster hadn't found anything obvious and so she had tasked Otto to dig a little deeper amongst her contacts.

'Did you find out what Spencer Auctions were covering up?'

'Of course I did. They were one of several houses that had unwittingly sold some Hebborns passing as a Matisse and a Reynolds.'

Aster shrugged, the name meant nothing.

'And?'

'Pah. Your education. Eric Hebborn was a notorious forger who duped everyone.'

'In your league?'

'Clearly not. He was discovered!'

Aster tried not to laugh. Otto's pride on this subject was monstrous, but also warranted. Luckily for Aster, Otto carried on talking, so Aster was spared having to hide the smile in her voice. 'It's a matter of public record, but Spencer Auctions have done a very good job of keeping their name out of most of the reporting. They were lucky that they were relatively smaller players, whereas Sotheby's and Bonhams caught most of the media attention.'

'Right,' said Aster thinking quickly, 'that's our way in. Gather a team together. All we need to do is cast sufficient doubt on the authenticity of the painting and point out that Spencers have fallen for forgers before.'

'I agree. But we need more. We need to control the telephone bids as well.'

'Bugger, you're right.'

'Of course. But I have already found a solution.'

As Otto explained her solution, the miles sped away and Aster drove along the motorway back to London, delighted that everything was falling into place. Now maybe she could devote a little time to identifying her rescuer. Every day she found herself thinking about him and realised she was beginning to get obsessed by the man. Seeing him that time at the auction house had given her fresh memories and she had found that he had increasingly taken up too much of her attention. He was all she saw at night when she went to sleep and the first person that came to mind when she woke up. There was nothing she hated more than an unsolved puzzle and she knew that she would have to run a facial recognition program soon. The problem was that felt like cheating.

'Did you hear me?'

'Yes. Of course.' Aster quickly rewound the conversation. Otto had been talking about the team she would bring in to work. 'You'll knock out all bids except for your own.'

'Correct. Now, I need to work and talk to people that are paying attention. Goodbye.'

And with that admonishment, she hung up. Aster grimaced and then imagined his face smiling down at her, her thoughts racing away from her.

Enough. She had work to do.

Chapter Fourteen

Aster strode through the bustling London streets, her trainers moving quietly against the pavement. The crisp spring air did little to cool the fever pitch of her thoughts as she walked towards the gleaming office building where Jessica Smith worked. Driving back from Birmingham, she knew she had to focus on the nightclubs, she had been avoiding it and that caused her greater shame. She had behaved like a coward and because of that, other girls had suffered. The past two days had been spent solely on drawing up a plan of action to destroy Marcus Barrie. Today was about honouring the women whose lives had been so violently disrupted by a predator still moving unchecked through the city.

The sleek glass and steel building loomed ahead, all sharp angles and cold modernity. Aster took a moment to square her shoulders and steady her breathing before crossing the polished lobby to the reception desk. The efficient-looking woman behind the counter raised a perfunctory eyebrow at Aster's request.

'Jessica Smith? Yes, she's expecting you. Third floor, conference room B.'

Aster thanked her with a tight smile and made her way to the lifts, her reflection distorted in the mirrored walls as she ascended. She emerged into a hushed hallway, all muted greys and inoffensive abstract art. Conference room B was at the end, a small, utilitarian space with a laminate table and a smattering of generic office chairs.

Jessica was already there, a tall brunette in her mid-twenties, nervously twisting her hands in her lap. She looked up sharply as Aster entered, her large brown eyes wide and unblinking in a pale face. Aster could see the shadows of sleepless nights etched under those eyes, the telltale signs of concealer hastily applied in an attempt to mask the toll of trauma.

'Jessica? My name's Jane. Thank you so much for agreeing to meet with me.'

Aster kept her voice soft and even, her movements slow and telegraphed as she took a seat across from the visibly anxious young woman. Aster wanted to keep her details out of this and was determined that nothing would be traced back to her and in turn, the Hiverton Estate. She would prefer not to have everyone know about her incident, but she absolutely didn't want anyone to know just how good she was at hacking into computers and the like. The Hiverton Estate didn't need that sort of exposure.

'Your e-mail said… you said you had information. About what happened to me that night at the club.' Jessica's words came out haltingly, her gaze skittering away to the window, the door, anywhere but Aster's face.

Aster leant forward slightly, her expression grave. 'I do. But before I show you, I want to warn you that this footage may be very upsetting to watch. If at any point you need me to stop, just say the word.'

Jessica nodded shakily, wrapping her arms around her middle in a self-comforting gesture. Aster flipped open her laptop and angled it so they could both see the screen. With a few deft keystrokes, she pulled up the relevant video file.

The scene that unfolded was chillingly familiar - the deep bass thrum of club music, the crush of bodies on the dancefloor, the clamour of overlapping conversations and clinking glasses at the crowded bar. Aster watched Jessica's face closely as the camera zoomed in on her laughing with a group of friends, her cheeks flushed and eyes sparkling in the pulsing lights. Jessica's breath caught as she watched her on-screen self detach from the group and make her way up to the bar to order a drink.

Aster saw the exact moment realisation hit, the colour draining from Jessica's face as she watched the situation play out on screen. A man's arm reached over her shoulder, depositing something into her glass whilst her back was turned. The movement was quick, almost imperceptible. If Aster hadn't known to look for it, she might have missed it herself.

'I don't recognise him,' Jessica whispered, her voice trembling. 'There's nothing…' She trailed off, pressing a hand to her mouth as the scene continued to unfold.

On-screen, mere minutes had passed, but the change in Jessica was horrifyingly apparent. Her lively animation had given way to a slumped, glassy-eyed daze as the man wrapped a supporting arm around her waist and guided her stumbling form towards the exit. Bile rose in Aster's throat as she watched, remembering with visceral clarity her own experience of confused, drugged helplessness.

Unable to watch any more, Aster reached out and gently closed the laptop. Jessica was shaking now, silent tears coursing down her ashen cheeks.

'I'm so sorry, Jessica. The truth is, the same thing happened to me.' Aster's voice was rough with barely suppressed emotion as she reopened the computer to pull up the footage of her own drugging. She watched as Jessica's eyes widened in horrified recognition.

'That's him! It's the same man.' Her voice shook with suppressed rage. 'He's done this to other women? But I don't understand… I reported what happened to me. I went to the police the next day. They said… they said there was little they could do. I had a rape test and blood screen test and both were positive. But without any security footage, and without my memory-' Jessica's words were punctuated by hitching breaths as she struggled to compose herself. 'But they did have the footage all along. Why would they lie?'

'The usual reasons. Incompetency. Laziness. Back covering. I imagine being involved in a police investigation is bad for business.' Aster leant forward, her gaze intent. 'I'm gathering that evidence, Jessica. You're not the only one. I've tracked down several other women I believe to be his victims. With your permission, I want to compile everything I have and take it to the media. I want to expose this predator for what he is and ensure he can never do this again. We can also target every venue that failed to provide the video evidence in an attempt to save their own skin.'

Jessica recoiled as if slapped, fresh tears spilling over. 'Go public? Have everyone know what happened to me, what he did? I can't… my job, my family, everyone will…' She shook her head vehemently, her breathing growing rapid and shallow.

Aster reached out slowly, giving Jessica time to pull away before gently resting a hand on her arm. 'I completely understand. But this is not your shame. It's his. Believe me, the last thing I want is to violate your privacy or cause you more pain. If we move forward with this, I promise you I can destroy your video. You don't have to be involved. You have my word.'

Jessica sniffled, swiping at her tears with trembling fingers. 'What about the other girls? Do they know you have these videos of them?'

Aster sighed heavily, feeling the weight of responsibility settle over her. 'Not yet. You're the first one I've approached. I've only been able to identify a few potential victims so far. My hope is that by going public with this, more women will find the courage to come forward to the police. There's strength in numbers, even if their individual identities are protected.'

Jessica was quiet for a long moment, her gaze distant as she processed Aster's words. Finally, she straightened her spine and met Aster's eyes dead on, a flicker of steel beneath the surface.

'I've been seeing a therapist. She says it will help me to talk about it. I want him stopped. What he did to me, what he did to you, what he's probably still doing… it's not right. It's not fair. Use my footage. Use whatever you need to take him down. I'll sign whatever you need me to sign. Just promise me one thing?'

'Anything,' Aster vowed.

'Promise me you'll nail the bastard to the wall.'

A fierce grin tugged at Aster's lips, a match for the determined fire kindling in Jessica's eyes. 'That's a promise.'

The tension in the room seemed to ease a fraction as the two women shared a moment of perfect understanding. Aster knew all too well the impotence of rage with no outlet, the haunting spectre of violated autonomy. She would not let Jessica's bravery be in vain.

'Are you seeing a therapist?' asked Jessica hesitantly. 'Talking to anyone?'

Aster shook her head. 'My sisters know, but my situation is different to yours. Someone else noticed I was drugged and took me home and kept me safe.'

Jessica moaned when Aster said 'safe' and then broke down crying. Dirty ugly sobs wracking her frame. Jumping up, Aster went over to the side table, poured Jessica a glass of water and grabbed a napkin, handing both to the woman.

An idea occurred to her then, a small way to offer some modicum of solace. 'Jessica, I know there's nothing I can say or do to undo what happened to you. But if you'll allow me, there is something I'd like to offer. My family, we run a sort of… retreat centre, in Cornwall. It's a peaceful place, beautiful, right on the coast. We established it as a way to help people who have experienced trauma find some healing in a safe, supportive environment. I'd like to arrange a stay for you there, as my guest. All expenses paid. You could take some time away, rest and regroup.'

Jessica blinked rapidly, fresh tears welling. But this time, Aster saw a glimmer of something like hope underneath the sheen of pain. 'You… you'd do that? For me? After everything you're already doing. Why?'

Aster smiled softly. 'It's the very least I can do. You're incredibly brave, Jessica. What you're agreeing to, it's no small thing. Let me help in this way. Please. Even if you say no to me sharing your video, the holiday is still yours.'

The taller woman seemed to crumple again. Aster rose and moved around the table, gathering Jessica into a careful embrace. She felt her own throat tighten with emotion as Jessica clung to her, but she took care not to pull away first. Whatever this woman needed, Aster would provide.

When she finally pulled away, Jessica's face was splotchy and damp, but her eyes were clear. 'Thank you, Jane. For everything. I don't… I didn't know how I was going to get through this, but now… I feel like maybe there's a chance. A chance for justice, or at least something like it.'

Aster squeezed her hand. 'We'll get justice, Jessica. I swear it. He picked the wrong women to mess with. We're going to take back every scrap of power he tried to steal from us. He has no idea what's coming for him. This isn't our shame, it's his.'

With final words of encouragement and a promise to be in touch soon with details about the Cornwall retreat, Aster left Jessica to compose herself before returning to work. As she exited the building into the busy London street once more, Aster felt a renewed sense of determination settling over her like armour.

No more distractions, no more delays. She would see this through to the end, whatever it took. She merged into the thronging crowd, just another unremarkable figure going about her day. But inside, a reckoning was brewing. Jessica's tear-stained face and hesitant spark of hope played on a loop in her mind.

'Nail the bastard to the wall,' Jessica had said.

And nail him Aster would. With relish.

By the end of the day, Aster had met three more women and had appointments to meet four more the following day. Two hadn't replied and she would approach them directly. By the time she went public, it would be with the approval of the ten women or she would delete their footage. She couldn't offer the same to the unknown women, all she could offer them was a possible way to step forwards and name their attacker. Marcus Barrie was not only about to face the full weight of the law, but also that of public opinion. By the time she was finished, there wouldn't be a single person in the country that didn't know who Barrie was and what he had done.

Chapter Fifteen

A week later, Aster woke up smiling. Immediately after interviewing the girls, she had got to work. As the days progressed, she found a sense of satisfaction as her plan fell into place. Chatting with the other girls, she discovered a strange strength in bringing them together. She knew they were in touch with each other and she hoped that this would be the first step in their recovery.

Last night she had spent a few hours accessing her fake online profiles. Like her e-mail server, there was no trace back to her sitting in a house in London. Any attempt to track her posts or e-mails down ended up pinging around VPNs set up in the Bahamas and Taiwan. There was still a long way to go, but last night she had uploaded all her evidence to the online channels. She had also submitted the evidence anonymously to the police. Now she would wait and see who dealt with the situation faster. The police or social media.

She bounded out of bed, her mind already buzzing with the final details of her scheme. Her hand drifted to her phone, itching to check the status of her video. She had spent hours piecing it together, exposing that vile bastard, Barrie. Meticulously edited and distributed through channels that ensured maximum impact and minimal blowback on the victims, it should be detonating across the internet any moment now.

She had also been busy digging into the business peddling the imitation muslin and had yielded some very interesting leads that she was eager to follow up on. But those projects would have to wait. Today was all about the painting.

Today was the auction and the fate of the painting was in her hands. No conman looking for a quick profit was going to get the better of her. Today it would be back in the hands of its rightful owners, if Aster had anything to say about it. And she had quite a lot to say.

She dressed with care, selecting an outfit that struck just the right balance of affluent art aficionado and unassuming blender-into-the-crowd. The key was to be memorable for her words and actions, not her appearance. She'd leave the peacocking to Otto's plants, the carefully selected actors she'd peppered through the auction attendees to help sway opinion in the desired direction. As she looked in the mirror, she was pleased with her appearance and wondered if the man from the nightclub would also be present. Should she approach him? He would recognise her without her burqa to disguise her. Would he remember her? Would he approach her? It was a variable she couldn't control. In the end, she decided there was nothing to be done but see how things played out. She had no active role in today's proceedings, Otto was in charge. Aster was simply there to get the ball rolling and see that everything went according to plan.

Aster arrived at the auction house with plenty of time to spare, melting seamlessly into the milling crowd of prospective buyers, curious spectators, and self-important art snobs. She exchanged pleasantries and air kisses with a few familiar faces, the picture of a well-connected junior collector excited for the day's offerings. The one thing she didn't know was the identity of Otto's people. It was best for all parties to not know who was involved, but each party had their own brief. They even had allowances to submit bids later in the day to cover their presence.

A group of people were standing in front of the large painting. Aster sidled up to a cluster of intent viewers, and prepared to insert herself into their conversation. However, an older woman was chatting to her companion, allowing the others to eavesdrop.

'It's a striking piece, isn't it?' said Aster. 'Such a shame about the provenance, though. I heard a rumour it might not be all it seems.' She let the words hang in the air, an unsubstantiated seed of doubt that would spread like a weed through this particular grapevine.

One of the men in the group, a portly gentleman with a monocle, turned to her with a raised eyebrow. 'What do you mean, not all it seems? Surely the auction house has done its due diligence.'

The woman looked him up and down.

'This was a private conversation.' Tapping her companion on the arm, they drifted away, leaving everyone else frowning. The man with the monocle harrumphed loudly.

'Some people say the most ridiculous things, Spencers is the finest of establishments. Their probity has never been questioned.'

'Well, not in the past twenty years, anyway,' said Aster with a shrug. 'Before my time, obviously, but wasn't there an issue with a Lowry a few years back?'

He blinked and inhaled deeply. Aster could tell a lecture was incoming when a couple walked past and the woman tapped on her brochure.

'Lot Fifty-Eight, darling, don't you want to look at that?'

Her companion laughed. 'Absolutely not. Proper cut and shut that one. All that dirt, someone's trying too hard. If that's an old master, I'll give in and sell the bloody Mondrian and buy you the place in St Kitts.'

'Oh darling, will you really?'

The pair drifted off and Aster simply looked at the man and shrugged, her expression artfully neutral. 'One would hope. But you know how these things go. Corners get cut, paperwork gets "lost". I'm just saying, I'd want to be very sure of what I was buying before I raised my paddle, that's all.'

She drifted away before he could press her further, leaving the little knot of collectors to murmur and speculate amongst themselves. She could practically feel the doubt radiating off them now, the first threads of uncertainty unravelling their confidence in the lot.

Aster meandered over to another group, this one clustered around a severe-looking woman with an imperious air who was also opining on the painting. She was holding forth on the Madonna's brushwork, dissecting its composition with the cool assurance of an expert.

'And of course, the use of chiaroscuro here is simply masterful, the play of light and shadow elevating the piece from mere religious iconography to true artistic sublimity. It's a prime example of the Baroque style at its most transcendent.'

Aster waited for a lull in the woman's pontificating before chiming in, her voice pitched to carry to the surrounding hangers-on. 'It is a marvellous effect, isn't it? Although I did hear someone just mention that this should be Lot Fifty-Seven, as it's a bit of a mutt.'

The self-styled expert whirled on Aster, her eyes narrowing in displeasure. 'And where, pray tell, did you hear such scurrilous gossip? I can assure you, I have it on good authority that this painting has been treated with the utmost care and professionalism.'

Aster widened her eyes in affected chagrin, holding up a placating hand. 'I'm sure you're right. It's just some chatter I overheard, nothing substantiated of course. Far be it from me to impugn anyone's integrity. Still, one wonders where all the documentation is, the provenance trail. A bit thin for a work of this supposed importance, don't you think? There's no attribution. It's been in a religious establishment for donkey's years and yet has no paperwork? I thought that lot had paper files going back to the Reformation.' She laughed at her own joke and was pleased to see others laughing along. 'Still, you're the expert. I'll just go with my gut, and my gut says I don't have that sort of money for a punt.'

Heading away, the crowd had broken up around the self-proclaimed expert and she had returned to the painting to stare at it more closely. Her frown was a picture in its own right.

'There's a lot in interest in that picture, isn't there?'

Aster turned and looked up to see a man in his late twenties was talking. He was wearing a quarter-zip, blue chinos and brown brogues. If he wasn't a city trader, Aster would eat her hat.

'It's quite large, isn't it? You get a lot for your money,' said Aster artlessly.

'Art's not about size, you know,' he winked at her, 'not that I've ever been bothered!'

Biting her cheek to avoid sneering at him, she smiled, fluttering her eyelashes.

'Really? Only I heard,' she dropped her voice and leant towards him, 'that that painting is a sleeper.'

She was rewarded with a patronising chuckle. If he patted her on the head, she would roll up her catalogue and impale him in the eye with it.

'That's not the sleeper. That's a ringer.'

'A ringer?'

'Something pretending to be what it's not.'

'Seriously?'

'Swear down.'

Aster almost winced. *Swear down.* Who did he think he was, some sort of city gangster?

'You mean it's a fake?' she whispered, looking around the room.

'Wouldn't swear to it, but ask the mug that buys it and then cleans it what they find.'

'Wow. So, which one is the sleeper?'

He tapped the side of his nose. 'Now, that would be telling. Why don't we go and grab a drink after the auction, and I'll show it to you?'

She smiled and giggled, trying not to vomit, told him she would catch him later, and then drifted off to look at a small painting of a blue apple on a red chair.

'Like this one, do you?'

Aster counted to three. If he was intent on following her around, it might not be a bad idea. He would act as a camouflage. No one would pay attention to her when he was talking. She knew the sort. She turned and smiled at him brightly.

'I like it. It's funny.'

'Come on, let me show you the good stuff.'

Taking her elbow, he steered towards a small Caravaggio, the star piece of the auction.

'See that woman over there?' He pointed to the woman who had been declaring Aster's painting a masterpiece earlier. 'That's Hortense Jones. Well-respected art critic. You could pick up a few tips from her. Let's see what she says about the Caravaggio.'

As they approached, he stepped ahead of Aster and greeted Hortense fulsomely.

'A bit tame for you, isn't it?' he said and pointed to the image of the Caravaggio. It was a study of some flowers, rather than the usual grisly depictions for which he was well known.

'If the price is right, I'd be happy to add it to my collection. Plus the attribution and provenance are excellent.'

'Unlike some!'

'Indeed,' she laughed. 'I was just saying that I pity the fool that drops fifty k on that eyesore over there.'

Everyone turned to look at the large painting that now seemed to be shunned by most of the room.

'Not a fan?' asked Aster's companion.

'Please,' said Hortense languidly, as if she hadn't been extolling its virtues only minutes before. Deciding she had done as much as she could, Aster made her excuses and headed towards the ladies before the auction started. As she passed an older couple, she saw the man draw a line through his catalogue and was delighted to see the nuns' painting being scratched from their selection. In the ladies', two women were chatting about the Lowry incident.

'If they're not careful, Spencers are about to get burnt again.'

The damage was done. The gleaming facade of credibility had developed a hairline crack. Fixing her lipstick in the mirror, Aster headed back into the showroom.

By the time Aster made her final round of the room, the very air seemed thick with intrigue and insinuation. The painting still drew the eye, but now it was with morbid fascination rather than covetous awe. Like rubberneckers at a motorway pileup, the punters couldn't look away from the impending disaster, even as they speculated gleefully about the carnage to come.

Chapter Sixteen

A buzzer announced the beginning of the sale and gradually the bidders made their way through to the saleroom. Aster moved quickly to a side seat towards the back. The last thing she wanted was that city creep to follow her out of the auction house.

The auctioneer gavelled the room to order, his brows already glistening with anticipatory sweat. Aster settled in to watch the show. She would bid for a few lots before and after the nuns' painting but would ignore the main event. Again, it was essential that she was not seen playing any part in this sabotage.

The bidding moved at a brisk pace and Aster was pipped to the post on a few pictures, shaking her head each time as the bids rose higher. She watched her would-be suitor bid on a picture and started to bid against him just to up the price, then pulled out at the last moment. Hopefully, he had paid more than he hoped. He had turned once to see who was bidding against him and she couldn't resist a little wave as his scowl turned to a gallant smile when she stopped bidding.

It was time for Lot Seventy-Eight. The auctioneer cleared his throat and began his well-practiced spiel about the rarity, the quality, the unmissable beauty of the Madonna. But his words rang hollow in the sceptical silence of the room. No paddles stirred, no eager voices called out opening bids. Even as he dropped the starting price lower and lower, trying to coax some flicker of interest from his recalcitrant crowd, he was met with nothing but shifting feet and averted eyes.

Looking down at his laptop in hopes of some bids, he tapped on his screen. Frowning, he placed his hand over his mike, called out to one of the various members of staff standing around. Aster watched with interest as a technician bounced up onto the lectern and tapped the screen and then shook her head. The auctioneer addressed the room.

'Apologies, we seem to have lost our connection to the online bids.'

His colleague whispered to him and he addressed the room again.

'No, we have one bid, no two bids have been salvaged.'

Aster groaned. The plan had been that only Otto's remote bid would make it through. If the other bidder was determined, she was screwed.

'I have forty-five thousand, who'll offer fifty?'

Aster winced. Her instruction to Otto was to bail at fifty thousand.

'Fifty thousand pounds, fifty-five thousand pounds?' The auctioneer looked out into the silent auction call, his alarm mounting at the sea of amused or hostile faces.

Aster listened in dismay as the bidding climbed. She was completely screwed, she didn't know who she was bidding and didn't know if she should start bidding. But if she did, it might wake the room up. The auctioneer looked up from his screen.

'And I'm out at fifty-five thousand pounds. Any takers in the room?'

The painting had made its reserve, but how would the room respond? Deciding she was going to have to bid just to secure the painting, she was about to raise her paddle when the auctioneer clearly decided the lot was cursed. He brought his gavel down quickly to spare himself any further embarrassment.

Aster took a deep breath and swore to herself. Who had bought the painting? How was she going to track it now? Furious, she wanted to storm out of the room immediately but need to remain discrete. Instead, she watched as the little picture of the blue apple soared past its reserve. Hortense and her suitor battled over it for a while but eventually it sold to a man in a pinstriped suit for an eye-watering quarter of a million.

As the auctioneer called a pause after the excitement, Aster slid out of the room and walked out into the fresh air. Pulling her phone out of her pocket, she was about to call Otto when a familiar voice interrupted her thoughts.

'What about that drink, then?'

She turned and looked up to see Giles or Rupert or whatever the hell his name was.

'No.'

She turned and was about to stride off when he laughed. Something in his tone was so carefree that she turned to look back at him. He bowed and smiled at her, then winked. 'The name's Jimmy by the way. Nice playing with you.' And he turned and walked off in the opposite direction, disappearing into the London crowds.

Had that been one of Otto's stooges? If it was, he had played his role brilliantly. She was almost tempted to chase after him and find out, but it would have to wait. She needed to find out who had bought the painting.

Her phone buzzed and she saw Otto's number on the screen. Walking briskly away from the auction house, she hit accept and got straight to the point.

'What went wrong?'

'I did warn you we might not be able to isolate all the other lines.'

'But they bid up to fifty-five thousand. Bloody hell, Otto, now I need to find out who bought it.'

'We did.'

'What?'

'We bought the painting.'

'But I told you to only go up to fifty.'

'I know, but I have a good feeling about this painting. In the greater scheme of things, what's five k here or there?'

Aster could hear the laughter in Otto's voice. Trying to find an argument, she realised she had none and joined in the laughter as Otto continued.

'Are you off to tell the nuns the good news?'

'Can't, this is one of their seclusion days. No visitors. No communications.'

'Mon Dieu. These women.'

'I don't know, sounds idyllic to me.'

'Very well, how do you plan to celebrate?'

Aster thought and shrugged.

'Get on to the muslin suppliers. Interview a few of our local connections. Get online, play a few games. I don't know, something along those lines. Oh, and I also need to line up an art restorer, can you send me some recommendations? I might get the painting delivered directly to them.'

'I shall do that. But Aster, go out and play! Celebrate.'

'Really Otto, are you fussing?'

'Of course not. What do I care?'

As they hung up, Aster saw a text come in from Otto. *More fussing?*

-Jimmy wants your number?

Aster stopped walking and thought about it.

-No

And she continued to walk, then paused and shrugged to herself. Otto would have pre-vetted him. She wouldn't have passed the message on if she didn't trust him.

-Tell him to give me his. And I'll call if I feel like it.

-Will do.

Considering the matter settled, she headed home.

Her phone pinged again and she saw Jimmy had already given Otto permission to share his number. She grinned to herself. Maybe a night out would be good for her? As she walked, she pulled out her phone and fired off a quick text to Jimmy.

-Drinks later to celebrate our triumph?

She hit send with a grin, already anticipating the verbal sparring match sure to ensue. Anyone who could keep up with her antics was worth getting to know better, in her book. Plus she liked male energy. They were so straightforward, easy to deal with. Today had gone brilliantly and her only disappointment was that her stranger hadn't been present.

To hell with it. If she never saw him again, so be it. Her video was gaining traction online and she hoped she would get justice for those girls. Her own search for answers would have to wait. She had too many other projects to focus on and they had to come first.

Chapter Seventeen

Aster practically skipped down the sidewalk, her heart light and her steps buoyant as she made her way to the convent. Last night's drinks with Jimmy had been fun and light-hearted and she realised how much she had missed that. Just a simple night out with a mate, no plotting, no angles, just celebrating a plan gone well.

And now she couldn't wait to tell Sister Bernard the good news - the painting was safe, back in the hands of those who would truly appreciate its value. She was also gratified to see her video was gaining traction. It wasn't properly viral yet, but it was gaining ground. The comments were universally horrified, some asking why anyone was surprised. Others saying they drank there, tagging friends. There were also links to various studies and reports about what an under-reported crime this was. Aster was pleased to see others pointing out that there was no point in reporting the crime if the victim was ignored or dismissed.

The convent came into view, its weathered stone facade a welcome sight. As she slid her phone away, Aster bounded up the steps and pushed the heavy wooden door. She checked quickly in the chapel. Seeing it was empty, she returned to the corridor and knocked on the convent door. A moment later, the visitor's grille slid open to reveal Sister Joan's smiling face peering out, her eyes as rheumy as ever.

'Aster, dear! What a lovely surprise.' The old nun beamed at her. 'Come in, come in.'

'I was hoping to have a word with Sister Bernard?'

'Let me see. She has a visitor, but I'll let her know.'

The grille slid back and Aster paced in the stone corridor, ignoring the benches as she waited for Sister Joan's return. She had envisaged sweeping in to share her good news with the Mother Superior, but now she had to pace and wait.

The door swung open and Sister Joan beckoned her forwards.

'Her visitor has had to take a call, so she can see you briefly, if it's important?'

Aster would have liked more time, but good news couldn't wait. Saying that would be fine, she walked behind Sister Joan, shuffled along the hallway, Aster practically hopping from foot to foot behind her.

Knocking on the door, Sister Joan swung it open, announcing Aster.

'I think she's in a fearful hurry to tell you something, Mother.'

Turning, she patted Aster on the hand and the shuffled back along the corridor.

'Goodness me, child. You are quite giddy.'

Aster raised an eyebrow, but the nun waved away her indignation, pointing to her chair.

'Out with it,' she said. 'I take it from your grin that you have some good news for me. Let's have it, and then I can share my good news with you.'

For the first time, Aster properly noticed the Mother Superior. She was also smiling, beaming in fact, and her cheeks were flushed red. Whatever her good news was, Aster couldn't wait to hear it, but she bet it didn't beat what she was about to tell her.

'Sounds exciting, but here's mine. I got your painting back!'

Sister Bernard stared at her in confusion as Aster ploughed on.

'Your painting, the Pietà, the one you sold. It went into auction the other day and I bought it back!'

'I don't understand. You bought it? But-'

Aster cut her off and carried on.

'I'm pretty certain it's an old master. I think whoever you sold it to also knew that and was ripping you off.'

'No, but-'

'But it doesn't matter. I've bought it back and I'm going to get it restored and then you can re-auction it and sell it for oodles of cash. Enough to help your orphanage for years to come. Although I will need the cost of the renovation back, my sister is furious with me.'

'Aster, will you let me speak! I have the money from the sale. Edward gave it to me just now. He bought the painting with the intention of re-selling it and donating the profits to the convent.'

'What?' Aster stared at her in confusion. None of this made sense.

'The man who bought it wasn't conning us. He didn't tell me his intentions, but he was acting out of the purest motivations.'

'Why didn't he tell you?'

'He said he didn't want to raise our hopes. But now you bought the painting and want to give it back to us. Oh dear, I can't have the money and the painting. I must give you the money back.'

The nun's face fell as she realised her own good news had just disappeared up the chimney.

'What, no, that's not what I meant,' said Aster staring at the nun in horror. How had this gone so wrong, she was certain that the buyer was a conman?

There was a knock at the door and the nun told the visitor to enter. Aster didn't bother turning around as Sister Bernard jumped to her feet, a picture of dismay on her face.

'Sorry about that, I had to take that call.'

Aster flinched, she would know that voice anywhere, it haunted her every waking moment.

'Oh Edward, there's been a terrible confusion. My great friend here bought the painting, thinking we had been conned.'

Edward, this was Edward, this was the man that had bought the painting.

Aster leapt up, her chair falling backwards, and swung around to face him.

Edward's eyes widened slightly as he took in Aster's appearance. A flicker of recognition passed over his face before it settled into an impassive mask.

'You,' he said, his deep voice a mixture of surprise and something else Aster couldn't quite place.

Aster felt her cheeks flush as memories of that night at the club came rushing back. His strong arms around her, shielding her from harm. The intensity in his steel-blue eyes as he looked at her with concern.

'I… I didn't realise…' she stammered, suddenly flustered under his intent gaze.

Sister Bernard looked between them, bewildered. 'You two know each other?'

Edward was the first to recover. 'We've met,' he said evenly, never taking his eyes off Aster. 'Though I didn't catch your name that night.'

Aster swallowed hard, her mouth suddenly dry. 'Aster. My name is Aster.'

Sister Bernard had also risen to her feet. 'Aster, my dear. This is Lord Edward Montclair, Duke of Peveril. Edward, this is Lady Aster Byrne Hiverton.'

A ghost of a smile played across his lips. 'Well, Lady Aster, it seems we have a lot to discuss.' His tone held a hint of amusement, but also an undercurrent of protectiveness that sent a shiver down her spine.

She had no idea what kind of man this Edward truly was – a conman, a hero, a bloody duke of all things, but as she held his gaze, one thing was certain: her life had just taken an unexpected turn, and he was going to be at the centre of it all.

'You're the man who put the painting in the auction?'

'I am.'

He moved into the room and picked up Aster's chair, inviting her to sit before he brought another chair and sat down.

'And Aster is the person who bought it,' said Sister Bernard, glancing back and forth between the two of them.

Aster placed her hands under her thighs and tried to calm her racing heartbeat. Edward was too large for this room of small prayer cards and crochet doilies on the furniture.

'You bought it!' He glared at her. 'Did you have anything to do with the sabotage of that auction?'

'Of course she didn't,' said the nun quickly. 'Aster is one of our most thoughtful and generous of patrons. You two have a lot in common.'

'I did,' said Aster jutting her chin out defiantly.

'Aster!'

'I did nothing wrong. Your painting was being sold off for a song.'

'The painting sold for fifty-five thousand pounds, hardly a song, and it could have been even more if someone hadn't started spreading rumours.' He broke off, laughing. 'My God, that was you in the burqa, wasn't it? On the viewing day. I knew I recognised your voice! You've been planning this for weeks.'

'Since I first realised the nuns had been hoodwinked, actually.'

Edward's face flushed. 'Now hang on a minute–'

'No, you hang on. Before we go any further, we need to discuss the painting and your mistake.'

'My mistake?' He raised an eyebrow and chuckled. 'I bought a painting that I thought would sell well on the open market and I planned to give all the money to the nuns. How exactly was that a mistake?'

Emboldened by his attitude, Aster pressed on. 'You made a mistake in not having it restored or authenticated. The painting is clearly a work of the highest quality. Yesterday, someone was about to walk out with a bargain.'

'I don't consider fifty-five thousand pounds a bargain.'

'Nor do I, but it was better than letting it get sold to someone that wouldn't give the nuns its true worth.'

'But I would. That was the plan.'

'And what? Someone could have picked it up for two hundred, half a million?'

He narrowed his eyes. 'That sounds like an impressive amount to me.'

'Not for a Raphael it doesn't, or a Caravaggio.'

'What!' Now he looked startled.

'If it's an authentic old master, it would be worth millions, but in your ignorance, you tried to make a fast buck.'

Sister Bernard gasped, her eyes widening. Edward, however, simply inclined his head thoughtfully.

'I see. Then it seems I owe you an apology…' His gaze flickered to Sister Bernard briefly before returning to Aster.

Aster rose to her feet. She could feel her hands shaking and her breath was becoming unsteady. Memories of the nightclub were flashing in her head and she began to sweat.

'Sister Bernard, I'll be in touch once the restoration is complete and we'll look at re-selling it. In the meantime, spend the money that this man has just given you.'

'But I can't-'

'Yes, you can,' said Aster. Her voice shook as a tsunami of emotions engulfed her. Just being this close to Edward in an emotional state was bringing on what felt like a panic attack. 'I have the painting, you have the money. Leave it with me. I have everything under control.'

Without looking at Edward, she turned and fled from the room. The urgency in her step morphed into a full sprint as she exited the convent. Behind her, she could hear Edward calling her name and his footsteps growing louder, echoing through the corridor.

Bursting through the front door, she was blinded by the bright sunshine. Dodging traffic, she heard him shout her name again, his voice carrying a mix of confusion and frustration. She sprinted for the tube station, her heart pounding in her chest.

Leaping the barrier, she raced down the escalators. A quick glance behind revealed no sign of him. She fled onto the first train that was leaving, the doors hissing shut behind her.

As the train jerked forwards, Edward rushed down the stairs, his eyes frantically scanning the platform. Her heart raced even faster, but as the train pulled away, she realised he hadn't made it. Relief washed over her. She had escaped.

She weaved through the crowded carriage, finding a secluded corner where she could finally catch her breath. As she slumped onto the prickly seat, she put her head between her knees and tried to calm her racing heart. Why had she run? Why did she completely overreact in his presence? The questions swirled in her mind, but for now, all she could focus on was the rush of adrenaline and the fleeting sense of dismay.

Chapter Eighteen

By the time she got home, Aster decided she had had enough of being scared. This whole fight-or-flight response was out of control. She had allowed her emotions to take charge and because of that she was screwing up. It was time to focus. Pulling her phone towards her, she called her sister.

'Hey you, I need your help about this fabric.'

Clem's voice was an instant tonic. Straight to the point and distracted. She loved Clem to bits, but of all her sisters, she was the least perceptive, which was just what Aster needed right now.

'What do you need?'

Aster grinned. No how are you, how have you been, just *what do you need*. So she replied in kind.

'First, is this the stuff the same quality as ours?'

'One hundred percent.'

'And can it be made anywhere else?'

'Really unlikely.'

'Okay, is this our muslin?'

'No, I don't think so. Aisha tells me how much is being produced and that's what we receive.'

'And Aisha is?'

'She's our UK based contact for the Indian co-operative. She used to live over there, but we now employ her here. It turned out she had an excellent head for business and wanted to leave home so we set her up here. Lots of her cousins work in the factory out there, so she knows the business inside out.'

'And you trust her?'

'No reason not to. You met her at last year's summer party.'

Aster shrugged, at the summer parties she only had time for her family and people she knew. She never bothered with the outsiders.

'Okay. I've had a look at the people who are distributing the other version and they are highly suspect. Tomorrow I'm going to interview Aisha. And see if I get any sense that she knows what's going on.'

'That's not a good idea,' said Clem slowly.

'Why?'

'Because she's excellent at what she does. I don't want you upsetting her.'

Aster laughed. 'That's your forte, not mine. I'm just going to talk to her and try to understand the supply route. Incidentally, I've just sent you some photos. Have a look and tell me if I'm looking at stolen or counterfeit gear. It's definitely hooky.'

'Will do.'

Aster could tell Clem was about to hang up, but she jumped in quickly with a more personal question.

'How are you doing?'

'Life's shit and I'm a failure. Other than that, just peachy. All I'm good for now is selling fabrics and dressing patterns.'

'Oh well,' said Aster artlessly. 'Everyone has barren spells. And I bet those sewing patterns will sell really well. Don't be too hard on yourself. Talent doesn't last forever, you know. Now let me know what you make of those photos I sent you. Bye.'

'Hang on a minute!'

Aster ended the call and switched her phone off. Clem had been building up a head of steam and Aster had no wish to hear her sister explode. Sighing to herself, she hoped that goading her sister like that would spur her into action. Clem thrived on strong emotions. Aster hoped this would fire her back into gear. She only wished that she could manipulate her own behaviour as easily. As soon as she put the phone back down, her mind had switched instantly to Edward and her earlier meeting. This morning she had woken up smiling, delighted to have saved the painting for the nuns, and now she was back to square one. Jittery and distracted.

Shaking her head, she opened her laptop and dug into the Hiverton files until she found Aisha's contact details and work address. She'd call on her first thing in the morning. Finally, an e-mail from Otto gave her the details of a restorer that was looking forward to working on the painting. Aster dropped a note to the auction house to have the painting delivered to the restorer's workshop.

Giving her video one final check, she saw the numbers were still rising, but as yet Marcus Barrie hadn't been identified. Closing the laptop, she padded over to the kitchen, poured herself a glass of rosé and headed out into the garden. As dusk fell around her, she focused all her attention on Edward.

Now she had a name, soon she would have an address. And then what? Knock on his door? Run away like an idiot.

As she watched the stars come out, she replayed his words in her head. Each sentence rolled around in her head as she remembered how he had looked at her. His surprise — and was that relief, when he first saw her? And then his arrogance, telling her off for spoiling the auction. She smiled when she remembered how she had schooled him and pointed out that he had potentially risked losing a great treasure. But when he took a step towards her and looked down at her, she had felt an overwhelming connection as their eyes locked and she panicked.

Now as she sipped her wine, she wondered about that panic. Certainly, he was tall and good looking. His size was almost a threat and in that small room, Aster had nowhere to escape to. That was it. She had felt backed into a corner. Her flight was a perfectly normal response. Relieved that she had put her sense of unease to rest, she finished her glass and smiled to herself as an owl hooted in the distance.

Chapter Nineteen

Nero's Oyster Bar was bustling as the lunchtime crowd began to fill up the booths and a long glass-topped oak bar. Two men sitting at one of the tables were attracting a lot of attention. A handsome man in his thirties with a floppy blond fringe and a broad smile was posing for selfies for a group of women that had come over, phones in hand. One woman even tried to encourage the man's companion to join them. Equally as good looking as his friend, he seemed happier to stay out of the limelight and good-naturedly declined their pleading invitations.

As the women left, a waiter brought over a tray of oysters and laughing with the blond man, left them to it.

'Honestly Gummy, what do they see in you?' asked Edward shaking his head in disbelief.

Aston Fox, star of various reality TV shows and major influencer, also known as "Gummy" to his oldest friends on account of losing his front teeth when he fell off a horse, laughed and knocked back an oyster.

'I believe it's my devilish charm and handsome demeanour. Or from the look of that lass, it's my dining companion.'

'Spare me!'

'Not tall and blonde enough for you? Tell me, how is the delightful Alessandra?'

'I am sure she is delightful as ever, but I haven't seen her in a few months.'

'Did she tire of waiting?'

Edward rolled his eyes. Gummy knew there was nothing between him and Alessandra, but that didn't stop him from trying to make a mountain out of a molehill. Gummy was always the same. He loved a bit of gossip and was always the first with a juicy morsel. What Edward thought was to his credit, and why he counted Gummy as his best friend, was that he never gossiped in public. None of his friends' private lives ever made it onto his social channels and Edward respected the privacy.

'If you must know, she is now very happily engaged.'

'She found someone richer than you!' Gummy placed his hands on his face in mock horror.

'Now, that's unfair. Alessandra was never about the money. We just didn't have enough in common to properly click.'

'Oh, I see. How wrong I got her. No doubt she is engaged to someone that works nine to five. No wait, someone on benefits. Yes, that's much more in keeping with Alessandra's quiet and demure countenance.'

Edward's lips twitched. Given that her new fiancée's father owned the largest chip brokerage company in Monaco, he didn't think either of the happy couple would be on welfare any time soon.

Gummy laughed at his expression, slapping the table and pointing at his friend's face. 'I knew it! Tell me more!'

Edward shook his head and helped himself to an oyster, savouring the lemony salty juices. 'There's nothing to tell. We were only ever friends and I hope now she has found what she's looking for.'

'A healthy bank balance?'

'Happiness, you cynic. You should know all about that. Just how is Jane?'

Jennifer Jane Ferguson, or JJ to her fans, was the light in Gummy's life and had been his wife for the past three years and his saviour from the day he met her. During those early days of reality star fame and fortune, Gummy had gone slightly off the rails. In fact, his carriage was in freefall crashing down the mountainside. Addictions of all shapes and hues were creating a tsunami of troubles for Gummy and no matter how much Edward and his other friends and family tried to intervene, nothing proved successful until Jane waltzed into his life and dragged him back to the straight and narrow.

Now Gummy smiled. Just thinking about her made him smile.

'That girl is a bona fide angel. We're off to the Cairngorms next week for a spot of hiking.'

After years in the special forces, Edward found hiking for fun a strange pastime, but he did concede there could be beautiful aspects to it. If one wasn't on an actual mission that was, or in the Balkans at the height of winter.

'Work or pleasure?'

'Bit of both. We'll be staying at Houghborough Hall for the start and end, promoting their fine establishment. And what about you? How's work?'

'The same as always, paperwork, paperwork and more paperwork.'

'The joys of being a landlord.'

'Precisely.'

'And work work?'

Edward paused. Gummy knew all about his other job, the work he did for the government, but Edward never shared the details and both sides appreciated that Edward could only talk about it in the vaguest of terms.

'Something's coming up, as it happens.'

'Will you be gone long? Only Jane wants to invite you over for the weekend. Just Jane, you understand. I told her I was sick of your ugly mug.'

Edward laughed and tipped another oyster back.

'How can I resist such a lovely invitation? Please tell Jane I would be delighted. I think I'm going to be out of the country for a week or so, but nothing more than that.'

'And will you be bringing a guest?' asked Gummy, a sly grin on his face as he drank his Virgin Mary.

Edward wondered what on earth Aster would make of a weekend in Gummy's company? She'd probably chew him up and spit him out within five minutes. She didn't seem to be the sort that was easily impressed, but he thought she might like Jane.

Gummy put his glass down and stared at Edward until he felt uncomfortable under the scrutiny.

'Have you met someone?' He paused, reading Edward's face. 'My God, you have, haven't you? Someone that you are actually interested in! Bloody hell, mate, tell me more.'

Edward raised an eyebrow and then sighed. Gummy would not stop until he had the whole story. However, Edward wasn't prepared to talk about Aster. Maybe a crumb would do.

'There is a girl. But I've only met her twice.' He stopped, remembering her in the burqa. 'Three times actually, but I barely know her and she doesn't care for me.'

He picked up his own virgin mary. Normally he'd have some wine, but despite Gummy's insistence, it always felt wrong to drink alcohol in front of a recovering addict.

'Is that it? She doesn't care for you? That is a long way from the whole story. Where did you meet? What's her name and why on earth doesn't she like you? Has she met you?'

'We met at Whistles.' He stopped and realised he didn't want to say anything more about that. Aster had been the victim of an assault, and he wanted to protect her from that event. It wasn't his story, and he wasn't going to tell it.

'Go on.'

'She was there reluctantly. When we met, she was checking out the bookcase.'

'Oh my God, Edward, only you could find a bookworm in a nightclub. So then what?'

'Nothing. We parted ways, but I met her again yesterday where she accused me of theft and called me a leech and a moron.'

Gummy rocked back in astonishment then laughed loudly, drawing the attention of several other patrons.

'A thief! The Duke of Peveril, a common criminal. I thought your ancestors gave up sheep stealing centuries ago.' Gummy was in his element, chuckling along at Edward's discomfort. 'A first from Oxford, the richest man in London, and she calls you a leech and a moron. I tell you what Edward, I'm beginning to really like this girl. What's her name and what were you trying to steal?'

Edward was laughing along now as well. It was ridiculous. Maybe that was her appeal, but each time he thought of her he felt an incredible attraction. That he was meant to be by her side. Listening to what she had to say, sharing news with her, keeping her safe. He shook his head. There was no point in mooning after her. Gummy would only notice and dig deeper.

'Her name is Aster and I wasn't stealing anything. I was trying to raise some funds for a convent, but I goofed up.'

'You. Goofed. Up? Oh my God, this is priceless. The infallible Duke of Peveril goofed up trying to,' he paused, choking on his laughter, 'trying to help a bunch of nuns.'

Tears were streaming down his face now and Edward had the grace to blush. Aster was right, he was a bloody moron. He grinned sheepishly.

'It wasn't my finest moment.'

'Now I have to know everything! What does she look like tall, blonde, drop-dead glamorous?'

Edward thought about it. Instantly Aster was in his mind's eye and he smiled, simply picturing her as he shook his head.

'She's none of those. She's short, really short, has plain brown shoulder length hair that she tucks behind her ears, she has a little band of freckles across her nose, a small face but large eyes. But glamorous?' He laughed. 'You know when you watch a wildlife documentary about octopus?'

Gummy chuckled. 'She looks like an octopus?'

'No, you idiot. I mean there you are, looking at a piece of coral when suddenly it reveals itself as an octopus in camouflage. That's Aster. You don't notice her until she twitches her lips or raises an eyebrow and suddenly, she's the only thing that you can see.'

'Sounds like you have it bad. When are you next seeing her?'

'If she has her way, never. And that's probably for the best. I don't need any distractions right now.'

'You protest too much.' He paused to take a sip of his drink and then looked Edward straight in the face whilst waving an oyster shell at him. 'Word to the wise. Next time you do see her, for the absolute love of God, do not mention that she reminded you of an octopus.' He laughed and then continued on. 'So, full details. You met in Whistles. What was she doing there? How did the evening end?'

At which precise moment Gummy's phone rang and he stared at in dismay. Groaning in frustration, he answered the call and Edward knew he was off the hook. Gummy would only answer a call if it was important.

Ending the call, he knocked back an oyster and grimaced.

'That was Jane. Tilly has broken her ankle. I have to go. But come for the weekend and bring Aster. I want to know everything.'

Leaving with a hug, Gummy dashed out of the bar and Edward sat back down again. He could think of nothing he would rather do, but the chances of seeing her again were remote. He could certainly engineer another meeting now he knew who she was, but he wasn't certain if his ego could cope with another session in her company. As he finished his oysters in silence, he found himself smiling and by the time he left the bar, he was also whistling.

Chapter Twenty

The following morning, Aster drove to the Hiverton warehouse near Heathrow. The personnel files she'd pulled on Aisha painted a picture of a capable, dedicated employee. Originally from a small village in India, Aisha had jumped at the opportunity when Nick offered her a position coordinating the muslin production. Now married with two small children, her performance reviews were glowing, praising her efficiency and attention to detail.

As Aster pulled into the car park, she noted with approval the high security fencing and the sturdy gate that required a key code for entry. Her own pin didn't work, a clear sign that her advice about regularly changing access codes had been heeded. A far cry from the laughably lax security at that other warehouse she'd broken into a few weeks back.

She pressed the intercom buzzer, announcing herself. After a brief pause, the gate swung open with a mechanical hum. Aster drove through, parking her car in one of the designated visitor spots.

The warehouse loomed ahead, a huge, nondescript building that gave little indication of the treasures housed within. Aster made her way to the personnel entrance, where a security guard was waiting to buzz her in.

'Morning, miss. ID please?' The guard, a burly man in his mid-forties, held out his hand expectantly.

Aster handed over her driver's licence, watching as he scrutinised it carefully before cross-referencing it with something on his tablet. Satisfied, he handed it back to her with a nod.

'You're all set, Miss Byrne. Aisha is expecting you in the main office. Just follow the yellow line.'

Aster thanked him and stepped into the cavernous space of the warehouse proper. The air was cool and carried the faint scent of new fabric and packing materials. Overhead, the fluorescent lights hummed, illuminating row upon row of towering shelves stacked with bales of fabric.

As she walked, Aster took in the organised chaos of the place. Forklifts zipped to and fro, their beeping reverberating off the high ceilings. Workers in Hiverton livery bustled about, pulling items from shelves and packing them into neat stacks on pallets.

She passed a section dedicated to their licensed products, the ones inspired by the precious textiles unearthed in their family archives. There were tablecloths and napkins, curtains and cushion covers, all bearing patterns and motifs that had once graced the grand estates of the aristocracy. Seeing them mass-produced and ready for distribution to department stores across the country gave Aster a little thrill of pride.

But it was the far corner of the warehouse that drew her eye, the area cordoned off and marked with large signs proclaiming: 'Authorised Personnel Only'. Even from a distance, Aster could see the bolts of gossamer-fine muslin, their delicate folds seeming to glow under the industrial lighting.

That ethereal fabric, so painstakingly recreated from centuries-old seeds and weaving techniques, was the reason she was here. She needed to find out who was flooding the market with the cheaper muslin of suspicious origin, undercutting Hiverton's prices and potentially jeopardising the fledgling micro-industry they'd worked so hard to establish in India.

Aster tore her gaze away from the muslin and hurried on towards the offices. She needed answers, and Aisha was her first port of call. The woman oversaw every stage of the muslin production process, from the fields to the factories to the final product that arrived here in England. If anyone could shed light on where the hooky fabric was coming from, it would be her.

Aster reached the door marked 'Main Office' and knocked briskly. It was time to sort this mystery out, to protect both her family's business interests and the livelihoods of the artisans in India who depended on the muslin trade. She squared her shoulders as the door swung open, ready to face whatever revelations lay ahead.

Aisha greeted Aster with a warm smile, but her eyes held a flicker of nervousness. She ushered Aster into her office, offering her a seat and a cup of tea.

'Thank you for coming, Miss Byrne. I understand you have some concerns about the muslin production?' Aisha's voice was steady, but her hands fidgeted with a pen on her desk.

Aster leant forward, fixing Aisha with a probing gaze. 'I do. We've discovered some imitation muslin on the market, and it's eerily similar to ours. I was hoping you might have some insight into where it could be coming from.'

Aisha's brow furrowed. 'I'm afraid I'm at a loss, Miss Byrne. The fabric you mentioned, it's truly of a similar quality to what we produce?'

Aster nodded, pulling out a swatch of the counterfeit muslin and handing it to Aisha. The woman scrutinised it, her frown deepening.

'This is… disconcerting. The weave, the texture, it's nearly identical to ours. But I assure you, every yard of muslin that leaves our factories is accounted for. I oversee the process myself.'

Aster studied Aisha's face, noting the genuine confusion and concern. She didn't believe the woman was directly involved, but there was something she wasn't saying.

'Aisha, if there's anything else, anything at all that might be relevant, I need to know. The livelihoods of a lot of people depend on getting to the bottom of this.'

Aisha hesitated, worrying her bottom lip. Finally, she sighed and met Aster's gaze.

'There have been some… irregularities, back in the village. People leaving abruptly, without explanation. My family there, they've been tight-lipped about it. I've tried to ask, but they brush me off, change the subject.'

Aster sat up straighter. 'Leaving? Do you know who, or why?'

Aisha shook her head. 'No one will give me a straight answer. Our own production hasn't been affected, thankfully. We've been able to train new workers to replace those who left. But the whole thing has left me uneasy.'

Aster digested this information, her mind whirring. Aisha was right to be concerned. These unexplained departures, combined with the sudden appearance of the imitation muslin… there had to be a connection.

'Thank you for telling me this. I know it can't be easy, feeling cut off from what's happening back home. But you did the right thing in sharing your concerns. I promise, I'm going to clear this up.'

Aisha gave her a grateful, if strained smile. 'I appreciate that, Miss Byrne. If there's anything else I can do to assist, please ask.'

Aster assured her she would be in touch and took her leave, her mind already racing ahead. It was clear now that the key to unravelling this mystery lay in India, at the source of the muslin production.

She pulled out her phone and dialled Nick's number. Her sister picked up on the second ring.

'I need to go to India as soon as possible.'

Nick, to her credit, didn't waste time with unnecessary questions. 'Okay. Leave it with me. I'll have your travel arranged within the hour. Just send me the details of where you need to go and who you need to see.'

Aster felt a surge of affection for her ever-efficient sister. 'Will do. Thanks, Nick.'

As she ended the call and slid behind the wheel of her car, Aster couldn't suppress a thrill of anticipation mixed with trepidation. She was one step closer to the truth, but she had a feeling that the real challenges lay ahead, in the dusty villages and sprawling cities of India. But she was ready. She would unravel this tangle of secrets, no matter where the threads led her.

An hour later, true to her word, Nick phoned back.

'I've got you sorted,' she said without preamble. 'There's a British trade delegation flying out to India in a couple of days. Jones has got some big event going on over there. I pulled some strings and got you added to the delegate list.'

'Should I know who Jones is?'

'The Foreign Secretary. Honestly Aster, for someone as switched on as you, you are completely dead to politics.'

'That's because they come and they go and they don't do anything.'

'Well, Anthony Jones is doing loads. I swear that man's department never sleeps. And because they are so busy, they happen to be announcing some initiative or other and I've been able to get you a spot on the delegation.'

Aster grinned, picturing her sister's satisfied expression. 'Brilliant. Thanks, Nick.'

'They're all travelling business-class. Are you happy to go with them, or did you want to fly economy?'

Aster scoffed. 'Economy? Please. I'll go first-class.'

There was a beat of silence on the other end of the line. 'Aster,' Nick began, her tone a warning. 'Need I remind you that you just spent an unauthorised packet on a painting? Fifty-five k pounds to be exact.'

Aster winced, remembering Nick's fury when she'd discovered the charge to the Hiverton account. 'That was for the nuns, Nick. You know how important they are to me. To all of us.'

Nick sighed, and Aster could picture her pinching the bridge of her nose. 'I know. They did so much for Da when he was a lad. I've got a soft spot for them too. But Aster, you can't just go around making huge purchases like that without running it by me first.'

'I know, I know. I'm sorry. But I really believe that painting is worth far more than what I paid. It's going to do a world of good for the convent when we get it restored and reappraised.'

'It had better,' Nick grumbled. 'Fine. First-class it is. But Aster, please try to keep a low profile on this trip? The last thing we need is any more unexpected expenses cropping up.'

Aster grinned, knowing she'd won. 'I'll be a model of discretion,' she promised.

Nick snorted. 'I'll believe that when I see it. Your tickets and itinerary will be in your inbox within the hour. Keep me posted on what you find out over there, yeah?'

'Of course. And Nick? Thank you. I mean it.'

'Yeah, yeah. Just get to the bottom of this muslin mystery, will you? And Aster?'

'Yes?'

'Be careful. I know you can handle yourself, but we don't know what kind of hornets' nest you might be walking into over there.'

Aster sobered, recognising the genuine concern beneath her sister's brusque tone. 'I will. I promise.'

Deciding to bite the bullet, she spoke quickly before she could chicken out.

'On another subject, Nick, have you ever heard of a Duke of Peveril?'

'Edward Montclair? Owns half of London. Is that who you mean?'

Aster could hear that she had piqued her sister's interest.

'I think so. What do you know about him?'

'Not much. Something of a party animal, at least he appears as much in *Tatler* as he does in the *Financial Times*. Massively wealthy, but not reckless. Why do you want to know?'

'No reason,' said Aster appearing disinterested. 'I saw an article about him and just wondered if you knew him.'

Nick hummed and Aster knew her sister was still curious about her query.

'Anyway, India. Let me know when I'm good to travel. I want to get out there as soon as possible.'

As she rang off, Aster leant back in her chair, her mind already whirring with plans and possibilities. India. She'd been there before, during her post-university travels. She remembered the vibrant colours, the pungent spices, the crush and clamour of humanity. It had been an assault on the senses in the best possible way.

Growing up on a multicultural street in London, Aster had picked up bits and pieces of various languages. She could get by in Hindi and a smattering of other Indian dialects, a skill that had served her well on her previous visit. She was looking forward to putting it to use again.

Her computer pinged with an incoming e-mail notification. Her tickets, no doubt. Aster smiled. In two days, she'd be winging her way back to the subcontinent, chasing down the secrets behind the mysterious muslin. She could hardly wait.

But first, she had a video to boost. The damning montage of evidence against Marcus Barrie was already out there, picking up attention, but she needed it to go viral, to reach as many eyes as possible.

An idea struck her, and she reached for her phone, scrolling through her contacts until she found Jimmy's number. They'd had such a laugh at the auction house. Perhaps he could give her some tips on how to boost the video's reach.

She hit the call button, a smile playing about her lips as she waited for him to pick up.

'Jimmy,' she said when he answered. 'It's Aster. Listen, I need a favour. And I think you're going to like it. Fancy a night out? I'll buy the first round.'

She could practically hear his grin through the phone. 'Aster, love, you had me at *"I need a favour."* What are we getting up to this time?'

Aster laughed. 'Let's just say it's for a good cause. I can't give you all the details just yet, but trust me, you'll be doing a real solid for some people who deserve justice. Meet me at Whistles in an hour?'

'I'm intrigued and I'm in. See you in an hour.'

As Aster hung up, she felt a thrill of anticipation. With Jimmy's social media savvy, that video would be inescapable by morning. Barrie wouldn't know what hit him.

Smiling grimly, she closed her laptop and headed out to meet Jimmy. One more wrong to right before she turned her attention to the mystery waiting for her in India.

Chapter Twenty-One

Aster arrived at the Smelly Badger, one of the places featured in her video. Originally named Skunk's in an attempt to be hip and edgy, a patron had had a look at the sign of a skunk smoking a spliff and had immediately dubbed the pub the Smelly Badger. Despite a massive branding drive for Skunk's, the name stuck and the new landlord had even replaced the sign with a picture of a mucky badger.

Like all the venues featured in her video, Badgers had originally claimed no footage existed of the crime taking place. After that denial, Aster considered them fair game.

Now she scanned the crowd, her eyes seeking out Jimmy's familiar face. She was also making sure that Marcus Barrie wasn't in the building, she wasn't sure how she would respond if he was. Recently her emotions had been all over the place and she no longer trusted her ability to stay calm. Tonight she wanted to focus on increasing the reel's views not on her reactions.

The video she'd posted was gaining traction, but she really wanted it to take off, to reach as many people as possible. She hoped he would have some ideas on how to make that happen.

Relieved that she couldn't see Barrie, she quickly spotted Jimmy at a table near the back, his eyes lighting up as he caught sight of her. He stood, moving to greet her, his arms outstretched as if to pull her into a hug, his face angling for a kiss on the cheek. Aster quickly stepped back, offering a small wave instead. She liked Jimmy, but she didn't want him getting the wrong idea. This wasn't a date, and she wasn't a fan of physical contact. People were too touchy-feely for her liking.

She'd dressed accordingly, in jeans and a long-sleeved t-shirt emblazoned with the logo of a heavy metal band. Casual, comfortable, and decidedly unromantic. Jimmy, to his credit, took the hint gracefully, gesturing for her to take a seat as he settled back into his own chair.

'So, this video you mentioned on the phone,' he began, leaning forward conspiratorially. 'What's it all about?'

Aster glanced around, ensuring no one was within earshot before replying. 'See for yourself.'

Jimmy's eyes gleamed with interest. 'Let's have a look, then.'

Aster pulled out her phone, queuing up the video. As Jimmy watched, his expression morphed from curiosity to disgust to outrage. The montage showed footage from various clubs and bars, each clip depicting the same scenario – a single man spiking a woman's drink when her back was turned.

When it ended, Jimmy looked up at her, his face grim. 'This is bloody awful. That bastard has been doing this all over the city. And look, there's footage from right here at Badgers.'

Aster nodded. 'Every venue featured in this video has denied having any footage when asked. And yet, here it is, plain as day.'

Jimmy shook his head in disbelief. 'Unbelievable. And it's the same guy in every clip. Has anyone identified him yet?'

Aster kept her expression carefully neutral. She knew the man was Marcus Barrie, but his name hadn't come up in the comments yet. 'Not that I've seen. But someone out there must know who he is.'

Jimmy's jaw tightened. 'Well, whoever he is, he needs to be stopped. And whoever put this video together must have some serious skills, to get their hands on all this when the clubs were claiming it didn't exist.'

Aster shrugged. 'I suppose they must. The important thing is, it's out there now. And we need to make sure it's seen by as many people as possible.'

'If only we knew who to thank?' said Jimmy, pulling out his own phone. 'I think she's clearly quite the operator.'

'Or him. Although I do appreciate your gender bias.'

He looked at her and winked.

'Indeed. Now, watch and learn.'

He opened his TikTok account and checked in, making a quick video of himself at Badgers, panning around to show the bustling crowd. Aster watched, impressed, as he posted it, the likes and comments rolling in almost immediately. He clearly had quite a following.

As they waited for the views to climb, Aster probed a bit deeper into Jimmy's social media savvy.

'So, how did you get into all this?' she asked, gesturing to his phone. 'The influencer game, I mean.'

Jimmy leant back, a reminiscent smile playing about his lips. 'It started as a lark, really. I've always been a bit of a clown, love making people laugh. One day, I just started posting my antics online, and people seemed to enjoy it. It snowballed from there.'

Aster nodded, intrigued. 'And now you use your platform for more serious stuff too, like this video.'

'Exactly. I figured, if I've got this audience, might as well use it for good, you know? Shine a light on things that matter, things that need to change.'

Aster felt a surge of respect for the man sitting across from her. Beneath the cheeky exterior, there was a core of genuine decency, a desire to make a difference.

Their conversation was interrupted by a ping from Jimmy's phone. Half an hour had passed, and it was time for the next phase of the plan.

He posted again, this time with a more serious expression. 'I've just seen a really disturbing video,' he told his viewers. 'It's a montage of footage from clubs all over London, including right here in the good old Smelly Badger. The same man, spiking women's drinks, over and over. Funny how all these places claimed they had no security videos when asked, and yet, here we are. I think everyone needs to see this.' He shared Aster's reel, his face solemn as he urged his followers to spread the word.

Shortly after, two girls approached their table, barely sparing a glance for Aster as they focused on Jimmy.

'Jimmy, darling!' the taller of the two exclaimed, air-kissing his cheeks. 'Fancy seeing you here!'

'Chantelle, Lila, my favourite dynamic duo,' Jimmy greeted them warmly. 'Out on the town, I see. Featuring Badgers in your latest vlog?'

Chantelle giggled, flipping her long, platinum hair over her shoulder. 'You know it, babe. Our followers just love a good club recommendation. Speaking of which, what's this video you just posted? It looks serious.'

Jimmy's expression sobered. 'It is serious, love. Have a look.' He handed his phone over, the video cued up.

The girls watched, their perfectly made-up faces morphing from curiosity to horror. Lila gasped, her hand flying to her mouth.

'Oh my God, Jimmy. That's well bad.'

Jimmy nodded grimly. 'Afraid so, love. And every single one of these clubs denied having any footage when asked.'

Chantelle shook her head, disgust evident in her expression. 'We can't let this slide, Jimmy. We have to spread the word, warn people. And we need to find out who this creep is.'

'My thoughts exactly,' Jimmy agreed. 'I was hoping you girls might share the video, get it out to your followers.'

'Too bloody right,' Lila said firmly.

She paused, a thoughtful look crossing her features. 'You know, whoever put this video together must be really clever. To get footage that the clubs claimed didn't exist. That's impressive. You sure it's not fake?'

Jimmy glanced at Aster, a knowing look in his eyes. 'It's not fake. Let me just say I trust the source. Someone very dedicated to the truth, and totally legit.'

The girls huddled together over their phones, their fingers flying as they presumably shared the video with their own extensive networks. Jimmy sat back, a satisfied look on his face.

'That should do it,' he said, turning to Aster. 'Those two have a massive following. Combined with my lot, that video will be all over the internet by morning. And hopefully, someone will put a name to that face.'

Aster felt a rush of gratitude and relief. 'Thank you, Jimmy. Really. This means a lot.'

He waved away her thanks. 'Happy to help, love. Men like that, they deserve to be exposed. And those women deserve to know they're not alone, that people are outraged on their behalf.'

Aster clinked her glass against his, a silent toast to justice and solidarity.

Aster was about to respond when a large, imposing figure loomed over their table. She looked up, her heart jumping into her throat as she recognised Edward. Two days ago, his very presence had provoked a panic attack. She was relieved to find that today she could look up at him without overreacting. If only her heart rate would slow down.

He was even more striking than she remembered. Tall and broad-shouldered, with chiselled features and intense blue eyes that seemed to see straight through her.

Without a word, Edward reached out and snatched Aster's drink from the table, his eyes never leaving Jimmy's face. 'Who are you?' he demanded, his voice a low, menacing growl. 'And what are you doing with her?'

Jimmy blinked, taken aback by the sudden hostility. 'Mate, what's your problem? We're just having a drink.'

Edward's jaw clenched. 'I asked you a question. Who are you?'

Aster found her voice, outrage overriding her initial shock. 'Edward, what the hell are you doing? Put my drink down, now.'

He ignored her, still glaring at Jimmy. 'Answer me.'

Jimmy held up his hands in a placating gesture. 'Look, mate, I don't want any trouble. I'm Jimmy, I'm a friend of Aster's. We were just chatting, that's all.'

Aster stood, placing herself between the two men. She knew Edward, knew what he had done for her that night at the club, but his intensity, his protectiveness, still caught her off guard.

'Edward, stop it. Jimmy is a friend, and we're just having a conversation. You have no right to come over here and start making demands.'

Edward finally looked at her, his expression a mix of concern and something else, something intense and unreadable. 'Aster, we need to talk. Privately.'

Aster's heart raced. She had so many questions for him, so many blank spaces in her memory that only he could fill. She needed to know what had happened that night, needed to retrace her steps and reclaim the hours she had lost.

But she couldn't do that with Jimmy here. She needed him to leave, needed to talk to Edward alone.

She turned to Jimmy, an apologetic smile on her face. 'Jimmy, I'm so sorry about this. Would you mind letting us talk privately? I promise I'll explain everything later.'

Jimmy looked between them, confusion and concern warring on his face. 'Aster, are you sure? I don't feel right leaving you alone with him.'

Aster placed a reassuring hand on his arm. 'I appreciate your concern, Jimmy. But I know Edward. He's... he's not a threat to me. Please, I need to speak with him. Alone.'

Jimmy hesitated, clearly torn. But the pleading look in Aster's eyes seemed to sway him. With a sigh, he nodded.

'Alright, love. If you're sure. But you call me if you need anything, yeah? I mean it. Anything at all.'

Aster smiled, genuine warmth and gratitude flooding through her. 'I will. Thank you, Jimmy. For everything.'

With a final, concerned glance at Edward, Jimmy gathered his things and stood. 'I'll talk to you tomorrow, Aster. Stay safe.'

As Jimmy headed off through the crowd, he turned and looked at her, pointing to a group of people all looking at their phones. He raised a thumbs up to her as he turned and left. The plan was already working, and she was delighted, but now she had to deal with Edward. Aster turned to him, her heart pounding, her mind whirling with questions. But before she could speak, Edward held up a hand, his expression grave.

'Aster, before we go any further, there's something you need to know. Something that's come to my attention.'

Aster frowned, a sense of unease creeping up her spine. 'What is it?'

Edward glanced around the crowded club, then leant in closer, his voice low and urgent. 'A video. It's been circulating online. It shows… it shows women being drugged. Here, in this pub, as well as others.'

Aster's blood ran cold. The video. The one she had helped create, had helped to spread. But how did Edward know about it? She schooled her features into a mask of surprise. 'What? That's… that's horrible.'

Edward nodded, his jaw tight. 'There's more. Aster, you… you might be in the video. Your face is obscured, but I recognised you. From that night.'

Aster's heart hammered in her chest. She had taken great pains to obscure herself and yet he recognised her. How had he done that?

'I don't understand,' she said, her voice carefully controlled. 'How can you tell it's me?'

His expression was kind as he smiled at her gently.

'The video, all the incidents are dated and time stamped. I was there. It would be too much of a coincidence. Besides, there are two girls in that clip and the one who takes the drink is considerably shorter.'

Aster nodded, his deduction was perfect and he did have additional information, but she was keen that no one else worked it out. But why was he here?

'What does this have to do with you?'

Edward sighed, running a hand through his hair. 'I own some of those places in the video. Including this one.'

Aster's world tilted on its axis. Edward, the man who had saved her, who had shown her such kindness and care… he was responsible for this? For the lies, the cover-ups?

Acidic fury surged through her veins, her mouth flooded with bile. She stood abruptly, her chair scraping against the floor. 'You own this place? This place that lied about having security footage? That covered up for a predator?'

Edward's eyes widened, his hands coming up in a placating gesture. 'Aster, wait, let me explain-'

'Explain what?' she snapped, her voice rising. 'How you could be party to something so vile? How could you sit back and let it happen?'

'It's not like that,' Edward insisted, his own frustration clear. 'I don't own the business, Aster. I own the property. The building. I had no idea what was going on here, I swear.'

Aster stared at him, confusion warring with anger. 'What do you mean, you don't own it?'

Edward sighed, pinching the bridge of his nose. 'I'm a property investor, Aster. I buy buildings, I rent them out to businesses. Badgers, like Whistles is one of my tenants. But I have no say in how they run their operation.'

Aster's mind raced, trying to process his words. She already knew this, Nick had said as much. But the hurt, the sense of betrayal, still stung. 'You should have known,' she said, her voice quieter but no less fierce. 'You should have been paying attention.'

Edward's shoulders slumped, guilt and regret etched into every line of his face. 'You're right. I should have. And I'm sorry, Aster. More sorry than I can say.'

Aster looked away, blinking back the sudden sting of tears. She didn't know what to think, what to feel. The man who had been her saviour, her protector… he was tangled up in this mess, even if unknowingly.

'I need to go,' she said, grabbing her bag. 'I can't… I can't do this right now.'

Edward reached for her, then seemed to think better of it, his hand falling back to his side. 'Aster, please. Don't go. Not like this.'

But Aster was already moving, weaving through the crowd towards the exit. She couldn't be here, couldn't be near him. Not now. Not with her emotions in such turmoil, her thoughts such a jumbled mess.

She burst out into the cool night air, gulping in deep breaths. Her phone buzzed in her pocket – it was from an unknown number. Opening it up, she stared at the following message.

- Portman House, Portman Lane. 12:00. Edward. Feel free to bring a friend.

Aster took a deep breath, giving the driver her address. She had come looking for answers, but had only found more questions. More complications.

But one thing was crystal clear. The mystery of that night, of her lost hours… it was inextricably tied to Edward. And whether she liked it or not, she knew she would have to face him again.

But not tonight. Tonight, she would go home, would try to clear her head and steady her heart. She had a trip to India to prepare for, a case of textile fraud to unravel.

Chapter Twenty-Two

Aster woke with a start, her hand instinctively reaching for her phone on the bedside table. She'd never been one for sleeping with her phone nearby, valuing her privacy and peace of mind above all else. There was a time, not so long ago, when she'd revelled in the freedom of disconnecting from the world, of leaving behind the constant buzz and chime of notifications.

She remembered that trip vividly, a solo trek through the lush, mist-shrouded mountains of Kyrgyzstan. For two glorious weeks, she'd switched off her phone, deleted her social media apps, and simply lived in the moment. She'd woken each morning to the soft trilling of exotic birds, spent her days hiking ancient trails and her nights marvelling at the brilliance of stars untouched by light pollution. It had been a revelation, a glimpse of a simpler, more profound way of being.

But then, upon her return, reality had come crashing down. Nick, her unflappable, always-in-control sister, was in the midst of a crisis. Her company was on the brink of bankruptcy, targeted by a malicious campaign of sabotage and slander. And where had Aster been? Off finding herself in the mountains, blissfully unaware whilst her family needed her.

The guilt had been overwhelming, a lead weight in her gut. Never again, she'd vowed. Never again would she prioritise her own desires over the needs of those she loved.

Now, her phone was always within arm's reach, a constant tether to her family and their wellbeing.

Blinking away the remnants of sleep, Aster squinted at the screen. A text from Jimmy caught her eye, urging her to check her social media. Opening up her apps, her eyes widened. Her feeds were in a frenzy, her video going viral in a big way.

Marcus Barrie's name was everywhere, plastered across posts and comments, tagged in shares and reposts. The court of public opinion had clearly found him guilty, and they were baying for blood. Aster felt a grim sense of satisfaction. The bastard was finally getting what he deserved.

As she scrolled further, another piece of news caught her attention. Badgers, along with three other clubs implicated in the video, had posted statements claiming they were currently closed until further notice. No further details were forthcoming. Had Edward been part of that? He said he owned the premises and he was aware of the video.

Aster sat back against her pillows, her mind whirling. The progress was heartening, a sign that her efforts were paying off. But her satisfaction was tinged with anxiety as she remembered her upcoming appointment with Edward at noon.

She thought of his revelation that he owned the property that housed Whistles, of the hurt and betrayal she'd felt at the realisation. A part of her dreaded facing him again, of reopening those raw wounds. But another part, the part that remembered his kindness, his protection that night, knew she needed answers. Needed closure. Glancing at the clock, Aster saw she had a few hours yet before she had to confront that particular demon. Enough time to savour her victory with the video, to revel in the knowledge that she'd helped bring a predator to justice.

She swung her legs out of bed, padding towards the bathroom. As she went through her morning ablutions, her mind continued to churn. The social media storm, the club closures, it was all a step in the right direction. But Aster knew it was only the beginning. Until those women got justice and Marcus Barrie was in jail, she wouldn't be satisfied.

Happy that she had got the ball rolling, she logged into the TikTok account she had created to launch the video and deleted it. She had created it using the free library internet, so the IP wasn't traceable and she'd faked a library card, so even that couldn't be traced back to her. Now that the video was viral, she could remove all traces of the original post. She knew that would add more intrigue to the story - who was the original poster? - but that couldn't be helped. She didn't want to be part of the story. Every other girl featured had agreed and she hoped that today would be the first step towards justice. She knew the police were unlikely to take action if no one came forwards, but she hoped that with the evidence she had compiled someone would feel confident enough that the system would support them.

Decisively, she silenced her phone and set it aside. She had research to do, logistics to arrange. Pulling out her laptop, she lost herself in the task, poring over travel advisories, weather forecasts, and cultural guides. The hours slipped by, the outside world fading away as she immersed herself in the intricacies of her impending journey.

It wasn't until her alarm chimed, jolting her out of her concentration, that Aster realised how much time had passed. She glanced at the clock and gulped. 11:30 AM. Half an hour until her meeting with Edward.

A sudden wave of nerves washed over her, her stomach twisting into knots. She'd been so focused on her trip, on the mystery of the muslin, that she'd almost forgotten about this other looming confrontation.

Shaking her head, Aster snapped her laptop shut and rose to her feet. She wouldn't let fear rule her, she faced challenges head-on, no matter how daunting.

The address Edward had given her was burning a hole in her pocket. Portman House, Portman Lane. Less than a mile away. She left the house before she could talk herself out of it. As she walked, a nagging sense of familiarity tugged at her. These streets, these buildings - she'd been here before. It wasn't until she turned onto Portman Lane that it hit her. She and Paddy, they'd walked this very route, that day they'd scoured Mayfair for any trace of her lost memories. But even then, even retracing her steps, Portman House had rung no bells. The revelation sent a chill down her spine.

As Aster approached the imposing facade of Portman House, she spotted an unexpected sight that stopped her dead in her tracks. There, sitting on the front steps, was Edward, a flask and a picnic basket by his side.

He looked up, catching sight of her, and a warm smile spread across his face. He raised a hand in greeting as Aster slowly approached, her confusion and nerves momentarily forgotten in the face of this bizarre scene.

'Aster,' he called out. 'I thought you might be more comfortable sitting outside. It's such a lovely day.'

She blinked, taken aback by his thoughtfulness. But then her gaze flicked to the surrounding houses, the immaculate facades and perfectly manicured gardens. This was Mayfair, one of the most affluent areas in London. What would the neighbours think, seeing them picnicking on the front steps like a couple of bohemians?

'Edward, I'm not sure this is a good idea,' she began, her voice low. 'People might talk.'

But Edward just shrugged, his smile never wavering. 'Let them. I don't give two figs what they think. You're more important.'

Aster felt a flush creep up her neck. It was a kind gesture, a considerate one. But the idea of being the centre of attention, of curious eyes and wagging tongues, made her skin crawl.

'I appreciate the thought,' she said, choosing her words carefully. 'But I think I'd be more comfortable inside, away from prying eyes. If that's alright with you.'

Edward's eyes softened, understanding dawning in their blue depths. 'Of course. Whatever makes you comfortable, Aster. That's all I want.'

He stood, gathering up the picnic accoutrements, and gestured for her to precede him into the house. Aster climbed the steps, her pulse thumping and crossed the threshold into the cool dimness of the entryway. She hesitated and waited for a sense of dread or recollection, but she felt nothing. The hall was familiar, but only because she'd seen it on the USB stick. There was nothing else.

She heard the door click shut behind her, heard Edward's footsteps on the hardwood floor. This was it. No more delaying, no more distractions. It was time to face her demons, to uncover the truth of that lost night.

'Cup of tea?'

Aster nodded but couldn't summon a smile.

Edward led Aster into a spacious, well-appointed kitchen. Sunlight streamed through the large windows, illuminating the gleaming marble countertops and high-end appliances. As Edward filled the kettle and set it to boil, Aster found herself drawn to the view outside.

The kitchen overlooked a stunning, meticulously landscaped garden that wouldn't have looked out of place at the Chelsea Flower Show. Soft drifts of planting in varying shades of green, purple, and white created a soothing, almost dreamlike atmosphere. Water features were artfully placed throughout, their gentle bubbling and splashing adding to the tranquil ambiance.

A winding gravel path meandered through the garden, inviting visitors to explore the different areas. Aster could make out a secluded seating area nestled beneath a pergola draped in fragrant wisteria, its delicate lavender blossoms swaying in the breeze. The garden was a masterpiece of design, each element carefully chosen and placed to create a harmonious whole. It was the sort of space that Ariana would approve of.

Aster watched as a pair of butterflies danced among the blooms, their delicate wings catching the sunlight. The scene was so idyllic, so removed from the turmoil of the past few days, that for a moment she almost forgot why she was here.

The whistle of the kettle jolted her back to the present. She turned to find Edward watching her, a small smile playing about his lips. 'Beautiful, isn't it?' he said, nodding towards the garden. 'It's my little slice of paradise in the city.'

Aster nodded, suddenly feeling awkward. The domesticity of the scene, the casual intimacy of being in Edward's home, was throwing her off balance. She needed to focus, to remember why she'd come.

'Edward,' she began, as he poured the boiling water into a teapot. 'About last night, at the club. The way you acted towards Jimmy… it wasn't right.'

Edward stilled, his hand hovering over the teacups. For a moment, Aster thought he might argue. But then he sighed, his shoulders slumping slightly. 'You're right. I overreacted. I was having a bad day, and then I saw you with a strange man and I just… I was worried. After what happened to you, I couldn't bear the thought of history repeating itself.'

Aster softened slightly at the genuine concern in his voice. But she wasn't ready to let him off the hook just yet. 'I appreciate your concern, Edward. But Jimmy is a friend. A good one. He deserves an apology.'

Edward met her gaze, his blue eyes sincere. 'You're right. I'll make it right with him, I promise.'

Aster nodded, satisfied for now. She watched as Edward poured the tea, the familiar ritual soothing her frayed nerves. As he handed her a steaming cup, she remembered the news she'd read that morning.

'I saw several clubs have been shut down,' she said, blowing gently on her tea. 'In the wake of the video going viral.'

Edward's jaw tightened, a flicker of anger passing over his face. 'Yes. I visited all the properties I own that were featured in that video. I cancelled their leases on the spot. I was livid, Aster. They'd all denied having security footage, had covered up these crimes. It was unforgivable. I've forwarded all their details to the authorities. The police will be able to formally request those video files.'

Aster scoffed, a bitter edge to her voice. 'The police? They'll probably just file it away and forget about it. They've never been particularly helpful or proactive in cases like these.'

Edward sighed, understanding her frustration. 'I know it feels that way, Aster. The system is far from perfect. But we have to try. We have to use every avenue available to us.'

He leant forward, his elbows resting on his knees. 'Look, some forms of justice can be swift. Like cancelling leases, cutting ties with those who enable this behaviour. Or posting videos that expose the truth, that rally public outrage. We've seen the power of that in just the last twenty-four hours.'

Aster nodded, acknowledging the point. The video had indeed sparked a swift and fierce reaction, a groundswell of anger that couldn't be ignored.

'But other forms of justice,' Edward continued, 'they take time. They require due process, evidence, a chance for the accused to defend themselves. It's slow and it's frustrating, but it's necessary. For true, lasting change.'

Aster sat back, she knew he was right. Vigilante justice, satisfying as it might feel in the moment, wasn't always a long-term solution. They needed the weight of the law behind them, the legitimacy of the courts. But she was surprised by his relaxed attitude towards people taking the law into their own hands. But then, she had often noticed that those with the most wealth and power thought the law didn't apply to them.

Edward leant back in his chair, a thoughtful expression on his face. 'You know, whilst some things need to go through legal channels, there are other, more indirect routes that can certainly get the ball rolling.'

Aster raised an eyebrow, curious. 'What do you mean?'

A small smile played at the corners of Edward's lips. 'I noticed you took your video down. The one exposing Marcus Barrie.'

Aster's heart skipped a beat, but she kept her expression carefully neutral. 'I don't know what you're talking about.'

Edward's smile widened, a knowing glint in his eye. 'Don't you? It's okay, Aster. I put it together last night. Only someone involved in the spiking incidents could have compiled that footage. But they'd need to be ruthless, determined, clever… and with a scant regard for the law.'

He paused, holding her gaze. 'And then I thought, I've recently met someone just like that. Someone who orchestrated that brilliant deception at the auction.'

Aster sat in bemused silence, her mind racing. How had he figured it out? She'd been so careful, so meticulous in covering her tracks.

As if reading her thoughts, Edward chuckled softly. 'Don't worry, your secret's safe with me. In fact, I'm in awe of what you've accomplished. The risks you've taken to bring that man to justice.'

Aster finished her tea and stood, her expression frosty. 'I appreciate the compliment, Edward. But I really don't know what you're talking about.'

She moved towards the front door, her steps measured and deliberate. Edward followed.

At the threshold, Aster paused, turning to face him. 'Thank you for giving me your address. It's helped me understand my route that night, to fill in some of the blanks. But I think our acquaintanceship has run its course.'

Edward's smile never wavered. 'Has it? I rather think it's just beginning.'

Aster's eyes narrowed. 'I hope not.' She winced as she heard how stilted her speech had become, but there was something about Edward that brought out the very worst in her. 'I think it's best we go our separate ways.'

She stepped out into the sunlight, her head held high. Edward watched her go, a mix of amusement and respect playing across his features.

'Tell me, have you made any progress with the painting?'

Aster paused, he had no right to know how things were going but she understood his interest. She shrugged, tipping her head to one side.

'No news yet.' So far, all she knew was that the bills were mounting up. Nick was sending her weekly accounts of the amount of money that was being sunk into the restoration.

Every text was more terse than the last and Aster knew that her financially astute sister was running out of patience. On the other hand she was receiving texts from Otto saying that it was all very exciting and passing every test being set. 'We're hopeful of a positive outcome,' said Aster turning to leave. 'Now, thank you and goodbye.' Taking a deep breath she walked down the steps and wondered at her reluctance to leave.

'We'll meet again, Aster Byrne,' he called after her. 'I promise you.'

Aster didn't look back, didn't falter in her stride. But as she walked away from Portman House, she couldn't help wondering: was that a promise, or a threat?

Chapter Twenty-Three

Aster swept through Heathrow's Terminal Five, her carry-on bag rolling silently behind her. She'd timed her arrival precisely, aiming to minimise interaction with the trade delegation before the flight. The upgrade to first-class had been a necessary extravagance, ensuring a reprieve from forced small talk and prying questions.

As she approached the first-class check-in desk, Aster smiled as the attendant checked her in.

'Good afternoon, Lady Aster. Checking in for the flight to Mumbai?'

Aster nodded, handing over her passport and booking reference. As the attendant processed her paperwork, Aster's gaze drifted to the nearby business-class desk, where a small gathering of people wearing matching lanyards were huddled.

'Lady Aster Byrne!' A shrill voice cut through the airport noise, laced with a hint of resentment.

Aster turned, her face an impassive mask, to see a short, plump woman with frizzy red hair marching towards her. The woman's lanyard bounced aggressively as she moved.

'I'm Penelope Hardwicke, the delegation coordinator,' she announced, a touch too loudly. 'We were expecting you to check in with the group, Lady Aster.' The emphasis on Aster's title carried a note of disdain.

'Ms Hardwicke,' Aster replied coolly, 'I'm afraid my schedule didn't allow for that. I'm sure you understand.'

Penelope's eyes narrowed, her lips pursing. 'Well, now that you're here, we need to go over the itinerary and protocols. The minister is joining us in a few days and I can't stress how important it is that things run smoothly and everyone plays their part.' The last words dripped with barely concealed disdain.

'I'm certain all necessary information will be provided on the flight,' Aster responded, her tone glacial. 'Now, if you'll excuse me.'

Before Penelope could retort, a tall, lanky young man with thick-rimmed glasses approached. 'Lady Aster! It's an honour to meet you. I'm Ethan Croft. I've been working with your sister Nick on Hiverton's tech initiatives.'

Aster's expression thawed ever so slightly at the mention of her sister. 'Mr Croft. Nick has spoken of your work.'

Ethan beamed. 'She's brilliant, isn't she? The way she's integrated blockchain technology into the muslin supply chain is revolutionary. I'm hoping to expand on that during this trip.'

A ghost of a smile played at the corners of Aster's lips. 'Indeed. Nick's always one step ahead'

Penelope, clearly miffed at being sidelined, interjected. 'Yes, yes, very nice. Now, Lady Aster, about the delegation protocols—'

'I'm sure Mr Croft can brief me, if necessary,' Aster cut her off smoothly. 'Now, I have some urgent matters to attend to before we board. Good day, Ms Hardwicke. Mr Croft, I look forward to hearing more about your work with Nick in Mumbai.'

Penelope, clearly frustrated by Aster's dismissive attitude, pressed on. 'Lady Aster, I must insist we go over your schedule. We have a series of engagements planned—'

'I'm afraid that won't be necessary,' Aster interjected coolly. 'I'll be travelling on to Kolkata directly after our arrival. I won't be available for any Mumbai events.'

Penelope's face reddened. 'But that's not possible! As part of the delegation, you're expected to attend all events. Especially the High Commissioner's black-tie gala!'

'As I've said, Ms Hardwicke, it won't be possible,' Aster repeated, her tone brooking no argument.

Penelope's eyes narrowed. 'The gala is on the final night. You'll be back in Mumbai to catch the return flight the next morning. There's no reason you can't attend.' She paused, then added with a hint of triumph, 'Nick assured me you would be there.'

Aster felt a flicker of surprise, quickly masked. She nodded curtly, realising she'd been outmanoeuvred by her sister. Nick had found a way to make her pay for the first-class upgrade, after all.

'If you'll excuse me,' Aster said, her voice cool and controlled, 'I believe they're boarding first-class now.'

Without waiting for a response, she turned on her heel and strode towards the first-class gate, leaving behind a smugly satisfied Penelope and a bemused Ethan.

As she walked away, Aster allowed herself a small, rueful laugh. Nick had played her masterfully, ensuring she couldn't completely avoid her obligations to the delegation. It was a reminder that her sister was always thinking several moves ahead.

Boarding the plane, Aster was momentarily distracted by the opulence of the first-class cabin. Soft lighting glowed off polished wood and buttery leather, creating an atmosphere more akin to a luxury hotel than a plane. Each seat was a private pod, a cocoon of comfort and exclusivity.

As she settled into her plush seat, Aster's mind drifted to her wardrobe crisis. The emerald silk dress was lovely, but hardly appropriate for a High Commissioner's gala. Perhaps an emergency shopping trip in Mumbai? Or maybe she could convince Clem to overnight something suitably glamorous…

So engrossed was she in mental fashion logistics that she barely registered the presence beside her until a familiar voice broke through her reverie.

'Well, if it isn't my favourite auction saboteur.'

Aster's head snapped up, her eyes meeting Edward's twinkling gaze. He lounged in the adjacent seat, looking unfairly handsome and entirely too pleased with himself.

'Edward?' Aster spluttered, composure momentarily deserting her. 'What the hell?'

He grinned, clearly enjoying her discomfort. 'Why, I'm part of the delegation too. Complete coincidence, I assure you.'

Aster's eyes narrowed suspiciously. 'Oh really? And what's your role in all this?'

'Just some work with a small government agency,' Edward replied airily. 'Looking into a few… issues.'

'How conveniently vague,' Aster muttered.

She glanced around desperately, hoping to spot an empty seat, but the cabin was full. With a huff, she reached for the partition between their seats, slamming it closed.

Edward's voice drifted through moments later, addressing a flight attendant. 'A glass of champagne for myself and my lovely companion, please.'

The partition flew open again, Aster fixing Edward with a glare that could melt steel. 'I am not your companion,' she hissed.

Edward merely winked at the flight attendant, who giggled at their antics.

Aster glared at her.

'I'll have a grapefruit juice, please.' Sliding the partition closed again, she waited until the attendant brought her glass around to her side. Aster was amused to see she was served by a different attendant. No doubt it was policy not to annoy or upset the first-class passengers. The first attendant's giggling had been very unprofessional in Aster's eyes.

Annoyed with herself for being so easily bothered, she pulled out her phone and sent Nick a quick message seeing if she could duck out of the function. The response was quick and brutal. If she failed to attend, she would let the family down. Aster hissed. Every time, Nick was one step ahead.

'Problems?'

Edward's disembodied voice drifted through the partition.

'No.'

'Maybe I can help?'

'With my lack of problems?'

'I heard a hiss. Maybe there's a snake on board. Should I call an attendant?'

'For a snake?'

'Who knows? Apparently, Hollywood made a successful film on that very premise.'

Aster's lips twitched. She liked the sense of ridiculousness.

'And what if you start a panic?'

'Well, the source of that hissing needs to be located.'

Aster smiled at the humour in his voice and slid open the screen.

'If you must know, I was trying to get out of this ball at the end of the week.'

Edward raised an eyebrow. 'Not one for social engagements?'

'Hardly.'

'Maybe you could bring a book?'

Aster frowned trying to work out why that was familiar.

'A book? We've joked about books before, haven't we?'

For a moment, a deep scowl flashed across Edward's face. Then it was gone, replaced by a warm smile like a sunny day.

'It was in the nightclub. We both agreed the music was dreadful and that the very least the club could do was to provide a quiet reading spot.'

'Ah, right.' Aster nodded and then looked out of her window. A silence fell between them and she turned back awkwardly. She had nothing to fear from him. 'Thank you. I think what I hate most about that evening is the lack of memory.'

'Not feeling powerless? You strike me as someone who would hate that.'

'Oh, I do,' she laughed ruefully. 'But even when I've seemed to be in a powerless state in the past, my brain has been working overtime to develop solutions, things I can do or get others to do to improve the situation. But that night…' She sighed. 'That night, I wasn't even present. I didn't even know I was powerless, that I was in danger. I mean-' She trailed off, biting her lip. 'Anyway. Every scrap of memory that I can claw back from that evening and the following day is a godsend, and even if I can't remember it, it's good to know about it.'

Uncomfortable at having said so much, Aster looked out the window again.

'So, about this ball. Apart from the desire to be anywhere but there and no books to read, have you any other objections?'

Aster was about to reply, but broke it off laughing. Her answer sounded inane. As she looked at Edward, his eyebrows shot up and she realised how rarely she laughed.

'It's just, and I know this sounds insanely dumb, I have nothing to wear.'

'Then I think your solution is obvious.'

'Buy a dress?'

'No. You don't want to go. So don't go.'

'I have to go.'

'You don't have to do anything.'

'Of course I do. My sister said so.'

'And…'

'And clearly you don't have any siblings.'

'I don't, but if I did, I still wouldn't do things just because they said so.'

'We have a different sense of family. I will do anything for mine.' She stared hard at him. 'Anything. What if your parents asked you to do something? You'd do it for them, wouldn't you?'

'I guess, but they died when I was twenty.'

Aster had been leaning towards him, engaged in the conversation but now she recoiled. It was too much. She was overwhelmed. He had no family. Nothing. And the pain of losing her own folks suddenly came crashing down on her as she contemplated losing her sisters as well. The plane began to taxi.

'Are you okay?'

Lost in her own thoughts, Aster shook her head, trying to dismiss the uncomfortable bond between them.

'Yes. I'm sorry about your family.' She picked up a book and nodded towards it. 'Look, I'm just going to read now. Excuse me.'

Closing the partition between them, she took a sip of her grapefruit juice, but it tasted too sour. She put it to one side and wondered just how much more this flight could screw up.

Chapter Twenty-Four

Aster was dozing off when she heard muttered voices from the cubicle next to her and she woke with a start. Despite the airline bed offering every level of comfort, she was finding it difficult to properly relax. The attendant seemed to ask Edward something and then left. Checking her phone, Aster could see it was still only ten. Not late at all. She was about to settle down again when a new man's voice began talking to Edward. His voice was oily and overfamiliar. Aster listened in, grinning. She hated when people talked to her using that voice and wondered how Edward would respond.

'Lord Peveril, can I just say what a pleasure it is to be travelling with you this week?'

'Thank you, Charles. How can I help? The attendant said you needed a word?'

Aster smiled that he hadn't told him to call him Edward. Did that mean he stood on his title, or was he just not letting this Charles person get overly chummy? In the past when she had asked people to simply call her Aster, on the whole, it went well but every so often there was a certain type that seemed to think this imbued them with special privileges. The idea of anyone thinking they were close to Aster was bad enough, that they thought they were even closer to her was abhorrent. This Charles struck her as one of those types.

'I just wanted to say that I'm pretty much an old hand at trade in India. Anything you need a hand with, let me know.'

'I think I'll be okay.'

Aster almost sniggered out loud as Edward then spoke in fluent Urdu, thanking Charles for his kind offer. There was a moment of silence and then Charles chortled loudly.

'Ah, I see you have the lingo. Well, good for you. Very clever. Yes. Very clever indeed. Lady Aster-'

Charles had raised his voice and then yelped suddenly. The next voice she heard was Edward's, dark and angry.

'Lady Aster is not to be disturbed.'

'No, of course. Not. Forgive me. Maybe you could let go of my hand?'

Had he been about to slide open her privacy partition? Aster was appalled at his nerve. Thank God Edward had the wit to stop the oaf. If he hadn't, Aster would have been forced to engage with the newcomer and her engagement would not have been welcoming.

'Hello. Is everything okay?' The alert voice of an attendant had now joined the discussion and Aster slunk even further under her sheets. She wanted the ground to open up and swallow her. Though if it did, she'd need a parachute. She tried to smother a giggle, this was ridiculous. Any time in Edward's company and she reacted like an idiot, either snottily or giggling or just basically running away. She knew it was all tied to her initial drugging and wondered when she would learn to come to terms with it. Basically, he had saved her and she couldn't handle being beholden to him. But his voice just then had given her chills, he sounded furious with the other man. Now he was back chatting to the attendant in his normal tone.

'Everything is fine. Mr Brown was just returning to his seat.'

Aster listened as Charles Brown and the attendant headed away. A soporific silence descended once more over first-class and Aster settled back down again.

'Sleep well, Aster,' Edward spoke softly, careful not to wake her just in case she was sleeping. 'No one will disturb you.'

For the first time since the incident, Aster slept peacefully for eight hours.

Waking up to the voice of the pilot informing them they would be arriving in Mumbai in an hour, Aster began to get ready for the day ahead. She had an hour between connecting flights and then a four-hour flight to Kolkata. This time, she was travelling economy as there was no other option, but she didn't care. At least she wouldn't be bothered by the delegates. Feeling oddly shy, she mumbled a quick 'Morning', and smiled to herself when she heard Edward echo it. She was reluctant to refer to last night's incident and instead got dressed and called for a breakfast.

'Would you like a game of cards before we land?'

'Cards?'

'Yes. I thought you might be a card player. Ignore me. I like playing cards.'

'Go on, then. What games do you know?'

'Shall I slide back my partition?'

Grinning, she slid hers back at the same time. Beating Edward at cards seemed like an excellent way to kill the final hour. One hour later, Aster was wondering just how she had managed to lose so much money.

With each loss, Edward's grin had become ever deeper and she found herself warming to his delight, even if it was her expense.

'You clearly had a misspent youth?' remarked Aster tartly.

'I have had some lucky cards.'

'True. But even then, you made the very most of them.'

'I suspect if you had had them, you'd have maybe beaten me instead.'

'Beaten you?' said Aster, raising an eyebrow. 'I'd have thrashed you.'

As the plane touched down, Aster picked up her bag.

'At some point, we'll have to have a rematch and I'll win my money back.'

'I'll hold you to that.' He laughed at some inside joke. Aster frowned and hastened to her connecting flight. An hour later, she was happily ensconced in a window seat on the front row. Nick had done well, she had loads of space and so far, no one was sitting next to her. Of course, that wouldn't last, but until then she would enjoy the peace and quiet. Mumbai Airport had been manic, barely hinting at the chaos in the city beyond and she knew Kolkata would be no better and possibly worse. Still, Nick had assured her she had booked her a driver who would meet her at the airport and drive her out to the village.

'Round two?'

Aster turned away from the window and stared at Edward in astonishment.

'What the hell are you doing here?'

'Seemed the easiest way to get to Kolkata.'

'But you're with the Mumbai Trade Delegation.'

'No, I'm with the India Trade Delegation. And like yourself, I'm heading on to Kolkata.'

'And when you get there, where are you going next?'

He laughed loudly and caused several people to stare at him as she narrowed her eyes. Was this man following her? He sat down in the aisle seat and grinned across at her as he dug around in his carry-on bag.

'I'll be stopping in Kolkata, I assure you. Are you travelling on?'

'Yes.'

She was determined not to get dragged into a conversation. The passenger for the middle seat would arrive shortly and remove any further conversation.

'Well then, let's make the most of our time together.'

Pulling out a pack of cards, he began to deal, laying the cards down on the seat between them.

'What are you doing? Someone will be sitting there!'

'I bought both seats,' he said as he carried on dealing giving her a quick wink.

Aster slowly closed her mouth. The confidence in that wink, who the hell did he think he was?

'You booked both seats?'

'Yes. Pick up your cards.'

'That just happened to be next to me?'

'That's right. Your cards.'

'And when did you book these seats?'

'Must have been around the same time I booked the Mumbai seat. Come on.' He picked up his own cards and started looking through them.

'And when exactly did you book those seats?'

'I think that was when I was asked to pop over to investigate a few things. Now look, I have some pretty decent cards. I think you might struggle to beat me. Again.'

Aster pursed her lips.

'Exactly what is your job, that the British government asks some dilettante lord of the manor to help them out with? Etiquette issues at the governor's high table?'

He looked across at her, chuckling.

'Now, now. Don't believe all the gossip you read. Although I am surprised that you looked me up.'

'Surprised? I ended up in a stranger's house, who then also tried to fleece some nuns out of a priceless painting. Of course I was going to investigate you.'

'Was I trying to fleece them?'

Aster shrugged. 'As it happens, no. But at the time, I didn't know that, nor could I tell from the ham-fisted way you went about it that your intentions were honourable.'

He scrunched his face up. 'That's true. I didn't handle that well. I suppose that explains your sloppy investigation.'

Her eyelids shot open.

'I beg your pardon?' Not once in her life had she been accused of being sloppy.

'Your investigation into me. *Dilettante lord of the manor*, that's an epitaph worthy of a tabloid, but not you, Lady Aster. Now what about your cards?'

Aster snatched at her cards. How dare he accuse her of having the investigative skills of a tabloid hack? But she was mostly furious because she knew he was right. She had only listened to Nick's brief summation of him and Aster had extrapolated his entire character without doing any proper investigation. He had got under her skin from day one and it had clouded her reasoning. The minute she was off this plane, she was going to spend some serious time checking His Grace out.

She was just about to hand the cards back to him when she had a quick glance. Two aces, plus a running jack that she could develop and a useful eight. She paused. Maybe beating him would make her feel better. She laid her first card down.

By the time the attendants were bringing around the snacks, Aster had won back all her money and was now up on the deal. By the time they landed, she was openly laughing along with Edward as he groaned about her achievements.

Chapter Twenty-Five

The moment they stepped off the plane in Kolkata, Aster was assaulted by a wall of humid air, thick with the scent of spices, diesel fumes, and humanity. The stark contrast between the artificial chill of the aircraft cabin and the oppressive heat of the Indian summer was jarring. As they made their way through Netaji Subhas Chandra Bose International Airport, the cacophony of voices in a dozen languages, blaring announcements, and the incessant rumble of rolling luggage threatened to overwhelm her senses.

The airport bustled with a chaotic energy unique to India. Families with mountains of luggage jostled for space alongside backpackers and businessmen. Bright sarees and kurtas mingled with Western attire, creating a vibrant tapestry of colour against the sterile airport backdrop.

Edward's hand hovered near the small of her back, not quite touching but guiding, nonetheless. Aster bristled at the presumption. She turned and glared up at him.

'I am capable of walking through an airport by myself you know.'

'I have no doubt, but I can't help myself. You bring out the overbearing bear in me. I just don't want to see you get knocked about, this place is heaving.' At that moment, a family laden with a small train of suitcases barged between the pair of them, flapping their arms at Aster to get out of their way. Edward stepped into the middle of their procession. Grabbing Aster, he moved her quickly to his side.

'See? If you stand still in here, you'll get run over.'

At the immigration desk, Edward leant in close, his breath warm against her ear. 'Follow my lead.'

Before she could protest, he was striding forward again, his bearing regal and commanding. He approached an official, speaking in rapid-fire Hindi. To Aster's astonishment, the official nodded deferentially, ushering them towards a separate, blessedly empty queue.

As they emerged into the baggage claim area, Edward smoothly manoeuvred Aster towards a man holding a sign with 'Lady Aster' written on it. The driver stood out in his crisp white kurta, a stark contrast to the colourful chaos around them.

'Well, I think that's you, Lady Aster,' Edward said to Aster, nodding towards the sign. Then he began speaking to the driver in fluent Hindi.

'*If Lady Aster gets into any trouble, call me immediately,*' Edward instructed. '*You'll stay with her for four days and keep an eye on her. I'll pay the bill.*'

Aster's eyebrows shot up as she understood every word. She felt a flash of annoyance at Edward's high-handedness. Who did he think he was, arranging a babysitter for her? She debated whether to reveal that she had understood his instructions, but before she could decide, Edward turned to her.

'This is Nikhil. I've asked the driver to stay with you for the next four days,' he said, his expression earnest. 'He'll be available whenever you need him, and I've taken care of the payment. If you run into any trouble, he'll contact me right away.'

She was impressed that he had been honest about what he said to the driver, but still.

'Edward, I appreciate the thought, but this is completely unnecessary,' she protested, her voice sharp. 'I'm more than capable of handling myself in Kolkata. I don't need a babysitter.'

Edward's expression softened, but his eyes remained resolute. 'Aster, please. This isn't about your capabilities. I will always protect you. I feel responsible for your safety.'

His words hit her like a physical force, causing her to take a step back. 'You're not responsible for me,' she countered, but her voice lacked its usual conviction.

'Perhaps not,' Edward conceded, 'but I can't help feeling that way. Truthfully, I'd prefer to accompany you myself, but I have business I can't avoid.'

Aster felt her breath catch in her throat. The intensity of his gaze, the earnestness in his voice – it was all too much. She felt shaken, off-balance in a way she wasn't accustomed to.

Before she could respond, Edward leant in. His lips brushed her cheek in a whisper of a kiss, sending an unexpected shiver down her spine. He pulled back slightly, his eyes locked on hers, filled with an emotion Aster couldn't quite name.

'Stay safe,' he murmured, his voice low and intimate.

Then, without waiting for her reply, he turned and walked away, quickly disappearing into the bustling crowd of the airport.

Aster stood rooted to the spot, her cheek tingling where his lips had touched. She felt dizzy, overwhelmed by the whirlwind of emotions Edward's words and actions had stirred up.

Shaking off her daze, Aster turned to the driver, a mischievous glint in her eye. In fluent Bengali, she quipped, '*Are you waiting for your mother's permission, or can we leave?*'

Nikhil's eyes widened in surprise, then crinkled with delight. '*You speak Bengali!*' he exclaimed, clearly pleased.

'*Yes.*' Aster nodded, smiling. Then, her tone turning more serious, she continued, 'I speak both Hindi and Bengali, but I thought you might pay more attention to your own mother tongue. Now, listen, I appreciate your offer to stay with me, but it's not necessary. Could you just drop me off and perhaps recommend a reliable driver for my return journey? And… let's keep this between us, shall we? No need to inform Edward.'

The driver hesitated for a moment, then nodded, a conspiratorial smile on his face. 'Alright, madam. I know just the person for your return trip.'

As soon as the car pulled out of the airport, Aster got on the phone to Nick.

'Landed safely?'

'Yes, all fine, although something odd happened. Edward Montclair is part of the delegation and was sitting next to me on the flight.'

There was a moment of silence on the other end and Aster knew that Nick was drawing the same conclusions she had.

'That doesn't feel like a coincidence.'

'Agreed. Could you look into it?'

'I'll call you back.'

Hanging up, she settled back in her seat. It was a two-hour drive to the village, watching the bustling streets of Kolkata give way to lush countryside. The leather seats of the car were cool under the air conditioning and Aster smiled contentedly. The landscape transformed before her eyes, a kaleidoscope of life and colour. Ramshackle shops and crowded apartment blocks gradually thinned out, replaced by verdant rice paddies stretching to the horizon.

The air grew thicker with humidity, carrying the scent of earth, growing things, and the occasional whiff of smoke from distant cooking fires. Vibrant splashes of colour punctuated the green expanse - women in jewel-toned sarees working in the fields, their bangles catching the sunlight as they moved. As the heat encroached, Aster reluctantly closed her window.

As they passed through small villages, life unfolded in vivid tableaux. Ancient banyan trees provided shade for impromptu gatherings of elders. Chai wallahs did brisk business, their tiny stalls a hub of activity and gossip.

The road itself was a microcosm of Indian traffic - lumbering lorries festooned with marigolds shared space with rickshaws, motorcycles laden with improbable loads, and the occasional wandering cow, sacred and unperturbed by the surrounding chaos.

With each passing mile, the air grew heavier, saturated with moisture from unseen rivers and ponds. The vegetation became more lush, almost jungle-like in its profusion. Banana trees lined the roadside, their broad leaves creating a natural canopy. In the distance, Aster could make out the hazy outline of low hills, shrouded in a bluish mist.

Her mind, however, kept drifting back to Edward. His insistence on protecting her, the intensity in his eyes, the whisper of his lips on her cheek – it all left her feeling off-balance. She wasn't used to this, to someone caring so deeply about her safety. It was… unsettling.

Her phone rang and she answered before the second ring.

'Found anything?'

'Bits and bobs. Seems His Grace is not quite what he appears to be.'

'Peer of the realm, rich socialite and general good time guy?'

'Exactly, as well as all that and holding various titles, he appears to work for the government from time to time.'

'Yes. I know that. I just told you he was part of the delegation.'

'On paper he is,' said Nick dismissively, 'but this jaunt is a party political one and your Edward doesn't seem to be involved in that sort of politics. As far as I can see, he has links to MI6 and other government agencies.'

'Oh.'

'Oh, indeed. I couldn't get far. Firewalls and the like. But I made a few phone calls.'

'Gut feeling?'

'Don't trust him. I don't know why he's in India and I don't know if it has anything to do with you or our business. But as a coincidence, I'm not buying it.'

The car jolted over a pothole, jarring Aster from her thoughts. She hung up, promising to keep Nick updated. She shook her head, annoyed with herself for dwelling on Edward when she had work to do. The mystery of the counterfeit muslin waited for no one, least of all for her confused feelings about a man she barely knew. But damn it, his appearance presented a thousand red flags.

As they passed through a small village, children ran alongside the car, waving and laughing. Aster waved back, a smile tugging at her lips despite her tumultuous thoughts. This was why she was here – to protect the livelihoods of people like these, to ensure the legacy of their craft wasn't stolen or cheapened.

With renewed determination, Aster pushed thoughts of Edward aside. She had a job to do, a mystery to solve. Whatever was happening between her and Edward – if indeed anything was happening at all – it could wait. For now, she had bigger fish to fry.

The car wound its way deeper into the countryside. Aster leant forward, eager for her first glimpse of the village where it all began. The landscape had become a tapestry of tiny fields, each a different shade of green, separated by low earthen bunds. In the distance, she could see the silhouette of what looked like an old temple, its spire reaching towards the cloudless sky.

Whatever secrets lay hidden here, amidst this timeless landscape of rural Bengal, Aster was ready to uncover them. The car bumped along the increasingly narrow road, and she felt a thrill of anticipation.

Chapter Twenty-Six

The car's tyres crunched on the packed earth as it pulled into Bhasagram, kicking up a cloud of ochre dust that hung in the humid air. Aster stepped out, her legs stiff from the long journey, and took a deep breath. The air was thick with a tapestry of scents – earthy petrichor, pungent spices, and something floral she couldn't quite identify. The late afternoon sun cast a golden glow over the village, transforming it into a scene from a painter's imagination.

As she surveyed the scene before her, Aster felt a swell of pride mixed with a keen sense of responsibility. This was Hiverton land now, a significant investment by her family's estate. The success or failure of this venture would have far-reaching consequences, not just for the village, but for the Hiverton name as well.

Bhasagram sprawled before her, a living canvas of contrasts. Thatched mud huts, their walls a warm terracotta, stood alongside freshly painted concrete structures in vibrant blues and yellows. The village hummed with the sounds of life and progress – hammers striking nails, the whir of power tools, voices calling out instructions in rapid-fire Bengali, all underpinned by the distant lowing of cattle and the cheerful chaos of children at play.

A group of those children, who had been engrossed in a game involving much running and shouting, spotted Aster and raced towards her. Their bare feet kicked up small clouds of dust as they approached, their faces alight with curiosity and excitement.

'Hello! Hello!' they chorused in English, giggling as they came to a stop in front of her.

Aster smiled, charmed by their enthusiasm. 'Hello,' she replied. 'How are you all?'

This sent the children into peals of laughter, and they began chattering excitedly among themselves in Bengali. Their words came so fast, tumbling over each other, that Aster found herself lost.

She held up her hands in surrender, chuckling. '*I'm sorry,*' she said, switching to Bengali. '*I'm afraid that was too fast for me to catch. Could you slow down a bit?*'

The children's eyes widened in surprise and delight at hearing her speak their language. Before they could respond, however, a tall, distinguished man approached. He cut an impressive figure in a crisp white kurta over pressed trousers, a gold watch glinting on his wrist. His face was weathered by years in the sun, laugh lines crinkling around his eyes, but his gaze was sharp and intelligent.

'Lady Aster,' he said in English, his accent thick but precise. 'Welcome to Bhasagram. I am Amit Choudhury, head of the muslin consortium and local manager for the Hiverton Estate's interests here. I see you have already met our welcoming committee.' He smiled warmly at the children, who beamed back at him before scampering off, their laughter trailing behind them.

Aster shook his hand firmly. 'Mr Choudhury, thank you for having me. And please, just Aster is fine. There's no need for titles here.'

Amit's smile widened, but there was a flicker of something – nervousness? – in his eyes. 'Of course, of course. But you must understand, it is our way to show respect. We are most honoured by your visit, Lady Aster.'

Aster tried again. 'Really, Mr Choudhury, I'd prefer if everyone just called me Aster. I'm here to work, not stand on ceremony.'

Amit nodded, but Aster could tell her words hadn't quite landed. 'Yes, yes, as you wish… Memsahib.'

Aster sighed inwardly but let it go for now. She had more pressing matters to focus on. 'I'm eager to see how our family's investment has transformed the village,' she said, steering the conversation back to business. It had been her intention to not mention the problems of the fabric supply in the UK. She was certain the problem originated here in India, but she didn't want to warn anyone until she had a better understanding of the situation.

'Ah yes, of course,' Amit replied, his chest swelling with pride. 'The Hiverton Estate's involvement has been most transformative. We have come very far in a short time. But come, you must be tired from the journey. Let us get you settled, and then perhaps a tour of the Hiverton operations?'

As they walked through the village, Aster's keen eyes took in every detail. New roofs of corrugated metal gleamed atop old structures, their modern lines a stark contrast to the organic curves of traditional thatch. Fresh paint in a riot of colours adorned shop fronts and homes, lending a festive air to the streets. In the distance, she could see a group of children in clean, pressed uniforms hurrying towards a building that could only be a new school, its facade bearing the Hiverton crest.

They passed a half-constructed building, its skeleton of steel and concrete a testament to the village's growing prosperity. Workers called out greetings to Amit as they passed, their faces showing a mix of respect and affection. Amit responded to each by name, inquiring after family members or commenting on the progress of their work.

'The Hiverton Estate's investment has allowed us to improve infrastructure significantly,' Amit explained, his voice swelling with pride. 'New housing, better sanitation, improved roads – it is all part of the comprehensive development plan.'

As Amit spoke, Aster again noticed an undercurrent of tension in his manner. His eyes darted about as if watching for unseen threats, and his shoulders remained tight, despite his easy smile.

They turned down a side street, the packed earth giving way to a newly laid brick path. The houses here were a mix of old and new, some still mud and thatch, others freshly built with concrete and tile. Amit led Aster to a modest two-storey house, its walls a cheerful yellow that seemed to glow in the late afternoon light.

'This is the local Hiverton office,' Amit said. 'We have set up a room for you here during your stay.'

A middle-aged woman emerged from the house, her round face creasing into a smile as warm as the afternoon sun. She wore a simple cotton saree in a deep blue, offset by a red bindi between her brows.

'This is my wife, Priya,' Amit said, his voice softening with affection. 'Darling, this is Lady Aster from the Hiverton Estate.'

Priya stepped forward, clasping her hands together in greeting. 'Namaste, Lady Aster. Welcome to Bhasagram. I hope you will be comfortable here.'

Aster returned the greeting, touched by the warmth of her welcome. 'Thank you for your hospitality, Mrs Choudhury. And please, just Aster is fine.'

Priya exchanged a quick glance with her husband before responding. 'Of course, Memsahib. Please, let me show you to your room.'

Realising her request had once again been politely ignored, Aster resigned herself to the formality and followed Priya upstairs to a small but airy room. Sunlight streamed through a large window, illuminating the simple furnishings. A narrow bed with a crisp white sheet stood against one wall, a wooden desk and chair opposite. A ceiling fan spun lazily overhead, stirring the warm air. The walls were adorned with framed photographs – landscapes of lush countryside and portraits of smiling villagers, interspersed with images of Hiverton Estate back in England.

'I hope this will be suitable,' Priya said, gesturing around the room. 'There is a bathroom just down the hall, and I have left some fresh towels for you there. Please, let me know if you need anything at all.'

As Priya left, Aster sank onto the bed, her mind whirling with everything she'd seen and heard. The village's prosperity was evident, a testament to the success of the Hiverton investment. Yet something nagged at her. It was all too… perfect. Too rapid a transformation for a village that had, by all accounts, been struggling just a few years ago.

She could hear Amit and Priya talking softly downstairs, their voices a comforting murmur in the background. As she unpacked her small suitcase, Aster reflected on her first impressions of Amit Choudhury. He was clearly proud of what had been accomplished in Bhasagram, his eyes lighting up as he spoke of the improvements to the village.

Whatever secrets Bhasagram held, Aster sensed that Amit Choudhury was at the heart of them. This wasn't just about solving a mystery anymore – it was about protecting her family's investment and reputation. With a deep breath, she steeled herself for the days ahead, knowing that her investigation was only just beginning.

After a quick freshen up, Aster made her way downstairs to find Amit waiting in the living room. The space was simply furnished but comfortable, with colourful cushions adorning a well-worn sofa and potted plants adding splashes of green to the corners. A tray of tea and biscuits sat on a low table, the spicy-sweet aroma of masala chai filling the air.

'Ah, Lady Aster,' Amit said, rising to his feet. 'I thought you might like some refreshment before we begin our tour. Priya makes an excellent masala chai.'

Aster accepted a cup gratefully, savouring the complex flavours. As they sipped their tea, Amit outlined the changes that had come to Bhasagram in recent years.

'Three years ago, this village was struggling,' he said, his eyes growing distant with memory. 'Our young people were leaving for the cities, seeking better opportunities. Those who remained could barely make ends meet. But then, we successfully revived the cultivation of phuti karpas – the special cotton used in Dhaka muslin. Since then, our fortunes have improved dramatically.'

Aster nodded, her mind already racing with questions. But before she could voice any of them, Amit set down his cup and stood. 'Shall we begin our tour? I'm eager to show you the improvements we've made.'

They set off down the village's main street, the late afternoon sun casting long shadows across their path. The street was alive with activity. Women in colourful sarees chatted as they walked home with baskets of vegetables, men on bicycles weaved through the crowd, their bells tinkling merrily. The air was filled with sounds – the sizzle of food frying in roadside stalls, the bleating of goats, the distant chanting from a temple.

Amit pointed out various new buildings as they walked – a community centre with a small library, a medical clinic staffed by a young doctor from Kolkata, and a vocational training centre where young people could learn new skills.

'Education has been a key focus for us,' Amit explained as they passed the new school building. The sound of children reciting lessons drifted through the open windows. 'We believe it's the foundation for lasting prosperity.'

As they walked, Aster noticed how people reacted to Amit. Everyone they passed offered a respectful greeting, often accompanied by a warm smile or a friendly wave.

They paused at a small tea stall, where the owner insisted on serving them a cup of his special blend. As they sipped the strong, sweet tea, Aster observed the easy camaraderie between Amit and the stall owner. They joked and laughed, sharing village gossip and discussing plans for an upcoming festival.

They passed a small park where a group of young men were playing cricket. The players paused their game to greet Amit, who exchanged a few words with them about an upcoming tournament.

'Sports have become quite popular,' he said as they moved on. 'It gives our young people a positive outlet for their energy, and it's bringing the community together in new ways.'

As they neared the end of their tour, they passed a group of elders sitting in the shade of a large tree, engaged in an animated game of chess. Amit exchanged a few words with them, and Aster noticed how they deferred to him, their expressions a mix of respect and something else – gratitude, perhaps?

'The elders were initially sceptical of our plans,' Amit explained as they walked away. 'Change can be difficult, especially for those who have seen hard times. But now, seeing their grandchildren with opportunities they never dreamed of… well, it's made believers of them.'

The sun was setting as they made their way back to Amit's home, painting the sky in brilliant hues of orange and pink. The village was settling into its evening rhythm – lamps being lit in windows, the smell of cooking fires filling the air, the sound of children being called home for dinner.

Despite the smiles, Aster sensed an anxious community. Tomorrow she would inspect the factory and surrounding fields and maybe then she would begin to get some answers.

She was about to fire up her laptop when her phone rang and she recognised Nick's number.

With a sigh—Nick rarely called unless something urgent required handling—Aster picked up.

'Hello, Nick. What's on fire now?' Aster asked alert to any incoming problem.

Nick's voice was brisk, as always. 'Not a fire. Quite the opposite, actually. I have some news, and for once, it's not a disaster. Are you sitting down?'

Aster had been typing whilst chatting but now gave Nick her full attention. 'Go on.'

'The painting,' Nick said, her tone carrying a rare note of excitement. 'The one from the convent. The restoration is complete.'

Aster leant forward, holding her breath.

'And?'

'And, it's a Raphael.'

The words hit Aster like a jolt of electricity. For a moment, she was too stunned to respond. 'A Raphael?' she finally managed, her voice almost a whisper.

'Yes,' Nick confirmed, her tone brightening further. 'I just got the report from the restorers. The pigments, the techniques, even the underdrawings—it's all been authenticated. It's a bloody Raphael, Aster. Can you believe it?'

Aster stood abruptly, pacing to the window. She gazed out at the street, her mind racing. 'Five thousand pounds,' she murmured. 'That man walked away with a Raphael for five thousand pounds.'

'Correction,' Nick interjected. 'He walked away with it for five thousand pounds, and then we bought it back for ten times that.'

'And you nearly had a fit, remember?'

'Water under the bridge.' Said Nick laughing at her own doubt. 'When we auction it, the proceeds will go back to the convent and their projects. It'll be worth millions.'

Aster's mind spun as she absorbed the magnitude of the news. A Raphael. A treasure lost in plain sight for centuries, hidden under layers of grime in a small London chapel. And now, thanks to her—and, she grudgingly admitted, Nick—it had been given a second life.

'This is… incredible,' Aster said finally. 'But how did the restorers confirm it?'

'The usual methods,' Nick replied. 'X-rays, infrared imaging, consultations with art historians. Apparently, there's a small signature buried in one corner that matches known Raphael works. It's all documented. It's unequivocal.'

Aster let out a low whistle. 'Well, I suppose I owe you a thank-you for handling the restoration so thoroughly. I wasn't sure we'd ever find out its true worth.'

'Don't thank me yet,' Nick said wryly. 'We'll see how the auction goes. But for now, I'd say you've done a good deed. The convent's roof is fixed, and their future is secure. Not bad for a day's work, eh?'

Aster chuckled softly. 'Not bad at all.'

Nick's tone turned teasing. 'Though if you're planning any more good deeds, try to keep me in the loop next time. My wallet might not survive another surprise like this.'

Aster grinned. 'I'll think about it. Thanks, Nick. Really.'

'Don't mention it,' Nick replied. 'Now, see if you can manage another miracle. How's it going out there?'

The sisters chatted briefly as Aster outlined her concerns and promised to keep Nick informed and they ended the call agreeing to put the Raphael straight up for auction, once Ari was brought up to date.

As the call ended, Aster set the phone down and stared at the papers on her desk, though her thoughts were far from her itinerary now. A Raphael. The convent's sacrifice had unearthed a treasure, and she felt a profound sense of responsibility to see it through.

Taking a deep breath, she returned to her plans for the factory tour tomorrow. But now, the excursion felt different, infused with a renewed sense of purpose. Whatever had gone wrong, she would be able to fix it.

Somewhere in the back of her mind, she could hear Sister Bernard's laughter, delighted at the thought of a watertight roof and a chapel no longer plagued by buckets. She knew Nick would be calling the nun to update her, Aster would have loved to let her know but this needed to be done face to face and Aster was stuck in India. She would have to catch up with her when she got home.

She also had an insane urge to call up Edward and crow, imagining his face, the look of shock would be priceless. Instead she pulled her laptop towards her and continued to make notes, a large smile on her face.

Chapter Twenty-Seven

The sun had barely crested the horizon when Aster and Amit set out for the cotton fields. The morning air was cool and heavy with dew, a brief respite before the heat of the day set in. As they walked, Aster noticed a change in Amit's demeanour. Gone was the effusive pride of yesterday, replaced by a more reserved, almost cautious manner.

The path to the fields wound through the awakening village. Women in colourful sarees balanced water jugs on their heads, the metal vessels glinting in the early light. The aroma of wood smoke and cooking spices hung in the air, mingling with the earthy scent of damp soil.

As they crested a small rise, the cotton fields spread out before them, a sea of green dotted with white. The plants stood in neat rows, their leaves glistening with morning dew. Workers were already moving between the rows, their practiced hands plucking the precious bolls.

'This is phuti karpas,' Amit said, his voice quieter than usual. 'It is special cotton, growing only here. The river and our soil, they create perfect conditions.'

Aster nodded, her eyes scanning the fields. The plants looked remarkably healthy, their leaves a vibrant green, the cotton bolls fat and plentiful. 'How many harvests do you get in a year?' she asked.

Amit's pause was almost imperceptible. 'Just one. The growing season is short, plants are delicate. But quality… quality is unmatched.'

They walked along the edge of the field, Amit pointing out various features - the irrigation systems, the experimental plots where they were testing new cultivation techniques. Aster noticed that whilst he answered her questions, his explanations lacked the enthusiasm of the previous day.

As they approached a group of workers, Aster smiled and greeted them in Bengali. Their faces lit up, and soon she was engaged in conversation, asking about their work and their families. Amit stood back, his expression unreadable.

'How long have you worked here?' Aster asked one woman, whose weathered hands spoke of years in the fields.

'Since the beginning, Memsahib,' she replied proudly. 'When Hiverton came, everything changed. Now my children go to school, we have good food, good life.'

Aster nodded, touched by the woman's sincerity. But as she spoke to more workers, a pattern emerged. Whilst they all spoke warmly of the changes Hiverton had brought, there was a wariness in their eyes when she asked about recent events or staff changes.

One young man, when asked if he knew anyone who had left recently, paled visibly. 'No, no,' he stammered, his eyes darting to Amit. 'Everyone is happy here. No one leaves.'

She knew people had left, Aisha had told her as much when she spoke to her in London. Why were the villagers so keen to deny it? As they left the fields and made their way to the factory, Aster's mind was buzzing with questions. The unease she had sensed in Amit seemed to have spread to the workers, but its source remained elusive.

The factory loomed before them, a large, modern building that stood in stark contrast to the traditional village architecture. As they entered, Aster was struck by the hum of activity - the whir of spinning wheels, the clack of looms, the murmur of voices.

Workers looked up as they entered, their faces breaking into warm smiles. 'Namaste, Memsahib,' they called out, some even standing and bowing slightly.

Amit led her through the factory, explaining each stage of the process. The pride was back in his voice as he spoke of the incredible fineness of the thread, the skill of the weavers, the quality of the final product. But his eyes kept darting about, as if expecting trouble from some unseen quarter.

Aster paused at one of the spinning wheels, watching in fascination as a young woman drew out an impossibly fine thread from a tuft of cotton. 'May I?' she asked, gesturing to the wheel.

The woman nodded, moving aside. Aster sat down, attempting to mimic the spinner's movements. Her clumsy efforts drew laughter from the surrounding workers, breaking some of the tension.

As she chatted with the spinners and weavers, Aster tried to piece together the puzzle. They spoke enthusiastically about their work and the opportunities Hiverton had brought, but clammed up when asked about recent changes or absent colleagues.

One older weaver, his eyes clouded with cataracts, leant in close to Aster. 'Things have changed,' he whispered, his voice barely audible above the noise of the looms. 'Not all for the better. But we mustn't speak of it.'

Before Aster could press for more information, Amit appeared at her side. 'We should move on, Memsahib,' he said, a hint of urgency in his voice. 'There is much more to see.'

As they continued the tour, Aster's sense of unease grew. The quality of the work was undeniable - the muslin they produced was indeed incredibly fine, almost ethereal in its delicacy. But the numbers didn't add up. How could they produce so much from a single, short harvest?

Moreover, the tension in the air was palpable. Workers smiled and nodded as they passed, but their eyes held secrets. There were whispered conversations that stopped abruptly as Aster approached, meaningful glances exchanged behind Amit's back.

At the end of the tour, Aster thanked the workers, her mind whirling with all she had seen and heard - and all that remained unsaid. As they stepped out of the factory into the late afternoon sun, she turned to Amit.

'Mr Choudhury,' she said, her voice firm but kind. 'I think it's time we had a proper talk. There are some things that don't quite add up, and I believe you might have the answers I'm looking for.'

Amit's face tightened, a flicker of fear passing through his eyes before he composed himself. 'Of course, Memsahib,' he replied, his voice carefully neutral. 'Perhaps we could speak in the office?'

Aster nodded, and they set off towards the Hiverton office, the weight of unspoken words hanging heavy between them. As they walked, Aster steeled herself for the conversation ahead.

The sun was high in the sky beating down on her head and she could feel beads of sweat trickle down her nape. The shadows had been eradicated from the village. Dogs and chickens clung to the edges of the building or slept under bushes, trying to escape the relentless attack. Aster barely noticed the beauty around her. Her mind was focused on the task ahead. As Amit opened the door to the office, she took a deep breath. It was time to find out what the hell was going on.

Chapter Twenty-Eight

Aster watched Amit fiddle with a keyboard on his desk and adjusted his screen three times before she lost her patience.

'Where are your missing staff?'

He winced and waggled his head rapidly, a forlorn expression on his face.

'Please, Lady Aster, may I be inviting my wife? She has a good business head and has many ideas.'

Aster frowned, but nodded her head. Two against one wasn't an issue and if he needed moral support, then so be it. She couldn't imagine what he had done to drive his staff away, but there were clearly empty seats and the workers in the fields were also determined that she didn't pay attention to the newly planted crops.

Priya came into the room and immediately the atmosphere in the room changed. She stared at Aster boldly whilst her husband looked nervously between the two women. Then she nodded curtly.

'We will need tea.'

Amit jumped up, but she shook her head.

'You make it weak. We need strong tea for our words.'

Priya's English was highly accented, but she made herself plain in the words she used and the jut of her jaw. By the time they were all settled, Aster took a sip of the tea and nodded her thanks and then asked Priya to begin. She immediately deferred to her husband.

'We are extremely grateful to the Hiverton Estate. Everything we have achieved here is because of you.'

Aster held up her hand, denying Priya's unwarranted praise.

'We have certainly provided a catalyst. But this success is down to you, and we too have benefited from our arrangement. But recently, we have noticed a new competitor in the market and if you are working with them, then we need to know. This would be in breach of our contract.'

Husband and wife both blanched as Amit hurried to reassure Aster that they were not working with anyone else, that they greatly esteemed the Hivertons, that they hoped they would work together for generations to come.

'They are stealing our bushes.' Priya's words cut through Amit's gush of praise, her words landing heavy and angry. 'They are stealing our people.'

She glared at Aster, tears welling in her eyes as she struggled to gain her composure.

'Who is?'

'Bad men. They come in the night and take them.'

'And your workers. Are they paying them higher wages?'

'No. They are stealing them.'

'But the workers?'

'Stealing.'

Aster looked at Amit for clarification.

'What my wife says in so few words is the heart of our despair. Our villagers are being kidnapped. Their families are distraught. Our weavers are mothers, their children are crying for them at night. We tell them their mummies are on holiday, but they are not. They have been stolen.'

Aster's heart sank. That explained how they were being undercut on price. They were using slave labour.

'And the crops?'

'Last year, they dug up an entire field. The field you saw was a new set of plants.'

'This has been going on for a year?'

'No, no, no, no. They have only been taking the people this season.'

Which was hen the new fabric had started to emerge onto the market, thought Aster. Everything fell into place.

'But why didn't you tell us last year when the bushes were stolen?'

They looked at each other and then back at Aster.

'Because the following day a group of very bad men, wicked men, arrived in a jeep. They had many guns and they said if we told anyone, they would come back and burn the village down and kill everyone in it.'

Aster stared at them.

'So what did you do?'

'We replanted the bushes. We have been growing new plants ever since we began and have expanding into all the fields in the valley. Your sister has been buying all the land around here for us.'

'But what did you do about alerting the police?'

Priya made a derisory noise and then spoke quickly in Bengali. It was too fast for Aster to catch most of it, but Priya's body language spoke volumes and Aster caught the gist of it. The local police were based in Kolkata. They didn't care about the villagers. They would only come if the villagers paid. Now they had the money, but were scared by the threat. It was not unheard of for a militia to wipe out a village for various reasons. An investigation would be launched. Money would be paid and the victims would remain dead and unavenged.

Aster also learnt some very expressive turns of phrase that made Amit pull at his wife's sleeve as she cut him off with a slicing movement of the hand. Her eyes flashed in indignation as her chest heaved and Aster could see this had been festering for months. And now with the loss of their villagers, she could hardly blame the woman for her anger. As she petered out, Aster rubbed her chin, thinking what the best plan of attack was.

'Do you have any idea where they are based?'

They shook their heads.

'They could be anywhere. This is a big country.'

'But this plant only grows in this region.'

'It is a big region.'

Aster leant down to her bag and pulled out a sample of the rival cloth and passed it to the couple.

Taking it, Priya stood up and walked over to a microscope over by a display table and placed it under the lens. Aster and Amit sat in silence for a while as Priya played with the magnification and then turned back to them. She spoke slowly in English.

'This could be us. But us last year.' She switched to Bengali and Amit supplied the words in English that Aster struggled to translate. 'The thread is almost as fine as ours, but the cotton is still juvenile and the fibres haven't set as well. Of course, it could be that the weavers are less experienced, but I think this work is Shakila's. I recognise the way she does her leaves.'

She broke off then and choked back a sob. Amit jumped up and hugged her as the two wept together. Aster sat, uncomfortable in the face of such strong emotion, until Amit wiped his face and held Priya's hand. They returned to the table. Priya gripped the fabric and as she offered it to Aster, she told her to keep hold of it.

'Who is Shakila?'

Amit stared miserably at Aster and then dropped his head in shame. 'Shakila is our daughter.'

Chapter Twenty-Nine

The silence stretched out as Aster tried to come to terms with the depth of their misery. Too scared to approach the police, unable to explain to the Hivertons what was happening and desperate to do nothing that could harm their daughter and other members of the village.

Priya waved the fabric at Aster. 'This means she is still alive.'

'Absolutely. We're going to get your daughter back. And the others. Leave it with me.' She stood up and started pacing, then looked at her phone. It was early, but Nick wouldn't mind. Neither would Ari and both would already be awake.

'I need to call my sisters. Please carry on as normal.'

As Priya stood up to leave, Aster asked how many guns were in the village.

'One,' said Amit as he wagged his head morosely. 'I bought it last month, but I regret to say I don't know how to use it. I am very happy to say I have never fired a gun. But also, I am sorry that I have never fired a gun.'

Waving her hand, she already knew she was out of her depth and in a very vulnerable situation. She dialled both sisters, setting up a group call on the office laptop.

Calling Ari first, she explained the call was serious and she watched her sister get up and start calling out for Seb to mind the children. Telling her she would get back onto the call from her study, Aster then called up Nick, who was out on her bike. Pulling her bike across the kerb, she settled down next to a hedge.

'Problems?'

'Major, but Ari will be joining us in a-'

She cut off as Ari's face now joined the screen.

'What's wrong?'

Aster explained as her sisters interrupted occasionally to ask relevant questions and then Aster summed up.

'So basically, we need to free the kidnapped villagers. We also need to protect them from ongoing incursions and protect our crop.'

'We also need you to get to a place of safety,' said Ari. 'Can you get a lift back to the city?'

'Not a good idea,' said Nick.

'What?!'

'Nick's right. The road to this village is probably being monitored. We have to assume my arrival has been noted. If my driver left yesterday, he may have already been pulled over and interrogated. They'll want to know who I am. Which means if I try to get back to the city, I might not make it.'

'Jesus. Aster!'

'I'm okay. I have a whole village here. I don't think they'll make a move. But we need to hire mercenaries.'

'Christ,' said Ari, a hint of panic in her voice, 'we have to get you out now. I'm calling the embassy.'

'By all means. But I think mercenaries will be faster. Nick, how much can I spend?'

'Knock yourself out. Call in the SAS if you want. Jesus, Aster, call in the whole Indian army. Just get those villagers safe and take care of yourself.'

'Okay,' said Ari, her voice shaking. 'Here's the plan. Aster, ask the villagers if they know of any local…' She broke off and ran her fingers through her hair. 'Christ, I don't know. Off-duty police officers, retired soldiers? And call the Kolkata police force as well and ask for assistance. I know Amit says he has tried, but let's try again. Nick, find out who we can call on. I don't care how dodgy their connections, I want Aster safe. I'm getting on to the embassy. Any developments, raise another call, otherwise we call in again in an hour's time. Aster, I love you. Nick, crack on.'

Ari's face disappeared and Nick nodded to Aster. 'Spend whatever you need. And Aster—'

'Yes, I know, you love me.'

'I was going to say you've got this.'

'I know.'

'Also, I love you. Now get to work.'

Buoyed by her talk with her sisters, she headed out of the office in search of Amit. She knew the situation was bad, but she was here and could get stuff done. Her sisters were grappling with the fact that they were so far away and felt powerless. Hopefully, in an hour's time, they'd have some plans.

'Lady Aster.' Amit had been squatting across the way, but now he sprang up and came across to join her. In his wake was another man and she recognised Nikhil, her taxi driver from the day before. 'You should return to Kolkata. Here is not safe.'

'Neither is driving back on my own. I'm staying here.' She turned to her driver and frowned. 'And so are you, Nikhil.

But why are you still here? You were going to leave and find me a new driver from the village.'

'I did.'

'So why did you stay?'

'Me. I am your driver.'

'I thought we had an understanding?'

'We do, but also I had an understanding first with Mr Edward.'

Aster groaned but was actually relieved. She had hated the thought that he might have been intercepted.

'Very well, Amit. I need to call the police force here. Maybe I can pay them to come out.'

'It is a lot of money.'

'It doesn't matter.'

He looked worried and Aster paused.

'Is there more I don't know?'

'If you call the police, they may tell the bad men. They may be paying them already. May they stand in a shower of diarrhoea.'

Aster groaned. There was a lot of money tied up in this counterfeit ring. Amit was probably right, they had probably sewn everything up already. Including keeping a watch on the village for developments.

'Right. Look, there's no need to worry immediately.' Though she was worried that her arrival may have set off a chain reaction. 'I need your gun. I know how to use it, so it makes more sense if I have it. Do either of you know any mercenaries, men with guns that we can hire?'

'No, no, no. If they arrive, the men will kill our friends.'

Aster swore again. The situation was intolerable. Without knowing where the villagers were being held, their hands were tied. Life was cheap out here and she knew any witnesses would simply be killed rather than being allowed to incriminate them.

She was about to speak again when the sound of distant machine guns rent the air, sending flocks of birds up into the sky.

Chapter Thirty

Aster and the men stared at each other in horror and then other villagers ran out into the street.

'Amit, the gun. Now.'

Priya ran towards them.

'Priya, take Nikhil and get everyone out into the trees. Clear the village.'

Amit came running back with the gun and handed it to Aster, who tried to hide her dismay. This had likely been last fired in the Partition. Checking to see if it even had bullets, she was relieved to see a full round and snapped the barrel closed again.

'This is excellent. Now get the villagers out of here. I'll greet our welcoming party.'

'I will stand with you.'

'No.'

'Yes,' said Priya. 'You are our guest. My husband is right.'

Standing in front of her husband, they gently brought their foreheads together and Aster felt a lump come to her throat. What was love without sacrifice?

As the villagers fled, Aster's trembling fingers dialled her sisters. The weight of what might happen next settled heavily on her chest. She needed evidence, yes, but more than that, she needed to see their faces one last time.

The screen flickered to life, splitting into quadrants as each sister joined. Paddy's face appeared first, the familiar Cornish coastline stretching out behind her. Aster's heart clenched - were the children nearby? She pushed the thought away. There was no time for that now.

'Aster?' Paddy's voice was sharp with concern. 'Where are you? What's wrong?'

Before Aster could respond, Ari and Nick's faces filled the remaining squares, their voices overlapping in a chorus of worry.

'What's happening?'

'Aster, talk to us!'

Aster opened her mouth, but the words stuck in her throat. How could she tell them? How could she possibly explain?

A burst of gunfire in the distance made the decision for her. She flinched and saw the horror dawn on her sisters' faces.

'What the hell was that?' Paddy's voice cracked, fear bleeding through. 'Aster, why is there gunfire? Why is Ari crying?'

Ari's quiet sobs formed a devastating backdrop as Clem's face suddenly filled the final square.

'This had better be important,' Clem began, her customary irritation faltering as she took in the scene. 'What... what's going on?'

Aster forced a smile, but it felt brittle on her face. 'My turn to bring the drama, Clem. Sorry to upstage you.' The attempt at humour fell flat, twisting into something painful. 'Ari, Nick - I'm going to livestream what happens next. Please... please record it.'

Another burst of gunfire, closer now. Aster couldn't stop the involuntary jerk, couldn't hide the fear that flashed across her face.

'Oh, God,' Paddy whispered, her face ashen. 'Aster, please run…'

'I'm at the muslin plant in India,' Aster said, her voice surprisingly steady. 'The village is about to be under attack. I have a gun, and I'll do my best, but…' She swallowed hard, fighting back tears. 'I needed to see you all. To tell you I love you. I don't say it enough, and I'm sorry for that.'

The screen erupted into chaos, all four sisters talking at once. Their voices blended into a cacophony of love and desperation:

'We love you too-'

'Aster, please be careful-'

'We'll get help, just hold on-'

'Don't you dare die on us, you stubborn-'

Aster's vision blurred with unshed tears. Her finger hovered over the mute button, knowing she needed to silence them to stay hidden, but desperately wanting to cling to their voices for just a moment longer.

'I love you,' she said again, her voice thick. 'No matter what happens, please know that.'

With a shaking hand, she hit mute, cutting off their responses. The silence that followed was deafening. Aster allowed herself one shuddering breath, one moment of vulnerability, before squaring her shoulders and turning to Amit.

'Is there somewhere we can hide but watch as they arrive?'

As she spoke, Aster felt a strange calm settle over her. The adrenaline coursing through her veins sharpened her senses, making every detail of her surroundings stand out in stark relief. The warm breeze carrying the scent of dust and distant gunpowder, the rough texture of the ancient gun in her hands, the rapid beating of her own heart - all of it blended into a surreal tapestry of what might be her final moments. It wasn't enough - it could never be enough - but it would have to do.

Amit's voice, tight with tension, cut through her thoughts. 'It's too late,' he said, his finger pointing down the village's main street. 'They are here.'

Chapter Thirty-One

Aster turned, her grip tightening on the gun as she followed Amit's gesture. The street stretched out before them, lined with the colourful facades of village homes, now eerily silent and abandoned. At the far end, where the packed earth gave way to the lush green of the surrounding countryside, a lone figure was approaching.

He was tall, his stride purposeful and unhurried. Even from this distance, Aster could see the outline of a machine gun held casually in his hands. Her heart rate quickened and she raised her own weapon, the unfamiliar weight of it suddenly very real in her grasp.

'Amit, take shelter,' she ordered, her voice low and urgent.

But Amit shook his head, standing firm beside her. 'Respectfully, I will not.'

Aster turned to him, exasperation mixing with fear. 'Priya will kill me if anything happens to you.'

A ghost of a smile flickered across Amit's face. 'She will kill *me* if anything happens to *you*.'

For a moment, Aster was struck by the absurdity of their situation - arguing over who would face potential death whilst an armed stranger approached. She let out a short, humourless laugh. 'Very well. If it's just one man, maybe he has come to talk.'

'Yes, I am hoping this also,' Amit agreed, his eyes never leaving the approaching figure.

Aster raised her phone, using the camera to zoom in on the lone man. As his features came into focus, she felt as though the ground had suddenly shifted beneath her feet. A broken laugh escaped her lips, equal parts relief and disbelief.

Walking towards them, with an impossibly wide grin on his face, was Edward. He even had the audacity to give her a little wave, as casual as if he were greeting her at a London café rather than in the midst of a potential war zone.

Aster's mind whirled. How on earth had he found her? Why was he here? And more importantly, what did his presence mean for the danger they were facing?

With shaking hands, she turned the phone back to her own face, unmuting the call with her sisters. Their worried faces filled the screen, a chorus of concerned voices overlapping.

'Girls,' Aster cut in, unable to keep a note of bewildered amusement from her voice, 'I don't know what's going on, but I think the cavalry has arrived. Paddy, do you recognise him?'

Paddy's eyes widened in recognition. 'Is that-'

'Yes. It is,' Aster confirmed. 'Don't ask me how. I'm hanging up now, but I'll call you back as soon as I have details.'

She ended the call and slipped the phone into her pocket, her eyes never leaving Edward's approaching figure. Beside her, Amit shifted uneasily.

'Is this man a friend?' he asked, uncertainty clear in his voice.

Aster hesitated for a moment before answering. 'I believe so.'

As Edward drew nearer, his smile seemed impossibly to grow wider. He stopped a few yards away, close enough now that Aster could see the fine sheen of sweat on his brow, the dust coating his boots. He looked utterly out of place in his tailored trousers and crisp white shirt, sleeves rolled up to reveal tanned, muscular forearms. The only thing that belied his casual appearance was the very real, very deadly machine gun in his hands.

'Do you want to put your gun away?' Edward asked, his tone light, as though he were commenting on the weather.

Aster's grip on her own weapon tightened. 'You first.'

Edward's smile didn't waver. 'Not going to happen. Not until I know the threat has passed.'

'She is very threatening,' Amit interjected fervently. 'She can shoot you dead before you raise your gun. This I can promise you.'

Edward's eyes flickered to Amit, a hint of amusement in their depths. 'I don't doubt that, sir. But I meant the threat of the armed outlaws we chased on our way here. Some peeled off, we're chasing them down.'

Amit's face paled at this information. 'They'll be making for their compound,' he said urgently. 'They have captured several of our villagers. Don't let them hurt them.'

Aster had a thousand questions burning on the tip of her tongue, but Amit's words pushed them all aside. The safety of the villagers had to take priority.

Edward nodded, his expression turning serious. He unclipped a radio from his belt and began speaking rapidly in English, relaying the information about the captured villagers.

Aster listened intently, trying to piece together what was happening from Edward's side of the conversation.

As Edward listened to the reply, Aster watched his shoulders visibly relax. It was only then that she realised how tightly wound he had been, the tension in his body belying his casual demeanour.

Edward re-clipped the radio to his belt, a sigh of relief escaping him. He turned to Amit, a warm smile spreading across his face. 'We have your villagers. They're safe. The bandits are all dead, including the ones that were racing to Kolkata.'

The change in Amit was instantaneous. With a cry of joy, he rushed forward, enveloping Edward in a bear hug that seemed to surprise the taller man. Then, without a word, Amit turned and ran back into the heart of the village.

A moment later, the air was filled with the resonant sound of a gong, its deep tones echoing across the empty square. Amit's voice followed, calling out to the villagers in rapid Bengali, summoning them back from their hiding places.

Edward turned back to Aster, his eyebrows raised in amusement. 'Hello. You can put the gun down now.'

Aster stared at him, her mind still struggling to process everything that had happened in the last few minutes. Slowly, she lowered the gun, surprised to find her hand was shaking. The adrenaline that had been keeping her focused was ebbing, leaving her feeling oddly hollow.

'Hi,' she managed, her voice hoarse. 'I guess you were in the neighbourhood?'

'Something like that,' Edward replied, his eyes serious as they scanned her face, checking for any signs of injury or distress.

'How did you know we were in trouble?'

Edward's face grew serious. 'It's a bit of a long story,' he began. 'I was actually flown out here at the request of the British government. They had concerns about a very prominent member of the British establishment.'

Aster's curiosity was immediately piqued. 'Really? Who?'

Edward shook his head. 'I can't disclose that, I'm afraid. What I can tell you is that they knew this individual had significant interests in India. The government felt it would be better to investigate quietly abroad before focusing on his British activities.'

'And how does that relate to our situation?' Aster pressed, her curiosity piqued.

'As I investigated, I heard rumours that this person had interests in textiles. Then someone mentioned he was involved in something up in the area around your village.' Edward's expression darkened. 'Given what I knew about his other activities, I immediately feared the worst.'

Aster nodded slowly, processing this information. 'So, you just happened to have a team of mercenaries on speed dial?'

Edward's lips quirked in a half-smile. 'Something like that. Bill and his team have worked with me before. When I suspected you might be walking into danger, I called them in as a precaution.'

A shiver ran down Aster's spine at the thought. She looked at Edward, really looked at him, and felt a swell of gratitude. 'Thank you,' she said softly. 'I mean it. You saved a lot of lives today.'

Edward's expression softened, and for a moment, Aster felt as though she could see right through his carefully constructed facade to the man beneath. 'You're welcome,' he said simply. 'Though I have to admit, I'm relieved I could connect the dots in time. This whole situation is bigger than I initially thought.'

The implications of Edward's revelation were breathtaking. 'We'll need to discuss this further,' she said. 'But for now, let's focus on the immediate situation.'

Aster started to pace the office. She wanted to call her sisters, but until she knew the full situation, she held back. Instead, she tried to process her feelings for Edward. That was the second time he had saved her from a near-death experience and she was feeling decidedly ungrateful. She was not a damsel in distress, she was the knight in shining armour. She was the one who rode in and saved the day. Waiting for rescue was not in her DNA.

Now he was sitting typing rapidly into a satellite phone and Aster wondered who he was communicating with. If he left the phone unattended, she would have a look, but she knew satellite phones were notoriously difficult to unscramble.

Half an hour of nail-biting agony later, the thunderous roar of engines shattered the uneasy calm that had settled over the village. Three Land Rovers rumbled into view, their dark green paint dulled by a thick layer of dust. The vehicles were battered and scarred, telling tales of countless missions across unforgiving terrain. They lurched to a stop in the village square.

As the dust settled, the doors of the Land Rovers swung open with a synchronised precision that spoke of military training. The men who emerged were a far cry from the polished, uniformed soldiers Aster might have expected. Instead, they looked like a motley crew of hardened adventurers, each one radiating an aura of barely contained danger.

The first man to step out was a giant of a fellow, easily topping six and a half feet. His massive frame was squeezed into cargo trousers and a tight-fitting black t-shirt that did little to hide his muscular physique. A shock of red hair and a bristling ginger beard gave him the appearance of a Viking warrior transplanted into the modern day. He carried a high-powered rifle with the casual ease of someone handling an everyday tool.

Following him was a lean, wiry man with skin the colour of burnished mahogany. He moved with the fluid grace of a dancer, but his eyes were sharp and alert, constantly scanning the surroundings. A series of tribal tattoos snaked up his arms, disappearing beneath the sleeves of his sand-coloured shirt. A wickedly curved knife was strapped to his thigh, and Aster had no doubt he knew how to use it with lethal efficiency.

From the second Land Rover emerged a pair that could have been twins – both of medium height with close-cropped dark hair and identical grim expressions. They wore matching tactical vests over plain t-shirts and moved in perfect unison as they secured the perimeter. The only way to tell them apart was the jagged scar that ran down the left cheek of one of them.

The third vehicle disgorged a man who seemed oddly out of place among his comrades. He was older, with silver streaks in his dark hair and lines etched deeply around his eyes. He wore khaki trousers and a rumpled linen shirt, looking more like an absent-minded professor than a mercenary. But the way he carried himself, and the respect the others seemed to afford him, made it clear he was a key member of the team.

The team moved with purpose, each knowing his role without need for verbal communication. Some took up defensive positions, their weapons at the ready, whilst others began to efficiently unload equipment from the vehicles.

The air was thick with tension as the villagers, who had begun to cautiously emerge from their hiding places, watched these strangers with a mixture of fear and awe. The mercenaries' presence was both reassuring and intimidating – clearly a force to be reckoned with, but an unknown quantity in this small, rural community.

From the back of one of the vehicles, five figures were carefully helped down to the ground. These were the rescued villagers, looking tired and dishevelled but mercifully unharmed. For a moment, there was a hushed silence as the reunited families stared at each other in disbelief. Then, as if a dam had burst, the square erupted into joyous chaos. A young woman in her late teens, wearing a simple white tank top and a long red skirt, looked around the crowd. Hitching up her skirts, she ran barefoot across the earth road.

'Mami, Dadi!'

As she ran, Aster could see a bleeding wound around one of her ankles. Fresh blood poured over her filthy feet as she raced into Amit's and Priya's hug. As the three of them embraced, Aster nodded grimly. The mercenaries may have killed the kidnappers, but someone was still behind this enterprise and they had a debt to pay.

The air filled with cries of relief and happiness as family members rushed forward. Tears flowed freely as husbands embraced wives, parents clutched children, and friends greeted friends. The sounds of laughter, sobbing, and rapid-fire Bengali blended into a cacophony of raw emotion that was almost overwhelming in its intensity.

Amidst this outpouring of feeling, the mercenaries maintained their vigilance. Their eyes continued to scan the surroundings, hands never straying far from their weapons. They were islands of controlled calm in a sea of unbridled emotion.

Edward made his way through the crowd towards a short, stocky man with an eye patch who had emerged from the lead vehicle. Despite his diminutive stature, the man exuded an aura of authority that made it clear he was in charge. His remaining eye, a steely grey, seemed to take in everything at once.

As Edward conversed with the leader in low, urgent tones, Aster watched the mercenaries disperse. Some headed towards the outskirts of the village, no doubt to secure the perimeter. Others set up communications equipment, establishing a temporary base of operations in the heart of the village.

The contrasts were stark – these hardened warriors with their high-tech gear, moving amongst the humble dwellings and simple lives of the villagers. It was as if two worlds had collided, the modern and the traditional, the global and the local, all converging in this small, dusty square in rural India.

As Aster took in the scene, her analytical mind was already working overtime. Who were these men? How had Edward summoned them here?

She was pulled from her thoughts by Amit's appearance at her elbow. His face was flushed with excitement, his eyes shining with a mixture of relief and anticipation. 'Oh, my beautiful girl is home. She and her mother are weeping for joy. This is the most auspicious day. Never did I doubt you. There will be a huge celebration,' he announced, his voice barely containing his joy. 'Edward and his men will be our most honoured guests. We must prepare!'

As Amit hurried off again to oversee the preparations, Aster's gaze was drawn back to Edward. He looked exhausted and Aster wondered if he had more at stake than she knew.

Chapter Thirty-Two

Aster walked towards the office, her legs suddenly feeling like lead. As the adrenaline drained from her system, she stumbled, the world tilting alarmingly. In an instant, Edward was at her side, his strong arm supporting her waist.

'Are you okay?' His voice was low, concern etched in every syllable.

Aster looked up into his steel-blue eyes, suddenly very aware of his proximity. A confusing swirl of emotions washed over her – relief, gratitude, and something else she couldn't quite name. It was disconcerting, this feeling of safety in his presence. She, who had always prided herself on her independence, was finding comfort in the steady strength of this man.

'Aster? Are you alright?' Edward's brow furrowed as he studied her face.

His arm tightened slightly, ready to lift her if necessary. The gesture, both protective and presumptuous, snapped Aster back to reality. She quickly disentangled herself, straightening her spine.

'I'm fine,' she assured him, her voice steadier than she felt. 'Just a moment of relief, I think. I need to call my sisters now. I'll catch up with you in a minute.'

Making her way into the office, her heart beat an irregular rhythm that had nothing to do with their recent brush with danger.

Spinning away, she all but fled into the offices and pulled up a group call to her sisters. The moment she established the connection, all four sisters appeared on the computer's monitor and she gave them a shaky wave as they all shouted in relief.

Paddy's face was red and puffy and sitting beside her was Hal, his arm wrapped tightly around her waist. As soon as she saw Aster, Paddy began to cry again.

'I'm fine, Paddy. Everything is over.'

'What happened?' asked a pale-faced Ari. Seb leant over her shoulder and waved at Aster. 'Glad to see you're okay, I'll leave you to it and let's have you home as soon as possible.' Ari smiled gratefully at his departing back and then smiled tremulously at Aster.

'God, that was nerve-wracking. I'm so sorry we sent you out there. I should never have done it, if I'd realised the risks.'

'The situation in rural India is always a quagmire,' said Hal, then as Paddy sobbed again, he took a deep breath. 'Sorry. Look, let me call you back in a bit. I have some contacts in the area. I'm going to call around, see what we can do.'

As an ex-soldier, Hal's expertise in the field was a given thing and Aster cursed herself for not speaking to him before she had headed over.

'When are you back?' asked Paddy, sniffing.

'Two days. If this hasn't delayed matters. Nick has my travel plans.'

'Then I'll see you at Heathrow. Oh, Aster. I love you so much.'

Paddy sobbed again.

'I know. I'll call you later, okay? Kiss the children for me.'

As she signed off, Clem sighed loudly.

'I swear to God, Aster if you ever scare us like that again, I'll kill you myself.'

'I love you too, Clem.'

'Stop saying you love us. It's freaking me out.'

Aster laughed. 'Normal service will resume soon. If it helps, I am also still freaked out. What about you, Nick? Not a word so far?'

Nick's face was even paler than Ari's and she shook her head.

'Sorry. Still processing.' As she spoke, she was also texting and then smiled at the screen. 'Gabe sends his love. He was on his way back from Paris. Asks if he should reroute to Kolkata?'

Aster knew the offer was serious and considered herself incredibly lucky in the men that her sisters had brought into the family.

'Tell him I'd be leaving as he arrived. The flight is a killer.'

Nick started texting again and Ari cleared her throat.

'What happened, Aster? Are you ready to tell us?'

'I am, but I don't really know much yet. I was about to go out on a recce, but I wanted to call you all first. You know, because I'm soppy like that?'

The sisters laughed and Aster felt the tension begin to ebb away.

'Like I said, I don't fully understand it yet, but it seems that Edward turned up with a pile of mercenaries who drove down the rebels and then freed our villagers.'

'And no one was hurt?' asked Nick.

'Well, the rebels were hurt with extreme prejudice. There was a lot of shooting.'

'Christ.'

'Ari, it's like Hal said, it's wild out here. Look, I'm going to go and inspect the site where our villagers were held hostage and will report back. Chat in a few hours. Love you all, and can someone check on Paddy?'

'I've already booked a flight whilst we were talking,' said Clem. 'Hal is picking me up from the airport. I'm bringing my design books so Paddy and I can work together on ideas. Help focus her mind away from her pesky little sister.'

'I love you too.'

Ending the call, she headed out into the sunshine. After reassuring her sisters and making plans, Aster emerged from the office, blinking in the bright sunlight. The village square was a hive of activity, villagers bustling about in preparation for what promised to be a significant celebration. Her eyes were immediately drawn to Edward, deep in conversation with one of the mercenaries – the short, stocky man with the eye patch she had noticed earlier.

As she approached, Aster took a moment to really look at Edward. In the chaos of the past few hours, she hadn't fully registered the change in him. Gone was the polished businessman from the auction house or the teasing companion from their card games. This Edward was all coiled energy and quiet authority. His shirtsleeves were rolled up, revealing tanned, muscular forearms. A fine sheen of sweat glistened on his brow and a day's worth of stubble darkened his jaw. He looked rugged, capable, and, Aster had to admit, ridiculously attractive.

She shook her head, bemused by her own thoughts. Since when did she notice such things? But then, she reasoned, it wasn't every day a man swooped in to save her life. Perhaps a little appreciation was warranted.

Squaring her shoulders, Aster approached the two men. 'Aster Byrne,' she introduced herself, extending her hand to the mercenary. 'I owe you my thanks. Now, can you bring me up to speed?'

The man's single eye flickered to Edward, seeking silent permission. Edward nodded almost imperceptibly, but it didn't escape Aster's notice.

She bristled slightly. 'I am the one paying your bill,' she said firmly.

The mercenary's weathered face cracked into a grin. 'Actually, yer man here has already paid for today's action.'

Aster turned to Edward, a mix of gratitude and annoyance warring within her. 'I shall repay you in full, with our thanks,' she said, her tone leaving no room for argument. Then, turning back to the mercenary, she continued: 'Are you able to take me to their compound and update me on the situation as we drive? Edward, perhaps you'd come with us and explain how you knew we were in trouble. I'll ask Amit to join us as well, so he can assess their operation. How does that sound?'

The mercenary's grin widened as he looked between Aster and Edward. 'That works for me,' he said, amusement evident in his gruff voice. 'Name's Bill, by the way. Bill McTavish.'

As Aster went to fetch Amit, she heard Bill mutter to Edward, 'Quite the cool customer you've got there, mate.'

Edward's response was too low for her to hear, but she could have sworn she caught a note of pride in his tone.

Soon, the four of them were piling into one of the Land Rovers. Aster made to climb into the front passenger seat, but both Bill and Edward objected.

'No way, Miss,' Bill said, shaking his head. 'You're not secure up front. You go in the back with Edward.'

Edward patted his rifle, flashing Aster a grin that was equal parts reassuring and infuriating. 'Don't worry, I'll keep you safe.'

'This is very good,' Amit chimed in, clearly pleased with the arrangement. 'I will sit beside Mr Bill and see where the road goes.'

Outflanked by all three men, Aster bit back a retort and climbed into the back seat. As they pulled away from the village, she found herself hyper-aware of Edward's presence beside her. The Land Rover's cabin suddenly felt claustrophobic as it bumped along the rutted track, throwing her constantly against Edward's side. Each time she scooched further away from him, a bump in the road threw her back against him.

'Relax,' said Edward, 'I'm not bothered. But if you'd feel secure, you can sit on my lap?' He laughed at her expression, then attempted to adjust her seatbelt and placed a jacket between them. 'Better?'

Aster just glared at him, then returned to looking out the window whilst she hung onto the door handle.

As they drove, Amit provided a running commentary on the landscape. 'This land is very fertile,' he explained, gesturing to the lush greenery surrounding them. 'But it is low-lying, you see? There is always a risk of flooding. This is why it is not populated.'

'Perfect for hiding illegal operations, though,' Bill grunted. 'Remote, fertile for growing crops, and close enough to the village to exploit local labour.'

Aster nodded, filing away this information. The pieces of the puzzle were coming together.

As they rounded the bend in the earth track, the compound came into view. It was a sorry sight – a run-down factory building surrounded by a handful of ramshackle living quarters. The corrugated iron roofs were rusted, and many of the windows were broken or boarded up. It looked more like a setting for a post-apocalyptic film than a centre of textile production.

Bill pulled the Land Rover to a stop a short distance from the main building. 'Watch your step,' he warned as they climbed out. 'We've cleared the area, but there might be traps we missed.'

As the engine died down, the silence enveloped them.

'Stay in the car,' said Edward, opening his door. 'I'll let you know when it's safe.' He stared at her, waiting for her to comply. Seeing a discussion would be futile, she nodded her head.

As soon as he was out of the car, she undid her belt and got out on her side and walked across the compound.

Aster's eyes were immediately drawn to the bodies lying in the dirt – the casualties of the earlier firefight. She regarded them dispassionately, her analytical mind already at work. These men would have killed her without hesitation, so she didn't waste a moment in regret.

'I told you to stay in the car.'

Aster looked over her shoulder at him. 'I heard you.'

'But it could be dangerous.'

'You're right. Tell you what. You go stay in the car and I'll call you when it's clear.'

He glared at her. Then, conceding defeat, he moved to her side, his rifle at the ready. 'I just want to keep you safe.'

'I don't need you to do that.'

He ran his fingers through his hair, the humid air causing furrows in it. 'I know you don't need it. But I do. Humour me please, I just can't relax if I think you are in danger.'

Aster pursed her lips. She was unused to this feeling of protection. She knew her sisters loved her and looked out for her as they all did for each other. But this was much more tangible. Normally, she felt like she was the person who would take the bullet. Now she was facing someone actively demonstrating he would take the bullet for her, and she felt nonplussed.

What did she want from someone when she was in the process of helping them? She wanted instant compliance. If people just did what she wanted, life would be so much easier. Her lips twitched as she saw the ridiculousness of her situation. Edward had the rifle, he had the mercenaries. He had the knowledge and experience.

'I'm not going back to the car, but I'm happy if you want to lead.'

He sagged in relief. 'Thank you. Are you okay?' he murmured gesturing towards the corpses.

'They deserved it.'

As they continued their inspection, Amit's expression grew thoughtful. 'The crop,' he said slowly, 'we could keep it. But the machines, the looms – we should bring them back to the village. They are good quality, despite their poor condition. With proper care, they could serve us well.'

Aster nodded, impressed by Amit's practical thinking. 'That's an excellent idea. We'll arrange for everything to be moved as soon as it's safe.'

They picked their way carefully through the compound. Inside the main building, they found rows of looms and spinning wheels, not dissimilar to those in the village, but here, everything was grimy, poorly maintained. And at each bench lay a broken ankle manacle. The air was thick with dust and the lingering scent of unwashed bodies.

'My God,' Amit breathed, his eyes wide as he took in the scene. 'This is where they kept my daughter? It is… it is monstrous.'

Aster's jaw clenched as she imagined the villagers forced to work in these conditions. She recalled the bleeding wound on Shakila's ankle and knew that whoever was behind this operation was about to have their world destroyed.

Heading back to the Land Rover, Aster walked beside Edward. Despite the grim surroundings, she felt oddly at ease in his presence. It was a novel feeling for her, this sense of security with another person. She was used to relying solely on herself, keeping others at arm's length. But Edward… Edward had proven himself trustworthy in the most extreme circumstances.

'Thank you,' she said quietly. 'For everything. I'm not used to… well, to needing help. But I'm glad you were here.'

Edward's expression softened. 'Anytime, Aster. I mean that.'

As they climbed back into the Land Rover, Aster felt a subtle shift in her perception of Edward. He was still an enigma in many ways, but she was seeing beyond the polished exterior to the man beneath – brave, resourceful, and unexpectedly kind.

The drive back to the village was quiet, each passenger lost in their own thoughts. Aster's mind was already racing ahead, planning their next moves. There were still many questions to be answered, loose ends to be tied up. But for now, she allowed herself a moment of relief. They had survived, the villagers were safe, and they had dealt a significant blow to whoever was behind this operation.

As the familiar outlines of Bhasagram came into view, Aster straightened in her seat. There was still much work to be done, but she felt reinvigorated, ready to face whatever challenges lay ahead. And, she realised with a start, she was glad to have Edward by her side for whatever came next.

The village square was now jumping as preparations for the celebration continued. Climbing out, Aster caught Edward's eye. For a moment, they shared a look of mutual understanding – a silent acknowledgement of all they had been through and the bond that had formed between them.

Then the moment passed, and Aster was all business once more. 'Right,' she said briskly. 'Let's get to work. We have a village to rebuild and a mystery to solve. Who was behind all this? I need to call my sisters and get the ball rolling.'

Edward's face darkened and Aster was surprised by the sudden flash of anger in his eyes. Puzzled, she headed towards the office and filed that away to think about later.

Chapter Thirty-Three

Aster settled into her makeshift office, her fingers hovering over the laptop keyboard. The events of the day weighed heavily on her, but there was work to be done. She glanced at Edward, who leant against the wall nearby, his arms crossed and his face unreadable. Despite the tension of the situation, she couldn't help but feel a flutter of attraction. His presence had been a comfort, his actions nothing short of heroic. But now wasn't the time for such thoughts.

With a deep breath, Aster started the video call to her sisters. After a moment, Nick and Ari's faces appeared on the screen, relief clear in their expressions.

'Hello you,' Ari breathed, her voice cracking slightly. 'Thank God you're alright.'

'What's the situation?' Nick added. Aster smiled and nodded at Nick, she was grateful to be getting down to business. As she explained the situation of the black-market factory and the slave conditions, she could feel Edward's presence behind her, a palpable tension radiating from him.

'We'll need to implement regular security measures,' Aster concluded. 'This can't happen again.'

Nick nodded, her business mind already whirring. 'Agreed. We'll allocate funds immediately. I'm actually flying out tomorrow to oversee the expansion of the factory and village. Hal's recommended some private security options we should consider.'

Before Aster could respond, Edward stepped forward, his voice tight with barely contained anger. 'With all due respect, ladies, your security measures are long overdue. You relied far too heavily on Aster, and you nearly lost her today.'

The silence that followed was deafening. Aster turned to Edward, her eyes flashing with a mix of surprise and indignation. The warmth she had felt towards him moments ago cooled rapidly.

'That's not fair, Edward,' she said, her voice low and dangerous. 'You don't know my sisters or our family dynamics. You have no right to-'

'No, Aster,' Ari interrupted, her voice small. 'He's right. We… we did put too much on your shoulders. We always have.'

Nick nodded, her usual composure cracking. 'We've taken you for granted, Aster. Assumed you could handle anything. That stops now.'

Aster felt torn between defending her sisters and acknowledging the truth in Edward's words. But that he had spoken to her family this way, that he had overstepped so dramatically, ignited a fire within her.

'Stop it, all of you,' she snapped, her voice sharp. 'Edward, I appreciate what you did today, but you have no right to speak to my sisters this way. And Ari, Nick - you did not put me in danger. I chose to come here. I knew the risks.'

Edward's jaw clenched. 'Did you? Did you really know what you were walking into? Because from where I'm standing, you were woefully unprepared for the situation here.'

Aster stood, facing Edward directly. 'And who are you to make that assessment? You swoop in with your mercenaries and your government connections and suddenly you're an expert on my life, my work?'

'I'm the one who saved your life today,' Edward retorted, his voice rising. 'If I hadn't been here-'

'If you hadn't been here, I would have found another way,' shouted Aster, cutting him off. 'I always do.'

On the screen, Nick and Ari watched in stunned silence.

'Aster,' Nick finally said, her voice cautious. 'Maybe we should discuss this when emotions aren't running so high.'

Aster turned back to the screen, taking a deep breath to calm herself. 'You're right. I'm sorry. This isn't productive.'

'No, I'm sorry,' Edward said, his voice softer now. 'I overstepped. It's just… seeing you in danger today… it affected me more than I expected.'

Aster felt some of her anger dissipate at his words, but she remained wary. This man had the ability to get under her skin was infuriating.

'Look,' she said, addressing both Edward and her sisters. 'What's done is done. We need to focus on protecting our people and our interests. Can we all agree on that?'

There were nods all around. The tension in the room eased slightly, but Aster could still feel the undercurrents of unresolved emotions.

'Nick,' she continued, 'you mentioned flying out. When do you arrive? We'll need to coordinate our efforts.'

As Nick outlined her travel plans and the security measures Hal had recommended, Aster found her temper simmering just beneath the surface. She clenched her fists under the desk, her nails digging into her palms. How dare Edward criticise her sisters? He didn't know them, didn't understand their bond. That Nick and Ari seemed to agree with him only fuelled her anger further.

She glanced at Edward, who had retreated to his position against the wall. His face was a mask of carefully controlled emotion, but she could see the storm brewing behind his eyes. Good, she thought. Let him be uncomfortable. He had no right to interfere in family matters.

Aster opened her mouth, ready to further defend her sisters and put Edward in his place, when a sharp knock at the door interrupted her. Amit burst in, his eyes wide. 'The police are here,' he announced breathlessly.

Aster exchanged a quick glance with Edward before turning back to the screen. 'We'll have to continue this later,' she said hurriedly, her voice still tight with restrained anger. 'Nick, call me when you land.'

She ended the call and stood, squaring her shoulders. 'Let's go see what the police have to say.' Her tone made it clear that their previous discussion was far from over.

Outside, they found Bill already engaged in conversation with the police chief, a huge man whose uniform strained against his belly. The chief's demeanour was oddly casual, as if he were discussing the weather rather than a violent conflict.

'Ah, Miss Byrne,' the chief said as Aster approached. 'I understand there was some… excitement here today?'

Aster raised an eyebrow at his choice of words. 'You could say that,' she replied coolly.

Bill cleared his throat. 'As I was explaining to the chief, it appears a local band of militia turned on each other. Quite the bloodbath. We simply stepped in to rescue the hostages.'

The chief nodded, seemingly satisfied with this blatant fabrication. 'These things happen,' he said with a shrug. 'Criminals, you know. No honour among thieves.'

Aster caught Edward's eye, seeing her own disbelief mirrored there. Despite her anger towards him, they shared a moment of silent communication, both recognising the absurdity of the situation.

'Well, we're grateful for your prompt response,' Aster said diplomatically, pushing aside her personal feelings to focus on the matter at hand. 'We're planning to implement additional security measures to prevent any future... incidents.'

Bill stepped forward. 'If I may, I'd recommend a troop of private security. I know a reputable firm that specialises in rural protection.'

The chief's eyes lit up at this, and Aster wondered briefly if he was expecting a kickback. 'An excellent idea,' he said enthusiastically. 'You can never be too careful.'

As the conversation continued, Aster felt her frustration growing. The ease with which they were brushing off such a significant event was infuriating. She could feel Edward's presence beside her, a reminder of their unresolved tension, but for now, they presented a united front to the authorities.

After the police left, the celebrations began. As night fell, the village square transformed into a vibrant tapestry of colour, sound, and scent. Lanterns strung between houses cast a warm, golden glow over the festivities. The air was thick with the aroma of spices - cumin, cardamom, and saffron mingling with the sweet scent of jasmine flowers adorning the women's hair. The rhythmic beat of drums and the melodious strains of sitars filled the air, punctuated by bursts of laughter and animated conversation.

Villagers, dressed in their finest clothes, moved through the square in a swirl of jewel-toned fabrics. Children darted between the adults, their faces sticky with sweets, their laughter rising above the general din. The rescued villagers were at the centre of it all, surrounded by friends and family, their recent ordeal momentarily forgotten in the joy of reunion.

Aster stood at the edge of the celebration, watching the scene unfold. Under normal circumstances, she might have appreciated the beauty of the moment, the resilience of these people who could find cause for joy even in the wake of such danger. But tonight, she felt oddly disconnected from it all.

The fear, the anger, the rush of adrenaline - it all caught up with her at once, leaving her feeling drained and overwhelmed. The noise and bustle of the celebration, which should have been uplifting, only heightened her discomfort.

She had never been one for large gatherings, preferring the quiet of her own company or the intimacy of small groups. Now, with her nerves still frayed from the day's events, the press of bodies and the constant chatter felt suffocating.

Spotting Amit nearby, Aster made her way over to him. 'I'm afraid I'll have to retire early,' she said, raising her voice to be heard over the music. 'It's been a long day, and I'm quite exhausted.'

Amit nodded his understanding. 'Of course, of course. You must rest. We are all so grateful for what you have done.'

Aster managed a small smile, then turned to make her way back to her room. As she navigated through the crowd, she caught sight of Edward watching her from across the square. Their eyes met for a moment, and she saw him move towards her.

Quickening her pace, Aster reached the relative quiet of the building where she was staying. She had just reached the bottom of the stairs when she heard Edward's footsteps behind her.

'Aster,' he called out, his voice low and urgent.

She turned, one hand on the banister, to face him. In the dim light of the hallway, she could see the conflict on his face, his mouth opening as if to speak.

But Aster cut him off before he could utter a word. 'No,' she said, her voice sharp. 'I appreciate what you did today. Hiring the mercenaries, coming to our aid - I'm grateful for that. But what you said to my sisters was out of line.'

Edward took a step closer, his expression earnest, but Aster held up a hand to stop him.

'I'm tired. It's been a long day, and I need to rest. We can discuss this further tomorrow if we must.'

Turning, she climbed the stairs, feeling Edward's gaze on her back. As she reached her room and closed the door behind her, Aster let out a long, shaky breath.

The events of the day replayed in her mind as she prepared for bed - the fear, the danger, Edward's timely arrival with the mercenaries, the argument about her sisters. It was all too much to process.

As she lay in bed, the sounds of the celebration drifting in through the window, she rolled over with a sigh, pulling the thin blanket tighter around her shoulders. Tomorrow would bring new challenges, new decisions to be made. For now, she needed sleep. As she drifted off, Aster's last conscious thought was of Edward's face - not as he had looked during their argument, but as he had appeared when he first arrived to rescue them, a mix of relief and something else written across his features.

Chapter Thirty-Four

The day passed in a flurry of activity - overseeing the security setup, reassuring villagers, and making preparations for the future. As evening approached, Aster found herself exhausted, looking forward to a quiet night to process the events of the past few days.

She had received a text from Nick saying that she was sending her an outfit for the gala in case she herself couldn't make it in time. Nick had been very clear that Aster had to attend the High Commissioner's gala, despite everything that had happened. The Hiverton Estate needed as much goodwill as it could muster.

Aster glared at the screen. Unlike last night, she could not slink off.

The sound of an approaching vehicle drew her attention. Curious, she stepped outside just as a dusty Land Rover pulled up. Aster's eyes widened in surprise as a familiar figure emerged.

Despite her petite stature, Clementine Byrne commanded attention the moment she stepped out of the vehicle. Her wild mane of fiery red curls caught the last rays of the setting sun, creating a halo effect around her heart-shaped face. Clem's curvy figure was accentuated by a flowing bohemian dress, and her presence seemed to electrify the very air around her.

'Clem?' Aster gasped, shock and delight warring in her voice.

Clem's face split into a radiant smile as she spotted her sister. In an instant, she had crossed the distance between them, enveloping Aster in a fierce hug that belied her small size.

'You impossible, reckless, brilliant idiot,' Clem muttered into Aster's hair, her voice thick with emotion. 'Don't ever do that again.'

Aster laughed, the tension of the past few days melting away in her sister's embrace. 'I can't believe you're here,' she said, pulling back to look at Clem. 'How did you manage this?'

Clem's green eyes sparkled with mischief. 'You think you're the only one who can pull off a surprise?' She glanced around, taking in the village in the fading light. 'This place is incredible,' she breathed. 'I can already feel the inspiration.'

'I thought you might,' Aster grinned, still marvelling at her sister's unexpected presence. 'Planning to stay a while?'

Clem nodded, her wild curls bouncing with the movement. 'I'm going to spend the week here with Nick. Total immersion in the textile industry and design. These people, their craft… it's extraordinary.'

As they stood there, Aster noticed how the villagers passing by couldn't help but stare at Clem. Her sister always had that effect on people - her vibrant presence drawing all eyes, her energy infectious. It was a stark contrast to Aster's own tendency to fade into the background, and for a moment, she felt a familiar surge of pleasure that she was so unremarkable. It would kill her to have people always mark her passing. She wondered how Clem tolerated it, but then she remembered that Clem didn't give a fig what anyone thought of her.

Their reunion was interrupted by the sound of whistling. Edward rounded the corner, his expression unreadable as he took in the scene.

Before Aster could speak, Clem's eyes narrowed. 'You!' she snapped, jabbing a finger at Edward's chest. 'How dare you speak to Ari that way? Who do you think you are?'

Edward's eyebrows shot up, clearly taken aback by this sudden assault. 'I beg your pardon?'

'Don't play innocent,' Clem seethed. 'Ari told me what you said. She was in tears, thinking she'd put Aster in danger. As if Ari would ever do anything to harm any of us!'

Aster winced, recognising the blind spot in Clem's otherwise sharp perception. In Clem's eyes, Ari could do no wrong, her love for their eldest sister bordering on reverence.

Edward opened his mouth to retort, but Aster stepped in, placing a calming hand on Clem's arm. 'Clem, it's okay. It's been dealt with.'

'By you?! That just means you've found some clever way to see both sides. Don't tell me you approve of him shouting at Ari?'

'Jesus, Clem, you've been here five seconds, stop bloody shouting. We all screwed up. Me, Ari and Nick. Okay? We screwed up.'

'And now you're handling it.'

'We are.'

'So we don't need James Bond here to sort things out.'

Edward snorted at the nickname.

'Look, Miss Byrne.'

'Lady Clementine.'

Aster groaned, Clem only fell back on her title when she was squaring up for a fight. It was time to head her off.

'Enough. We were in the wrong. Edward did us a favour. He shouldn't have shouted at Ari or Nick. Happy? Now don't spoil our reunion. I take it your arrival has something to do with my new outfit?'

If there was one thing that was going to stop Clem in her tracks when she was building up a full head of steam, it was taking about clothing.

'I left it in Mumbai. I've checked the three of us into a suite. Nick arrives tomorrow.'

'So, I don't have to attend the gala,' said Aster hopefully.

'Not a hope. Nick wants a shock and awe campaign.'

'Not sure I supply either of those.'

Clem laughed. 'Don't worry, I'll provide enough for both of us.' She looked at Edward. 'Are you still here?'

'I'm heading back to Kolkata with the team now,' he said, his voice clipped. 'The security firm is in place. They'll keep things under control here. I just came to say goodbye.'

Aster nodded, a mix of relief and something else - regret, perhaps? - washing over her. 'Thank you, Edward. For everything.'

He held her gaze for a moment longer than necessary, then turned and walked away.

'I don't trust him,' said Clem. 'That's twice now he's been nearby when you've been – well – you know.'

'I know.'

She thought about it. The first time had been a coincidence, but had the second time?

Within the hour, Edward and the mercenaries had departed for Kolkata, leaving the village in a strange calm.

The sisters spent their final evening in the village, Clem absorbing every detail with an artist's eye whilst Aster made last-minute arrangements with Amit and the new security team. As night fell, they sat on the roof of Amit's house, looking out over the quiet village, each lost in their own thoughts about the events that had transpired and what was yet to come.

'Oh, I meant to say, have you been following the news?'

Clem turned and looked at her sister expectantly.

'I have been otherwise occupied.'

'Fair enough.' Clem pulled her phone out and waved it around. 'No bloody signal out here, anyway.'

She took a glug from her bottle and waved it at Aster.

'Marcus Barrie has been arrested.'

'What?'

'It's all over the papers. Innocent until proven guilty and all that rubbish. But lots of women have come forward. He's facing multiple charges. You did it!'

Clem leant over and chinked her bottle against Aster's as Aster smiled out into the night sky.

The following morning brought a flurry of activity as Aster and Clem prepared to depart. They bade farewell to the villagers, Amit's eyes shining with unshed tears as he thanked them once again for all they had done. Then they were off, the dusty roads of the village giving way to the chaos of Kolkata's streets and a four-hour flight back to Mumbai. Overnight, Aster had been composing messages to all the women that she had spoken to prior to her campaign and as they approached Kolkata her phone sprang into life and sent out those texts and e-mails. As soon as she had a signal, she started scouring social media and chat boards and was satisfied that he would not escape justice.

Clem smiled over at her. She put her phone away as they walked into the airport.

'You did a really good thing, you know.'

Aster shrugged.

'I was the right person in the right place. That's all.'

'Pah!'

Linking arms with her little sister, the two girls strode into the airport and headed towards Mumbai.

Chapter Thirty-Five

'I just don't trust him.'

Aster shook her head. She and Nick had been arguing this point for hours. Nick was deeply suspicious about Edward, not least because he wouldn't say whom he had flown out to India to investigate. Nick was certain that whoever it was, they were also behind their own troubles.

'Because he won't share his intel with you? That's not rational,' said Aster in exasperation.

'Well, you know my opinion,' chimed in Clem. 'Completely untrustworthy.'

Aster ground her teeth. The three sisters had reunited in their suite and Nick immediately hugged Aster, which they both endured for about two seconds before declaring they had had enough soppy stuff. Clem had unpacked Nick's evening wear and steamed all three outfits whilst Aster and Nick talked business with Clem adding her opinion every now and then.

'He is not untrustworthy,' snapped Aster. 'He's just not prepared to reveal his sources or share any intel with us.' Aster found herself in the strange position of defending a man that she was hardly enamoured with herself, but in this, Nick was determined.

'But Aster, don't you see? Someone was undercutting our business. They were responsible for kidnapping our employees and turning them into slaves. We need to know who they are, so that we can move against him.'

'I know all this.'

'And yet you're taking Edward's side.'

'How many more times, Nick? I am not taking his side.'

'How do we even know this wasn't his enterprise?' said Clem, applying her mascara and waving the wand for added emphasis.

'Because he didn't shoot me. That would be my clue. Really, Clem, this isn't helping. Edward has his faults, and I appreciate him playing his cards close to his chest must be killing you, Nick. But it doesn't matter.'

'You think what this person has done doesn't matter?' screeched Clem, but Aster could see that Nick was waiting patiently for her to carry on.

'It doesn't matter if Edward isn't prepared to tell us the name of the man in question because I'll find out for myself.'

Clem laughed loudly from the dressing table. 'That's my girl! When are you going to get started?'

'I started yesterday.' Aster smiled at her sisters and was gratified to see the worry dissolve from Nick's face.

'Gosh, you've had twelve hours and you haven't found it out yet?' asked Clem, teasing her little sister.

'After my last run-in, I'm moving with extreme caution.'

Nick's relief was complete. Aster stared at her sister and tried to hide the guilt that she had felt at scaring them this week.

'Well, Clem, now that you've made yourself look pretty, shall we go? And Nick, remember your promise.'

'You can leave as soon you've said hello to the High Commissioner.'

'Perfect. Then let's go!'

Laughing, the three girls headed down to their limousine.

As the three Hiverton girls stepped out of the hotel lobby to their waiting limousine, they attracted the attention of several passersby. At five foot ten, Nick led the way in one of Clem's couture creations emphasising her slim build and height. The long black gown was covered in small pearls and mother-of-pearl decorations. Clem had been inspired by the Cockney Kings and Queens and had then created a runway collection that had been fought over by royalty and A-list celebrities. This particular gown she had held back for something special and the need to impress the Indian authorities felt like the perfect occasion. It would attract a lot of publicity and goodwill for the High Commissioner's gala, for Water Aid, which everyone wanted to support.

Behind Nick came Clem, resplendent in a full-length saree in shades of green and blue, her long red locks pinned up into a topknot and then cascading down her back. The saree had been designed and made by Kavya Verma, an up-and-coming local designer, and Clem was keen to promote her work.

Finally, Aster brought up the rear, wearing a plain black tuxedo gown which Clem had made for her and fit her beautifully. The original version had braiding on the sleeves and lapels, but Aster had begged for even those flourishes to be removed.

Just as they got to the car, Aster surreptitiously stepped to the side where a security guard had left his motorcycle unattended. A second later, she climbed into the limo and they set off.

'Aster Byrne, where did you get them?'

Nick glared at Aster, who now appeared to be the proud owner of a pair of mirrored sunglasses and a walkie-talkie. Aster smiled sheepishly.

'What?'

'You know what.'

'Just in case there are photographers when we arrive.'

'There won't be any photographers,' said Nick reassuringly, only for Clem to butt in, muttering that there bloody well better be. Nick glared at Clem, but decided not to argue the point. Everyone knew Aster's aversion to publicity.

'Just make sure you ditch them before we enter the High Commission.'

'Deal.'

As the limo finally made it through the traffic, they pulled up into a queue of limos waiting to disgorge their occupants to an awaiting crowd of paparazzi. Aster immediately removed her frock coat and looked at Clem. 'I don't suppose you'd carry this for me, would you?'

'And spoil my outfit? Absolutely not. And neither will Nick.'

Aster turned to Nick. There was no way she was going to have her photo taken with her sisters.

'Come on, Nick, whoever heard of a security detail carrying a coat?'

'And go against Clem on a matter of fashion? Have you lost your mind?'

Knowing that the fight was over before it began, Aster folded the tailcoat over her arm and put on the sunglasses. She would make the best of it and pretend that maybe she had a concealed gun under the draped coat. Nick shook her head in despair as the driver opened the door.

Nick stepped out to a barrage of flashbulbs that practically exploded as Clem emerged, followed shortly after by a small security guard in black trousers and a white shirt. She was talking into a walkie-talkie and looking all around, canvassing the crowd. The photographers promptly ignored her and carried on taking photos of the two dazzling women now walking the line and telling photographers who they were and whose clothes they were wearing.

At the top of the steps, beyond the photographers, the smaller bodyguard leant over to one of the security detail and handed them a pair of sunglasses and walkie-talkie. She grinned at them, popped her tailcoat back on and then moved quickly to rejoin her sister, grinning from ear to ear.

'Happy?'

'Delighted. Now let's get on with the torture and then I can go home.'

Having been checked in through security and announced as the Ladies Clementine, Nicoletta and Aster Hiverton, the three girls moved into the throng and began to socialise. Nick was soon engaged in serious conversation, Clem was laughing and chatting to all and sundry and Aster was propping up a pillar. She had been introduced to the High Commissioner ten minutes ago and now waited to catch Nick's eye and make her escape.

'Is it possible that I saw you earlier acting as a security guard?'

Aster spun around to look up into Edward's smiling face. His eyes were sparkling with mirth as he looked down at her leaning against the same pillar.

'Lady Aster, working as private security? Seems unlikely.'

Edward barked a laugh.

'Seemed entirely likely to me. Now look, I've found something you'd like.'

Handing her a bottle of water with a sealed cap he grabbed her hand and pulled her along with him. 'Hurry. It's very special.'

Bemused but happy to be in his presence again, she looked over her shoulder to check that Nick and Clem hadn't clocked her departure and followed along after him. Tonight, he was in a dinner jacket and was looking every inch a lord. As he wove his way through the ballroom, she tried to see where they were going, but short of jumping up or dodging to the side she couldn't see past him. As they headed into a corridor, she caught up to him and he smiled down at her.

'You'll love this.'

As they got to the next turning, two security agents were standing barring the way further into the residence. They simply nodded their heads as Edward strode past, grinning at Aster conspiratorially. As they reach an elegantly carved mahogany doorway, Edward paused and released Aster's hand. Opening the door and looking in, he then pushed it open and invited Aster to step inside.

Aster raised an eyebrow, wondering what was so special. Edward was practically beaming with glee. She found his excitement infectious as she stepped into the room and was greeted by the most glorious library she had ever set her eyes on.

She was immediately enveloped by the comforting scent of old books, leather and beeswax. The library, whilst not vast, was impressively large and exquisitely appointed. Dark wooden shelves lined the walls from floor to ceiling, packed with leather-bound volumes in a myriad of muted colours. A massive mahogany table dominated the centre of the room, its polished surface adorned with antique reading lamps casting pools of warm light on open books and scattered papers.

Plush leather armchairs were strategically placed throughout the room, inviting readers to lose themselves in comfort and literature. At the far end, tall windows framed a breathtaking view of Mumbai's skyline, the setting sun casting a fiery glow over the city. Near the fireplace, which boasted an intricately carved mantelpiece, stood several glass-fronted cabinets housing what appeared to be rare first editions and ancient manuscripts. The entire space exuded an air of quiet elegance and centuries of accumulated knowledge.

'When we were in the nightclub, you said it needed a few bookcases. Was this what you had in mind?'

Aster was laughing and was already exploring the bookcases. Edward headed over to one of the armchairs and pulled out a pack of cards from his pocket.

'Fancy a rematch?'

'You want to lose again?' Aster peeled away from the shelves and came and sat down opposite him. With a grin, Aster watched as Edward shuffled the deck.

'Guess what?'

He raised an eyebrow, she knew her playful tone was unlike her but she couldn't wait to tell him about the painting.'

'How many guesses do I have?'

'One. But I will give you a clue. It's about you being really, really wrong.'

He narrowed his eyes and thought for a second.

'God damn. It's the painting isn't it?' An excited smile began to crease his face.

Aster stared back at him in mock confusion.

'What painting? Oh, the Raphael?'

Edward's jaw dropped.

'Holy Mary!'

'Amen!' laughed Aster.

'But that's amazing.' He suddenly groaned. 'The nuns. God! I nearly lost them a fortune.'

Aster nodded smugly. 'Indeed.'

As they both started laughing and celebrating, Edward filled Aster's glass with champagne and then began to deal as he quizzed her all about the restoration. Frustratingly, she had little to tell him. The last few days had been frantic and she hadn't had time to focus on the painting.

As he dealt, he cleared his throat.

'About your sisters.'

Aster glared at him. Why did he have to spoil things?

'I'm not going to apologise for losing my temper, but I am sorry that I hurt you by shouting at them.'

'I-' Aster paused. That was a deeply odd apology. 'The thing is, we all made mistakes. If you were going to tell them off, you should have been shouting at me as well.'

He groaned and ran his fingers through his hair.

'I know that. I could have throttled you for placing yourself in such a dangerous situation. But mostly I was furious with myself for letting you drive off into the Indian wilds with no more security than a taxi driver.'

'You're not responsible for me,' said Aster, confused. No one was. It was why she had been so angry for upsetting her sisters, they weren't responsible for her either. It had been her mistake and hers alone. She had failed to properly assess the threat and that was on her. She looked at Edward, trying to understand what he meant.

Edward set the cards down, his eyes meeting Aster's with an intensity that made her breath catch.

'Aster, you're extraordinary,' he began, his voice low and earnest. 'The way you see problems and fix them, it's... it's unlike anything I've ever seen. You're not constrained by laws or conventions, and yet you have this unwavering moral compass to do what's right. I can't tell you how much I admire that.'

He leant forward, his gaze never leaving hers. 'Your fierce intellect, the way you pieced together the muslin mystery, how you derailed the auction - it's all done without a shred of ego. You don't seek praise or recognition. You just do what needs to be done.'

Edward's voice grew softer, filled with admiration. 'I've seen you risk your own safety to protect others, like when you confronted Marcus Barrie. You exposed him, brought justice to those women, all whilst keeping yourself out of the spotlight. And the way you care for your family, your dedication to the nuns, your commitment to the villagers - it's remarkable.'

He paused, seeming to gather his thoughts. 'You're a force of nature, Aster. You're brilliant, fearless, and yet so compassionate. The way you handle yourself in any situation, whether it's outsmarting criminals or playing cards on a plane - you're always ten steps ahead of everyone else.'

Aster sat stunned. His words were mortifying, he was describing someone she didn't recognise and yet she couldn't stop him. She felt she was in thrall to him, confused and hypnotised. How closely had he been watching her, why was he saying these things? His expression softened, a warmth in his eyes that Aster had never seen before. He opened his mouth to speak again, his voice thick with emotion. 'Aster, I-'

The door to the library swung open and Aster jerked away from Edward's face as she looked up to see an English man striding into the room.

'Found you, you old bugger!'

For a second, Aster saw Edward's face tighten in fury and then a moment of concern before he leant across the table and bent to kiss her on the neck. As he did so he whispered urgently, '*Play along.*' And then he jumped to his feet, turning round to greet the newcomer.

'Tony! Can't a man find a quiet corner anywhere, you bloody reprobate?'

Stepping forwards the two men shook hands. The newcomer was in his fifties, but trim. He exuded the sort of confidence that came from unlimited wealth and power. Aster loathed him on sight, but she also recognised him. Her brain began to race as she began to put two and two together. He glanced at her briefly, then ignored her again.

'Good news. I've only managed to bag you a bloody spot on the shoot!'

'Mate!' said Edward in a tone that Aster couldn't reconcile. He had changed from an intelligent, humorous companion to a loud boorish Hooray Henry. 'The tiger?'

'Fingers crossed, but no, this will be mostly antelope. But who knows, hey?'

'Too bloody right,' laughed Edward, loudly matching the boisterous level of the newcomer. 'Oh God, where are my manners? Sabrina, this is Anthony Jones, our very own British Foreign Secretary, no less. We are honoured.' He punched Tony playfully on the arm. 'And my lovely companion is Sabrina Lecky, part of the trade delegation.'

Aster smiled vapidly at both men and then giggled. 'I've seen you on TV, haven't I?' This was going to be her safest approach.

The MP smiled at her benignly. 'For my sins! Now, where are my manners, interrupting your - conversation?' He raised an eyebrow and chortled knowingly. Aster silently cursed her flat shoes. A stiletto heel would be most useful at this moment, but she giggled instead and shrugged her shoulders as he continued. 'Well, I had best leave you.'

'Don't be bloody stupid, mate. I want to hear all about this shoot. Sabrina, why don't you get back to the party?'

Her admiration for Edward had climbed another notch as she considered her new name. Clearly, he also didn't want the Foreign Secretary to know her true identity. She pouted, but stepped away from Edward and headed to the door. Just as she got to the door, she heard Edward whisper loudly to Tony.

'Waste of time, mate. Honestly, you saved me from a very tedious mistake. Let me say goodbye properly before she sulks.'

The two men laughed loudly as Tony headed towards a bottle of whisky and some tumblers and Aster opened the door. Edward loped across the room and leant against the doorframe and leant down to kiss Aster's neck again. At least this time she was prepared for the shock of his lips on her skin, but she still felt a bolt of electricity course through her.

'Sorry about that,' he whispered against her neck, 'I just know how much you want to protect your privacy. See you in London.'

Did he really think she would buy that? That he was simply protecting her privacy. She was going to say something, but he had his back to her, shouting at Tony to pour him a double, and effectively dismissed her.

Heading back through the ballroom, her mind was churning. Across the room, she caught Nick's eye and waved goodnight. Clem was deep in a throng of party-goers and she would rely on Nick letting her know she was heading back to the hotel.

Hailing a taxi, she slipped onto the back seat, her mind spinning. As much as she wanted to focus on Edward's lips on her neck and the thrill that had given her, she had bigger fish to fry. His sudden change in personality hadn't fooled her. She sent Nick a private text. No point alerting Clem, who would go off like a rocket.

- Read my next text in private.

She hit send and then began typing again.

Chapter Thirty-Six

Stepping off the plane at Heathrow, Aster was happy with what she had achieved on the flight. Her sights were now firmly set on her quarry. He might think his position of power protected him, but he was about to find himself firmly on his arse.

Deep in thought, she left baggage reclaim and headed out into the arrival lounge, where she was immediately assaulted by two small boys dressed as medieval knights waving foam swords around and generally shouting her name in glee. Grabbing her nephews in a massive hug, she looked up to see Ari and Paddy running towards her as well. Behind them, Seb was waiting with Paddy's children, who were both smaller in age and gentler in temperament. Aster briefly wondered where Hal was, and then she was engulfed in her sisters' embraces.

Laughing, she eventually pushed them all off her and caught her breath.

'Where's Hal?'

'On his way to Mumbai. Left an hour ago.'

'We've been here forever,' piped up Leo.

'Forever,' echoed little Hector and then wriggled in Seb's arms to return to his mother. Paddy scooped Eleanor up and turned back to Aster.

'He's gone over to offer some advice regarding the security situation.'

Hal had been a soldier on active duty for several years out in the Middle East and had contacts in lots of strange places. It made sense for him to head out and Aster felt relieved that someone within the family was going out to help Nick. Clem would be away with the fabrics.

'Aster, I've got a new sword. Look!' Stabbing her in the calf, Leo and Will both mounted a full-scale assault until Aster roared at them as they ran off screaming in delight.

Eventually, Ari and Seb got everyone including Aster back under control and they headed home with Aster riding in Paddy's car. Even if there had been room in Ari and Seb's car, Paddy had barely let go of Aster's hand since her arrival and Aster was happy to go with the flow until Paddy was finally reassured that her little sister was truly safe.

'Are you heading back to Cornwall tomorrow?'

Paddy kept her eye on the road as they drove into London, but shook her head. 'No, we're heading up to Hiverton. Let the cousins play together for a bit. Michelle is running Kensey and I can take care of the admin from here. Plus I can run all the marketing for Hiverton from anywhere.'

'Relax. I know you have it all under control. I wasn't interrogating you.'

'I know. I just. God, I don't know. I just wanted to prove I'm pulling my weight.'

'Paddy. Stop it. You worked your butt off to put food on the table. You have always been the peacemaker and the glue that has held us all together and even now you are turning the House of Hiverton into a global brand whilst bringing up two adorable little angels.'

'But—'

'No. Stop it! Hey, Eleanor!

'Yes?'

'I think there's some chocolate mousse back at the house. Want some?'

'Yay!'

'And who's the best Mummy in the world?'

'Mummy!' shouted Eleanor, and Alice gurgled in agreement.

Aster looked at Paddy.

'There you go. You're doing fine. And so am I. Take a left here, it's quicker.'

Racing Ari home, the two sisters got there first to the delight of Eleanor and the dismay of Ari's boys who pulled up five minutes later.

The following morning, Ari and Paddy finally left with all their entourage and Aster breathed a sigh of relief. Their fussing was overwhelming her and she had work to do. Having spoken to Ari about her findings, she warned her not to do anything, especially any online searches. She wanted nothing to tip him off but she felt as head of the family, Ari needed to know what they were up against.

Finally, as she watched them drive around the end of the street, she headed back indoors and fired up the computer. As she sat down, her phone pinged and she saw a text from Edward.

– *Heading home tomorrow. Drinks?*

Aster looked at the phone for a few minutes. Twenty-four hours. That would be enough time to get things in place.

- *Come to mine. 10 AM.*

Checking he agreed, she put her phone down and fired up her computers. She had a trap to set.

'Shall we head out?' said Edward, standing at the front door. Today he was dressed in an open neck polo shirt and a pair of chinos. Every inch the relaxed millionaire, gadding about town. For a second, Aster caught her breath, having forgotten the impact he had on her every time she saw him. He was just so solid. She laughed to herself, it was hardly a complimentary description.

'Is everything okay?'

Aster chuckled and shook her head.

'Everything is fine. Come inside, we have things to discuss.'

Aster walked through to the back of the house and waved at him to sit opposite her at the kitchen table. Edward raised an eyebrow, and then settled down on one of the chairs as Aster opened her laptop.

'So, Edward, Duke of Peveril, owner of half of Mayfair, man about town, happy-go-lucky socialite, who exactly are you?'

Now Edward leant back in his chair, considering her challenging tone.

'I am exactly who you have just said.'

'Except you are a lot more than that, aren't you? You are also someone that His Majesty's Government turns to from time to time. According to your MI6 files, you are-'

Edwards eyes opened wide in alarm.

'Aster. Don't speak. You have to know any MI6 files are classified. You can't possibly know what is or isn't in them.'

'So I don't know about your time in Islamabad?'

'I was a soldier. It is public knowledge that we were stationed out there.'

'I'm talking about the following year.'

'That's classified. Hell, Aster, it's probably treasonous. How the hell do you know about that?'

'Like I said. I read the files.'

'But how? Aster, that's hacking. At the highest level!'

'Please. MI6 need a complete overhaul of their security protocols.'

'They are the tightest in the country.'

'They were until six months ago. When they upgraded their automated air-con system and gave the tender to the cheapest bidder. And that cheapskate piggybacked onto MI6's router but kept a standard password for their own router. All I had to do was hack that router and I had open access to the rest of the network.'

'But you'll have left a trail?'

'As if.'

She sat back and smiled at him. How he reacted now would tell her all she need to know.

'Mother of God!' And then he burst into laughter. 'You really are something special, aren't you?'

She continued to watch him carefully as he wiped away a tear from his eye. 'Aster, I swear, you are magnificent.' He stood up and walked over to the sink and poured a glass of water for himself and one for Aster before sitting back down.

'So, let's have it. Why have you been investigating me?'

'Because I wanted to see who you really were before I decide to work with you.'

'Who I really am?'

'Yes. You have two faces. The playboy dilettante and the Edward that I have met.'

Edward gazed at her. 'And they're different?'

'You know they are. The side I see feels real. You are clever, resourceful, determined.' She wanted to say that his presence made her feel safe. That she had a friend by her side. But she held back the words. 'I can work with this person. The dilettante? I don't know. So, which one is the real you?'

'They both are. A bit. But the side you see is the side I am most of the time, but don't get me wrong, I like a good party.'

'So how did you start working on what I'm guessing are covert operations?'

'I was approached back as a teenager. Could I cultivate a slightly unthreatening air?'

'But you joined the army?'

He shrugged. 'It's what my sort do. Public school, degree, armed services or the city. I was drawn to the action of the army. After all, it's not like I need a salary. I liked the idea of serving.'

Aster nodded along.

'And what do you do for the government?'

'It's classified.'

'I could look it up?'

He laughed again and shook his head. 'You know when I leave here, I will draw their attention to a possible breach.'

'Fair enough.' She knew that would be his response. 'And will you give them my name?'

'Of course not. But you knew that already, didn't you? You must know that I will never put you in harm's way.'

He smiled at her and leant forwards, stretching out his hand, but Aster felt uncomfortable at the intensity of his stare. This was getting off topic and she had a deadline.

'Okay. Let's get to work.'

Edward leant back in his chair, withdrawing his hand as Aster got up and flicked the coffee machine on.

'Work?'

'I have an idea how we're going to take down the Foreign Secretary.'

Edward shot to his feet.

'Absolutely not. You are not to go near him.'

He glared at her as she opened the fridge and removed the milk, paying him little heed.

'Besides,' he said, quickly realising he had just gaffed, 'why do you want to attack Anthony Jones?'

'Spare me. Milk?' Pouring some into his mug and leaving hers black, she returned to the table handing him his cup. 'You and I both know that Jones is the brains behind the counterfeit fabrics and kidnapping.'

'Did you find that out when you broke into the MI6 files?'

'No. The penny dropped when he walked into the library in Mumbai and your demeanour instantly changed. You suddenly became someone harmless and inconsequential. It was an act and one that Jones completely accepted, meaning that's how he always sees you. As I walked out of the room, I wondered again what you were doing on this business trip and it occurred to me that maybe you were there to spy on someone.'

Edward groaned. 'You worked all that out that quickly?' He waved his hand. 'Of course you did. I shouldn't be surprised. But Aster, he is much more dangerous than a simple counterfeiter.'

'Oh, I know. I mean, I went and looked at what MI6 had on him. Incidentally, MI5 systems. Tight as a drum.' She grinned as Edward groaned. 'Please never let them know. They'll never stop crowing.'

She sipped her coffee, then put the cup down. 'Not my problem. Jones is and by the look of what I found on him, I'm not the only one who needs to stop him.'

Aster had read his file in increasing alarm. As Foreign Secretary, he had moved from being a seriously corrupt businessman and used his new position to feather his nest in the worst ways possible. He had links to people smuggling, arms trading, slavery. The list went on, but it was also clear that the evidence against him was sketchy at best, just a long list of coincidences and witness statements from people who subsequently turned up dead.

'Aster, is there anything I can do or say to convince you to stay away from him?'

Tucking her hair behind her ear, she looked up at him and shook her head.

'With or without you, I'm going after him.'

He sighed and then broke out into a huge smile.

'Well, then. It looks like I'm on board. What do you have in mind?'

'I understand he's an art collector?'

Chapter Thirty-Seven

A month later, Anthony Jones sat in the back seat of his car, staring out the window as London's familiar streets blurred past. The morning sun cast long shadows, hinting at the busy day ahead. His driver, Peter, manoeuvred through the city's congestion with practiced ease, but the Foreign Secretary's mind was far from the traffic. He had a speech to deliver in the House of Parliament today, one that could significantly impact his political career. Yet his thoughts kept drifting back to India.

It had been a month since the disaster. The illegal venture that was supposed to fill his coffers had instead become a quagmire of unforeseen complications and financial haemorrhaging. Anthony clenched his jaw as he recalled the endless stream of messages from his associates, each one more alarming than the last. What had seemed like a foolproof plan to exploit cheap labour and smuggle people for profit had quickly unravelled. The theft of the new Hiverton cloth, meant to undercut competitors, had backfired spectacularly. Local authorities had become suspicious, and the operation was on the verge of being exposed. His partners, initially eager and co-operative, had turned into liabilities, either through their incompetence or their own greed.

The car hit a slight bump, jolting him from his reverie. His phone buzzed in his pocket. He fished it out, glancing at the caller ID. It was the auction house. He took a deep breath and answered.

'Mr Jones, good morning,' came the polite but businesslike voice on the other end. 'I'm calling to confirm that your financials have been verified, and your maximum bid of twenty-five million pounds is in place for the Raphael auction.'

'Thank you,' Anthony said curtly. 'Is there any news on other bidders?'

'I'm afraid we can't disclose specific details, but I can tell you that interest is very high. As you know, the Vatican is interested.'

Anthony's grip tightened on the phone. Of course, the Vatican. With its seemingly bottomless coffers, it was a formidable opponent in any auction. 'Understood. Please keep me updated with any developments.'

'Certainly, Mr Jones. Best of luck.'

Anthony glanced down at the auction catalogue resting on the seat beside him. Picking it up, he flipped through the glossy pages until he found the section on the Raphael. The rediscovered masterpiece was breathtaking. The detailed brushwork, the vibrant colours—it was a rare piece of history, something that could elevate his status in the art world immeasurably.

He knew the odds were against him. Competing with the Vatican was like David versus Goliath, only this Goliath had far deeper pockets and the backing of centuries-old prestige. But he was determined. The Raphael wasn't just an investment; it was a statement, a legacy. It was something tangible and beautiful, a stark contrast to the chaos and disappointment he had faced in India. It had been his first solo venture in a bid to show other parties that he was a serious player on the global stage, but it had all gone wrong.

The car slowed as they neared Parliament. Anthony closed the catalogue and straightened his tie. He needed to focus. Today's speech was critical. It was his opportunity to regain some control, to reassert his authority. The fallout from the Indian debacle had shaken his confidence, but he couldn't afford to show any weakness now. Being an MP was far from his only job, but it was the only one that most people were aware of, and it was an essential part of his other, more dubious businesses.

Peter pulled up to the entrance, and Anthony stepped out, the weight of his responsibilities settling on his shoulders. He nodded to the security officers as he made his way inside, the grand architecture of the building looming around him. The halls were buzzing with activity, a constant hum of voices and footsteps.

As he walked towards the chamber, he mentally reviewed his speech. It was meticulously crafted to address the current economic concerns, proposing new measures to stimulate growth and investment. He had spent countless hours refining it, ensuring that every point was backed by solid data and compelling rhetoric.

Yet, as he took his seat and waited for his turn to speak, his thoughts kept drifting back to the auction. The image of the Raphael hovered in his mind, a beacon of hope and achievement. He imagined it hanging in his study, a testament to his perseverance and success.

When his name was called, Anthony stood, smoothing the front of his jacket. He walked to the podium, the faces of his colleagues and opponents watching him intently. Reaching into his pocket, he turned off his phone, silencing the world outside, and began.

'Mr Speaker, honourable members,' he began, his voice steady and authoritative. As he spoke, he felt a familiar surge of confidence. This was his arena, where he could wield words and ideas like weapons. The frustrations of the past month faded, replaced by the clarity of his vision for the future.

Charlotte Jones moved through the sprawling house with an air of practiced calm. The elegant rooms, filled with expensive furnishings and carefully chosen art pieces, were a far cry from the modest apartment she had once called home. Despite the opulence surrounding her, a sense of unease never quite left her.

Marrying Anthony had seemed like a dream come true, at first. He was charming, influential, and had swept her off her feet. But it hadn't taken long for the dream to sour. His temper was volatile, and his fits of rage had left her walking on eggshells. She had heard whispers about his first wife, about how she had been quietly paid off and silenced with an NDA. Charlotte suspected that the woman had crossed her husband one too many times, and the thought terrified her.

As she rearranged a floral display on the mantelpiece, the phone rang, startling her. She left the flowers and hurried to the desk, where the phone's persistent ring echoed through the room.

'Hello, Jones residence,' she answered, trying to keep her voice steady.

'Mrs Jones, this is Amanda from the auction house. I'm calling to inform you that Mr Jones' financials have been verified, and his maximum bid is in place for the Raphael auction. However, we've been trying to reach him to discuss an urgent matter, and his phone appears to be switched off. Can you assist us with this?'

Charlotte paused, she knew better than to involve herself in his business but he had spoken of little else recently. If something went wrong and she was somehow responsible, she knew she would suffer. 'Oh, yes, he's at the House right now. What's the issue?'

'There's been significant interest in the Raphael, and to ensure Mr Jones remains competitive, we need to discuss the possibility of increasing his bid limit. Can you provide additional bank details to authorise a higher limit?'

Charlotte's hand trembled as she clutched the phone. She could only imagine Anthony's fury if his bid failed because she couldn't handle this. 'I'll try to reach him immediately. Please hold.'

She quickly dialled his number, but it went straight to voicemail. Panic set in. She couldn't let this fail. Not when the consequences of his anger loomed so large in her mind.

'He's not answering,' she said, her voice quivering slightly.

'I understand, Mrs Jones, but the auction is about to start. We need to complete the arrangements. Is there another account you can provide?'

Charlotte's mind raced. Another account? She remembered overhearing Edward mention a 'goodies account' once, a term that seemed to be tied to one of his savings accounts. Could that be the answer?

'Yes, there is,' she said slowly. 'Let me get the details.'

She rushed to Edward's study, her hands shaking as she pulled open a drawer in his desk. After rifling through papers, she found a small black notebook with various codes and account numbers. She located the one labelled 'Goodies' and recited the details to the auctioneer.

'Thank you, Mrs Jones,' Amanda said, relief evident in her voice. 'We'll process this immediately. You've been very helpful.'

Charlotte hung up the phone and exhaled deeply. A small smile crept across her face, a mixture of relief and triumph. She had navigated a potential disaster and ensured Anthony's bid would stand.

As she closed the notebook and put it back in its place, she hoped Anthony would never know how close they had come to missing out. She had taken a risk, but it had paid off. For now, at least, she was safe.

Walking back to the living room, Charlotte thought about how excited he had been about this painting. When he returned from his state visit to India, he had been in a foul mood, snapping at everyone, his temper barely in check. The venture in India had clearly gone awry, and the atmosphere at home had been tense and oppressive. But then the announcement of the lost Raphael coming up for auction had changed everything. Anthony had become like a kid with a new toy, his dark mood lifting almost overnight.

Every day since then, the house had been filled with his good mood. He talked endlessly about the painting, showing her articles and pictures, explaining its significance. For the first time in weeks, he seemed genuinely happy. He had even promised her a holiday somewhere top-notch soon, something she could barely remember him doing before. It had been a rare glimpse of the man she had fallen in love with.

The thought of his disappointment, of his anger if the bid fell through, was enough to make her hands shake again. But for now, she had done her part. The Raphael was within reach, and she had ensured that nothing would stand in his way. Maybe now, he would be happier.

Chapter Thirty-Eight

The grand steps leading into the auction house were bustling with reporters and photographers, their cameras flashing and voices mingling into a cacophony of excitement. Among the arriving guests, Lady Ariana, Countess of Hiverton, and her husband, Sir Sebastian Flint-Hyssop, stepped out of their sleek black car. Ari, as she was known to her family, looked every bit the aristocratic figure in a stylish yet understated ensemble, her chestnut hair perfectly coiffed. Seb, tall and dapper in his tailored suit, offered his arm as they approached the steps.

'Ari! Seb! Over here!' called one of the reporters, and soon the couple was surrounded by a throng of journalists.

A young, eager-looking reporter squeezed to the front, her microphone extended. 'Countess Hiverton, Sir Sebastian, could you tell us about your involvement in today's auction? We understand you recently purchased the painting now up for auction?'

Ari smiled graciously, her eyes sparkling with a mixture of amusement and confidence. 'Ah, yes. The painting was well known to my sisters and me. It's a piece that holds significant sentimental value.'

Another reporter jumped in. 'There's been some controversy surrounding the painting. Can you comment on that?'

Ari waved her hand dismissively. 'Oh, that's just silly nonsense. The picture was filthy and sold without provenance. Naturally, people were wary, but I had a gut feeling about it.

Sometimes you just know, don't you?' She gave a light, infectious laugh, and the reporters joined in, caught up in her effortless charm.

A more seasoned journalist, with a knowing smile, asked, 'And what about Lord Edward's purchase from the nuns? Any thoughts on that?'

Ari's smile widened. 'Oh, you know Edward. His heart's in the right place. Always trying to raise some money for the nuns.' The crowd laughed, understanding the irony behind her words. Lord Edward's reputation was well known among them.

'You weren't tempted to keep it, then?' another reporter queried.

'Absolutely not. I had it restored and gifted it back to the nuns,' Ari replied airily, as if it were the most natural thing in the world. 'They sold it in the first place to raise funds for their charitable works. Let's hope today brings them an absolute fortune.'

Making her excuses, Ari added, 'Now, if you'll forgive us, we must get inside. The auction is about to begin.' With a final wave, she took Seb's arm, and they gracefully made their way into the auction house.

Inside, the atmosphere was buzzing with anticipation. As they moved through the elegant hallways, Seb leant in and whispered, 'You handled that beautifully, darling.'

Ari smiled up at him. 'Thank you, Seb. Let's hope everything goes as smoothly inside. It felt wrong mocking Edward like that.'

'It was his own suggestion, remember.'

They entered the auction room, ready to take their seats among the elite art connoisseurs and bidders, their minds set on securing the painting that had caused such a stir.

Sister Bernard stood at the back of the grand auction house, her small frame dwarfed by the opulent surroundings. Dressed in her simple habit, she couldn't help but draw curious glances from the finely dressed patrons around her. But she paid no mind to the attention, today was a day of miracles. The air buzzed with anticipation, and Sister Bernard couldn't help but feel a sense of wonder. The painting—*their* painting—had been restored to its former glory, all thanks to the Countess Hiverton and Sir Sebastian. It was a gift she could hardly fathom, a blessing beyond measure. And now, here she was, about to witness the next chapter in the life of this treasured work of art.

As she stood there, eyes wide with awe, she spotted her young benefactors making their way through the crowd. Ari's elegant presence seemed to draw every gaze, but it was the warm smile she directed at Sister Bernard that brought tears to the nun's eyes.

'Sister Bernard!' Ari called out softly as they approached. 'You made it!'

'Oh, Lady Ariana, Sir Sebastian,' Sister Bernard said, clasping her hands together in joy. 'I can't believe I'm really here. This is all so… so wonderful!'

Seb smiled kindly at the nun, his voice gentle. 'It's our pleasure, Sister. We wouldn't have it any other way.'

Ari took Sister Bernard's hand, squeezing it reassuringly. 'It's Ari and Seb as you well know. And we're so glad you're here with us. The painting wouldn't be here without your care and devotion all these years. And of course, your diligent work in the convent archives. We never would have uncovered the painting's provenance without you.'

Sister Bernard blushed, feeling a mix of pride and humility. She had spent countless hours poring over the dusty old records in the convent's archives, determined to find any clue that could help authenticate the painting. When she finally unearthed a tattered ledger that documented the painting's history, it had felt like divine intervention. That discovery had been the key to proving the painting's worth, leading them to this very moment.

Shaking her head, she said, 'It was the least I could do. The painting is a gift from God, and you've helped it shine again.'

Ari beamed, and the three of them stood together for a moment, sharing in the quiet joy of the occasion. Sister Bernard couldn't help but marvel at how everything had come together—how what once seemed like a distant dream had turned into this miraculous reality.

As they prepared to take their seats, Sister Bernard whispered a prayer of thanks. Today was a day she would never forget, a day when the impossible became possible, and she was grateful to be a part of it.

The female auctioneer, poised and confident, stood at the podium with an air of authority. Her voice rang out around the room as she began the proceedings. Several lots were up for bid before the main event, but everyone knew what today's main attraction was.

'Ladies and gentlemen, we will start with Lot Thirty-Seven, a fine example of eighteenth-century portraiture. Shall we open the bidding at ten thousand pounds?'

Paddles went up, and the bids followed in quick succession. The auctioneer skilfully guided the room through each lot, her voice steady and engaging, keeping the momentum alive as each piece found a new home.

With each sale, the tension in the room grew, the audience's collective focus gradually shifting towards the final lot—the rediscovered Raphael. Sister Bernard could feel the energy building, her eyes flicking anxiously to the auction catalogue in her lap. She knew the moment everyone was waiting for was fast approaching.

The auctioneer smiled as she concluded another sale, her eyes sparkling with the thrill of the competition. 'And now, ladies and gentlemen, we come to the moment you've all been waiting for—Lot Forty-Three, the Raphael masterpiece.' The room fell silent, all attention now firmly on the podium. The air seemed to hold its breath as the bidding for the main event began.

Chapter Thirty-Nine

In the small, dimly lit room miles away, Aster finished her phone call, her voice perfectly mimicking the professional tone of 'Amanda' from the auction house.

'Thank you, Mrs Jones,' Aster said, maintaining the calm, measured cadence that had put Charlotte at ease. 'We'll process this immediately. You've been very helpful.'

With that, Aster slowly replaced the phone in its cradle, letting her fingers linger for just a moment. As she did, she heard Edward speaking quietly into another phone, his voice low and deferential. Aster couldn't make out the details, but she knew he wasn't speaking to just anyone. His tone, unusually respectful, hinted at the importance of the person on the other end.

When Edward finally finished his conversation and turned toward her, Aster couldn't resist a sly smile. 'So, am I going to meet your non-boss today?'

Edward looked at her, a grin tugging at the corner of his mouth, but his eyes remained guarded. 'Best not,' he said with a touch of irony. 'None of this is taking place, remember? And you definitely don't have clearance.'

Aster's smile faded slightly as she absorbed his words. The truth was clear, Edward wasn't in control of the operation. He was merely a conduit, a go-between for those pulling the strings behind the scenes and Aster, who was tasked with executing the plan. The shadowy figure at the other end of Edward's phone call was the real authority, someone with far more power than either of them, sitting in the heart of the British government.

Edward's expression turned serious. 'You've done your part providing the idea and the painting, and you've done it well. But now, we follow the script. This operation has been planned down to the last detail. We can't afford any deviations.'

Aster nodded, the gravity of the situation settling over her. The stakes were immense, and the margin for error non-existent. She watched as the operatives in the room continued their work, their fingers flying over keyboards as they began the process of accessing the MP's account.

Before she turned back to the screens, Aster spoke quietly, her voice laced with a hint of concern. 'Remember, Charlotte needs to be taken to a place of safety until this is all resolved. She's served her purpose, now we need to make sure she's out of harm's way.'

Edward's gaze hardened, and he gave her a curt nod. 'Already taken care of. Officers are already on their way to her address. Don't worry.'

As Aster turned away, she couldn't shake the feeling of being a piece on a much larger chessboard, manipulated by unseen hands. The presence of Edward's 'non-boss,' lingering at the other end of that phone call, served as a stark reminder of the forces at play, forces far beyond her control.

The auction house was a battlefield. All eyes were on the stage, breaths held.

'Twenty million pounds,' the auctioneer announced. Her voice cut through the room, sharp and precise. The bid hung in the air, the excitement rising.

Ariana remained still. Her heart pounded. Across the room, a paddle went up. The bid climbed higher, pushing the tension to its breaking point.

'Twenty-one million pounds,' the auctioneer called out. Silence followed. The room was on edge. Who would dare to raise the stakes further? The auction house was a storm of tension. Every breath, every glance was charged.

'Twenty-two million pounds,' the auctioneer's voice rang out. The crowd, frozen, watched as the stakes soared higher.

Back in the small room, the operatives worked furiously. Fingers danced over keyboards, codes flashing across screens. They were close. Very close.

In the auction house, a paddle shot up. 'Twenty-three million,' the auctioneer declared. The room buzzed with silent intensity. Who would fold first?

'Firewall breached,' an operative muttered, sweat beading on his forehead. The final layers of security were giving way. Another click, another keystroke. Almost there.

'Twenty-four million pounds,' the auctioneer's voice cut through the air. Ariana's gaze was steely, her nerves taut. The tension was unbearable.

'We're in,' one of the operatives whispered. The bank account details flashed on the screen. All eyes turned to Edward. He gave a sharp nod.

'Twenty-five million pounds,' came the auctioneer's next call. The room was a powder keg ready to explode. The bidders were on the brink.

'Transfer authorisation,' the lead operative said, his voice barely above a whisper. The countdown to execution had begun. Every second was critical.

The auctioneer's gavel hovered in the air. 'Going once… going twice…'

The operatives stared at their screens, breaths held. 'Initiate transfer,' Edward ordered.

'Sold!' The gavel came down with a resounding crack.

At the same moment, the operatives hit the final command.

The tension snapped like a wire pulled too tight and the auction house erupted. Cheers filled the air, a wave of sound that swept through the room. Ari laughed as Seb hugged her and then they both shook hands with a stunned Sister Bernard. The Sisters of the Divine Mercy had just received a life-changing amount of money and Ari knew that that money was about to be redistributed far and wide improving lives across London, Britain and many countries beyond.

Back in the small, dimly lit room, the atmosphere was far different. The operatives stared at their screens, tension still hanging in the air, until the confirmation flashed in front of them and Anthony's financial transactions filled the screens.

Edward leant back in his chair, a feral grin spreading across his face. His eyes gleamed with cold satisfaction as he looked at Aster. 'We've got him.'

The operatives continued their work, piecing together the tangled web of transactions. Each payment led them deeper into a labyrinth of corruption and crime, revealing connections that spanned continents. The account was a hub for laundering money, funding illicit activities, and facilitating deals that spanned everything from arms trafficking to human smuggling.

'Here's another one,' the first operative said, highlighting a particularly large transaction. 'This one links directly to a group flagged by Interpol for cybercrime.'

'And this,' the second operative added, 'is tied to an offshore account connected to a major European drug syndicate.'

Edward, watching over their shoulders, leant in closer, his expression hardening with each revelation. 'Keep digging,' he ordered, his voice like steel. 'I want every connection, every transaction tied down.'

The operatives worked with a grim determination, mapping out the MP's secret dealings, uncovering a dark and sprawling network. Each new discovery seemed more damning than the last, money flowing to and from organisations that dealt in death and destruction on a global scale.

'There's no end to it,' muttered a technician, almost to himself, as another series of transactions revealed links to a notorious African warlord. The room seemed to pulse with the enormity of what they were unearthing. This wasn't just a corrupt politician; this was a man deeply entrenched in a worldwide web of crime.

Edward stood back, absorbing the scope of their findings. His mind raced with the implications. The MP wasn't just compromised, he was the lynchpin in a much larger, far more dangerous game.

Anthony Jones reached the crescendo of his speech, his voice rising with passion. 'Let us not be divided by fear, but united by hope. Let us take bold steps forward, confident in our shared vision for a prosperous and secure future.'

The chamber erupted in applause, a wave of approval that washed over him. Anthony allowed himself a small smile as he stepped back from the podium, acknowledging the support with a nod. As he returned to his seat, he was greeted with handshakes and pats on the back. The speech had gone down better than he had hoped—he had played his part to perfection. In another year he'd make a challenge for the leadership. Nothing was going to stop him.

As the session concluded and members filed out, Anthony felt a surge of triumph. This was the boost he needed, a victory that would solidify his standing. His mind briefly drifted to the auction and the Raphael painting, imagining it hanging in his study as a symbol of his success. Everything was falling into place.

He left the chamber, still basking in the afterglow of his performance, and reached into his pocket for his phone. As he switched it on, the screen lit up with a flurry of notifications. He scrolled through quickly, dismissing the less important ones until he saw a message from Charlotte And his world stuttered to a halt.

- Can I give the auction house the details of your Treat account? They've asked for a higher limit to secure the bid.

Anthony's stomach twisted into a knot. He stopped dead in his tracks, the din of the surrounding crowd fading into the background. He opened the next message, hoping for a reprieve.

- Never mind. I found the details and passed them on. No need to worry.

His blood ran cold. The words on the screen blurred as panic set in. Charlotte had given them the Treats account details, the very account he had worked so hard to keep hidden from official sources, and Charlotte had just simply handed it over to the first person who asked. An account tied to deals, payments, and operations that could destroy him if exposed. His mind raced, his pulse pounding in his ears. He needed to act, and fast.

Anthony looked up from his phone, his eyes scanning the lobby of Parliament as he tried to compose himself. The usual bustle of politicians and aides seemed distant, almost surreal, as if he were watching from outside his own body. He forced himself to move, heading toward the exit, but something caught his eye, two men standing near the main desk, their eyes discreetly scanning the room. His breath caught in his throat. He recognised the look: undercover detectives, waiting, watching. They hadn't approached him yet, but it was only a matter of time. They were here for him. The walls were closing in.

Without a second thought, Anthony turned on his heel, walking quickly but not so fast as to draw attention. He made his way through a side corridor, heart racing as he sought an exit that wouldn't lead him directly past the detectives. Every instinct screamed at him to run, to get out before they could stop him.

Finding a side door, he pushed through it, searching for an escape. His eyes locked onto a car, a modest sedan with the keys still in the ignition. Anthony didn't hesitate.

He yanked open the door, slid into the driver's seat, and set off carefully, desperate not to draw attention to himself until he was out of the confines of the Houses of Parliament. At each barrier, he was waved through with a smile and a nod as he made a joke about borrowing the wife's car. He was well known amongst the security staff and had made it his habit to befriend all junior workers. Anthony had never once underestimated the power of the working classes. Now they waved him through and he headed out into Westminster. He had to get to his country house, the one place he could think clearly, away from prying eyes. His hands gripped the steering wheel, knuckles white as he navigated the London streets with reckless speed.

The city blurred past him as he merged onto the motorway, the needle on the speedometer climbing steadily. His mind was a whirl of thoughts, panic, anger, desperation. How had it all unravelled so quickly? Just hours ago, he was on top of the world, delivering a speech that could have launched him towards the premiership. Now, everything was slipping through his fingers like sand.

He pressed harder on the accelerator, the car surging forward at a hundred miles per hour. The trees along the side of the road became a green blur, the sky a streak of grey above him. He needed to think, to figure out his next move, but all he could feel was the cold grip of fear tightening around his chest.

He knew that once the people he had connections to discovered what had happened, his life wouldn't be worth a week's notice. The treat account held the darkest of his dealings—transactions that tied him to criminal organisations across the globe. He wasn't just facing a political scandal; he was staring down the barrel of a gun held by the very people he had once worked with. There would be no mercy, no second chances.

He spotted the familiar turnoff to his country house up ahead, but something made him hesitate. As he rounded the bend, his eyes caught sight of something that made his blood run cold. Police cars, discreetly parked just beyond the gates of his estate. They were waiting for him. They had expected this move.

His heart pounded in his chest as he realised that there was no safe haven left, no sanctuary where he could gather his thoughts. The net was closing in, and there was no way out.

A sharp curve loomed ahead, but Anthony didn't ease up on the accelerator. His mind raced through his options, but none of them offered salvation. There was no one he could trust, no way out that wouldn't end in disgrace or worse.

In the distance, he saw the massive oak tree ahead, standing tall by the roadside, its thick trunk unyielding. Without thinking, without hesitation, he yanked the wheel hard to the right.

The car swerved violently off the road, tyres skidding on the gravel as it barrelled toward the tree. The last thing Anthony saw was the looming bark rushing up to meet him, and then, in an instant, everything went dark.

There was a sickening crunch of metal and glass and then the world outside fell silent as the twisted wreckage settled, smoke rising slowly from the crumpled hood. The stillness of the scene was broken only the sound of a distant combine harvester bringing in the crops.

Aster sat quietly in the corner, listening to the events unfold at the auction house and the Houses of Parliament. From Clem's initial concern that someone was flooding the market with the new Hiverton muslin, this investigation had grown from broken warehouses in Manchester out to India and then back to a little room in London. Even for Aster, she felt that this was one of her greatest achievements. Certainly, some of her individual victories brought her great comfort, especially her recent triumph over Marcus Barrie, but nothing was on the scale of helping to break an entire chain of global smuggling and racketeering. But now she wanted to go home. She read a text from Ari saying the Vatican had just purchased the painting and would put it on public display for all to see. The nuns were delighted and Aster smiled, happy that all was going well. Shortly after that, Anthony put the phone down and walked over to her.

'That was the police stationed at Jones' house. His car left the road and hit a tree. Death was instantaneous.'

Chapter Forty

Ari's heels clicked as she walked along the stone pavement towards Harvey's, a popular restaurant with a great reputation for food. Part of its charm was in its lively vibe and it was the perfect venue to have a private conversation as everyone was too busy talking to listen to their neighbours. Checking her watch, she was pleased to see she was ten minutes early. This would give her time to gather her thoughts and decide on a plan of action. As she gave her name to the server, she was ushered towards a side table as requested and sighed when she saw Edward come to his feet as she approached.

'I'm afraid I was in the area earlier than expected,' he said warmly, pouring her a glass of water as she settled herself down and placed her order. The joy of a regular lunch spot was that she didn't need to bother with a menu.

'Looks like we both were.' She smiled politely and decided that this wasn't a power-play that she needed to engage in. He clearly liked to have the upper hand and she wasn't the sort to bother with ego, his or hers. Although she noted he mirrored her menu choice, so he wasn't that bothered about being in control. At least not over the small things. She suspected the rest of the conversation might not be so easy. 'Thank you for joining me for lunch today.'

'It was my pleasure.' He sipped his water and waited for her to proceed.

'I just felt that given how much you have recently been involved in our family matters, the least I could do was take you out for lunch to say thanks.'

'Well, I must admit I wasn't helping your family out so much as Aster.'

Seb had wanted to come to lunch as well, but Ari had felt the two men might become confrontational. Now, given Edward's tone, Ari knew she had made the right decision. She had realised since Edward had told her and Nick off that he was very unimpressed with them, but she wanted to see if it was simply because of their poorly executed business operations in India, or if there was more to it. She thought she knew the answer, but she had chosen this lunch to test out her theory.

'Yes, you've spent a lot of time with her recently, haven't you?'

'Our paths have crossed.'

This really was like pulling teeth.

'It has been quite the week, hasn't it? Sister Bernard is still singing. I found the whole event very exciting.'

Edward visibly relaxed.

'I would have loved to be in the room. You should have seen the look on Aster's face when she first spoke to me. She thought I was such an idiot, potentially losing all that money for the nuns.'

'Yes, she can be a bit black and white when you've made a mistake. It's not personal, she just holds people to a higher standard.'

'God's?' asked Edward confused.

Ari laughed. 'Hers. Aster is not religious.'

'That's what I thought. But she is very fond of those nuns, isn't she?'

'Extremely. And was furious when she thought someone had pulled a fast one on them.'

He put his hands up in defence. 'I was only trying to make them a quick buck.'

Ari raised an eyebrow and Edward groaned. 'I know. Not my finest hour.'

'No, I think that was rescuing Aster in the nightclub.'

His face clouded over again and Ari realised that if the conversation steered towards Aster in trouble, Edward became very closed and defensive.

'Still, it's been quite a newsworthy week, hasn't it? What with the Secretary for Foreign Affairs' fatal crash.'

She studied Edward, her eyebrow raised. Both knew the truth behind the headlines, but in theory Ari knew nothing about it, given how much the government were currently keeping a lid on things. Plus Aster had signed the Official Secrets Act, thereby forbidding her to discuss the matter with anyone without the correct clearance. Edward had watched Aster smile as she readily signed the document and it was all he could do not to roll his eyes. He wondered if the ink had even had time to dry before she was telling her sisters all about it.

Edward took a mouthful of crab linguine and nodded his head appreciatively, changing the subject.

'This is good!'

'It is, isn't it?' said Ari appreciatively. 'Since moving to Norfolk, I've become a real fan of crab. It was too much of a luxury growing up. Even tinned was out of our price range.

But on Mum's birthday, Da would always buy two fresh crabs from Billingsgate.'

'Your change in circumstances has been extraordinary, hasn't it?'

'It has, but the more things change, the more you see what lies at your core. In our case, it's each other.'

She took another forkful before returning to her previous conversation.

'With the death of Jones, I imagine there will be lots of overseas developments. Not just in India. Obviously, it's very sad when someone dies but it's an ill wind that blows no good.'

She couldn't make it plainer in the busy restaurant that she knew exactly the extent of Anthony Jones' vile criminal network, courtesy of Aster. Edward looked thoughtful and nodded his head.

'Although of course whatever those changes are, need to remain quiet whilst all the ramifications are brought to the surface.'

'Loose lips sink ships and all that jazz?'

'Quite.' His lips were pursed and Ari wondered how he would respond. 'When you said just now that at your core you sisters have each other?'

'Yes?'

'Do you think that's to your detriment?'

Ari's fork clattered on her plate as she coughed and then started laughing. 'It's our main strength.'

'Even if it means you treat some of the family still as children?'

The gloves were off now, and he raised an eyebrow. All sense of previous good humour gone. He might be still talking in allusions, but Ari tackled him head-on.

'If you think we have ever treated Aster as a child, you only display your ignorance.'

'You sent her to India, under prepared and outgunned.'

'And you think that's how we treat a child? Aster was in control of that decision. She failed to properly assess the situation and so did we. And you have no idea how many sleepless nights I have had since then for my total stupidity in not properly assessing the risk.'

She stabbed at her plate and chewed quietly as she felt her cheeks burn.

'But Aster could have died.'

Tears prickled Ari's eyes. 'I know, dammit.'

Edward swore quietly and then ordered two glasses of wine for the table whilst Ari composed herself in silence. Taking a small sip, she fixed her gaze on Edward.

'To reiterate. We have never treated Aster as a child, but we have protected her. Kept her out of the limelight. Allowed her to shine in her very special way and occasionally mopped up after her.' Ari shrugged. 'But those days are behind us now. Since she was a teen, she has been in control.'

Ari took a sip of wine as Edward watched her closely.

'Which is why that event at your club caused her such intense stress. Aster is always five steps ahead, always in control, has a perfect memory, and is never duped. Waking up in a stranger's house with no memory crushed her.'

'But she handled it so well, the way she got justice for those other girls.'

'That was Aster at cruising speed. You should see her when she's full guns blazing.'

'I think we witnessed that two days ago.'

Ari hadn't been fully involved in the takedown of the MP but she knew from what Aster had mentioned that it was a substantial operation. Although by her own admission, Aster's primary motivation was to protect the Hiverton Estate.

'Just so. If you don't mind me saying, you appear to have become very protective of Aster.' Her voice raised lightly and she tilted her head.

'Our paths have crossed a few times and I find her interesting.'

'She's not an exhibit,' said Ari sharply.

Edward flushed and now it was Ari's turn to wait whilst he composed himself.

'Have I been invited for lunch just for you to warn me off?'

'Not at all, but as head of my family it's my duty to take care of everyone.'

'As we have established, Aster is not a child.'

'No, but emotionally…' Aster trailed off.

Edward smiled softly to himself. 'Emotionally, she's just a bit more vulnerable.'

'Yes. And as such it's only fair to warn you that messing around with her will only hurt her, not you. Although I promise you my sisters and I would do much to redress that.'

Edward lifted his wine glass, smiling tightly.

'I promise you. I will never hurt Aster. And whilst I'm by her side, no harm will ever come to her.' He looked at her pointedly. 'From any source.'

Ari laughed. 'My tip to you. Never, ever ask Aster to side against her family. No matter what you think of us.'

Concluding her lunch, Ari stood up and smiled at Edward, putting her hand out.

'Nice to meet you and I do sincerely hope we meet again.'

As Ari left the restaurant, she dialled Clem.

'How did it go?'

'My God. He is so in love with her.'

'Genuinely?'

'Yes. Every time he mentioned her, he had this dippy look on his face. It was like watching a mountain melt.'

'Blimey. And what about Aster?'

Ari sighed. 'That is less certain. I think he is clearly on her radar, but it's Aster. Who knows? I think now we have to leave it in the lap of the gods. But if Aster falls for him, I approve.'

The phone rang just as Aster was settling down into the sofa. Her laptop was to one side and she was looking forward to planning her next trip away. So far, every time she tried, she found herself distracted, which seemed to have been her default state for the past three days and it was annoying her. Looking at the screen, she sighed and answered the call. At least Nick wasn't one for prolonged chats.

'I need a favour.'

'Shoot.'

'I want you to run a bit of a background check on someone, but they're well placed so we need to move carefully.'

Aster leant forward and pulled a pencil and her notepad towards her.

'Go ahead.'

'Edward Montclair.'

'What?'

'Well, don't you think he's too close to the family right now? Why was he out in India at the same time as you? I know he's working with the government. I mean, look how they all brought down the Foreign Secretary.'

'But-'

'Yes, I know they couldn't have done that without your help. Christ, you were the main driver. But don't you think he is too powerful to be so close to our business? I don't want a full root and branch investigation into him but I do want something on him. Something that I could use as a shot across the bows if he tried to get any closer.'

Aster's stomach churned. Her palms were sweaty. Her pencil slid out of her hand and back onto the sofa. She dried her palm on her thigh as she listened to her sister.

'Have you spoken to Ari about this?'

Aster had fully confided in Ari the extent of Edward's involvement with the government, but hadn't told Nick. Maybe she should have, but she had tried to uphold her promise to keep his reputation as a dilettante in place.

'Nick, I don't think he's a threat-'

'How can you say that? He's-' Nick's protest dried up as she suddenly groaned. 'I'm an idiot. Of course you don't want to do this.'

'What? Why?'

'Because of the drugging. I'm an idiot. Of course you probably feel obligated to him.'

'No. Hang on a minute. I'm quite capable of remaining detached.'

'Yes, but he literally saved you. No wonder you feel you owe him.'

'I don't. I just don't think he's a threat.'

'Of course he is. You see, your reasoning is compromised.'

'It is not!' There was a silence between the two sisters following Aster's outburst before she took a breath and continued. 'Okay. Maybe you have a point. I'll look into him.'

Aster bit her lip. She had already of course fully investigated Edward and had found loads of skeletons and suspicious events and activities, probably as many as she herself had. But sharing that information felt like a betrayal. She had found nothing in his actions that suggested self-promotion, or greed. She had only found noble intentions.

'Thank you,' said Nick, 'I'll tell Ari, she was concerned.'

'She was?'

'Bound to be. She was asking me what I thought about him the other day.'

'Did she say why?'

'No, Will and Leo started fighting, so she had to hang up, but it stands to reason. He has been closely involved with us, you in particular, and we know nothing about him. So, I just need to know if he's squeaky clean. And if he's not, I need to know what I can use against him in case he tries to blindside us. I'm never having a repeat of Harrington's again.'

'That wasn't your fault.'

'Hmm. Not strictly true.'

'You're not invincible, Nick.'

'Take that back!'

The two sisters laughed and then Nick carried on. 'Thanks for this. Are you sure that you aren't conflicted? God knows I understand that. My feelings for Gabe could have destroyed the family.'

'But he wasn't working against you or us. He's okay.'

'Really?' Nick's surprise was evident. 'Have your feelings towards him mellowed?'

'I suppose he can't help his father or those brothers of his.'

Aster was trying to keep the tone light, but her stomach was still churning. Investigating Edward was wrong, but she couldn't say why.

'Well, he'll be very relieved to hear that.'

'Why?'

'Because he worries you don't like him.'

'What does he care what I think of him?'

'Because you're my sister and I love you.'

'Oh, if you're going to be wet, I need to go.'

Nick laughed.

'Off you go, then, and see what you can dig up. Let me know as soon as possible.'

Hanging up, Aster stared at the phone for a bit longer and then looked out over the garden. Why didn't she want to do this? What was her issue? She already had the report. With one click of an e-mail, Aster could send the file to Ari and Nick. God knows there was enough to properly compromise Edward and even embarrass the government, although Aster knew instinctively that neither sister would go that far. But she still didn't want to share her knowledge.

She was startled when a fox ran across the lawn, switching on the security lights. Moths flew in and out of the dark. How long had she simply sat there, looking vacantly at the garden as the night had fallen around her? Getting up, she stretched her stiff limbs and headed to bed, where she lay with her eyes open until dawn broke. Her mind gyrating on one broken spindle over and over again. Making no sense, never resolving itself.

As the sun rose, she got in her car and drove to Hiverton.

Chapter Forty-One

Ari snuggled down under the duvet and placed her feet against Seb's nice warm calves. With a yelp, he jumped out of the bed.

'Oh, you're up,' said Ari with a devilish grin. 'Put the kettle on, will you?'

'Minx!' Padding over to the window, Seb threw open the curtains and looked out over the estate. 'What the hell?'

'What is it?'

She watched as he shook his head and then turned back to look at her in astonishment. 'I think you'd better look for yourself.'

Reluctantly getting out of bed, she joined her husband and gave a double take.

'Oh dear. That does not look good.'

Walking down the long drive towards Hiverton was Aster. She was walking slowly, her head was hanging down and her shoes were in her hand.

'Okay,' said Seb. 'I'll sort the children out and you sort out your sister. What the hell do you think has happened?'

Ari continued to stare. 'I've seen her do this before. When she was small, she really got into the concept of penitence. A way of physically atoning for having done something wrong. Once, she made Mum cry and she spent a whole week barefoot as a way to apologise.'

'I've said it before, but I'll never understand Aster.'

Ari watched as her little sister trudged towards the house. Even from this distance, she looked wretched and Ari felt her heart break.

'She's the easiest of all of us to understand. There is only black or white in her world. And she never thinks she's wrong. Except very occasionally.'

'And you think this is one of those occasions?'

'Evidently.'

'Shall I go and drive down to meet her?'

'God, no. You won't stop her from walking.'

Ari headed over to the wardrobe and got dressed. 'Can you keep the children well away? I'll take her through to my study.'

Seb came over and wrapped Ari up into his arms. 'It will be okay, darling. Whatever this is.'

Ari leant against him and sighed. 'I hope so. But this,' she looked out the window again. 'This is not good news.'

As Aster approached the front door, it swung open before she knocked and Ari stood on the doorstep staring at her, her arms crossed.

'Where did you leave the car?'

'At the top gatehouse.'

'Right you are. Well, let's go inside. Tell me what's happened.'

Aster trailed in after her sister and followed her through to Ari's study. Her feet were sore and muddy and she looked behind her as she left a trail of dirt. After she'd said her bit, she'd clean that up. That is, if Ari didn't send her away.

Walking into her sister's office, she looked around at the space. To the left was a large table with plans laid out across it. No doubt they were the road plans down at Tregiskey or one of a thousand other projects that the Hiverton Estate was overseeing. The wall was lined with files and document boxes and Aster thought Ari would soon need to move into a larger workspace. Her mind was already thinking about how to solve that problem when Ari cleared her throat and sat down, waving at Aster to take a seat.

'Sit down, then, and explain your feet.'

Aster remained on her feet and swayed slightly. The thought of what she had to stay steadied her back. 'I'll stand.'

Ari sighed and got to her feet. 'Well, so will I, then. Out with it and trust me. Nothing you say will make me think any less of you. I love you. You are my little sister and if you are in trouble, I will bring down the walls of Jericho to protect you.'

Aster swayed again and Ari dashed around the table and hugged her sister.

'Sit down, right now.'

As she scolded her sister, the door opened and Seb came in with a pot of coffee. Smiling at Aster, he closed the door again and left.

'Right, out with it. I'm not having my first coffee of the day on my feet. Now sit!'

Ari's hands pushed down on Aster's shoulders and she slumped into her seat. She hadn't slept a wink and then had driven the whole way, her mind turning over the same dilemma, and now here was the moment that she had come to say what needed saying and she was mute. Her feet were stabbing, her head ached, she felt sick, but that was nothing compared to how terrified she felt.

'I can't do it.'

She watched as Ari sipped her coffee, her expression puzzled.

'Do what?'

'Dig up dirt on Edward.' As soon as she said it, there was a rush of words. 'I can't. Well, I can. But I won't. Well, in fact I already have done. Here.' She opened her palm and in it lay a USB stick. 'On here there's so much dirt on Edward that it could completely undo him. But you can't have it.' She closed her palm and hitched back a sob. 'I'm-' She sobbed again. 'I can't.'

When she looked up, Ari was staring at her in confusion.

'Why would I want you to dish the dirt on Edward?'

'Nick said you did. But I'm sorry, I just can't and I know that's wrong, but I can't. He's like me. Does wrong things for good reasons. He would never be a threat to us. I just know he wouldn't. He's not like that. He's not.'

Ari held up her hand.

'Aster. Calm down.'

Drawing a deep breath, she stared at her big sister as she scrubbed her face with the heel of her palm and waited for Ari's judgement.

'I don't want you to snoop on Edward. We've discussed this before. I will confess to asking Nick what her feelings were about him and she said—oh…' Ari broke off and groaned. 'Oh, she must have thought I was concerned he was a threat, when that wasn't what I meant at all.'

Ari slammed her hand on the table in a rare display of annoyance.

'Damn it.'

Confused, Aster sniffed then glared at her display of emotion.

'So, you didn't want me to do this?'

'No, of course not. Especially when you are so clearly in love with him.'

The silence was total. All Aster could hear was the roar of blood in her ears as she stared at her sister.

'I am not.'

Ari rolled her eyes.

'Okay, let's break it down. You feel wretched because you have decided to say no to me, correct?'

Aster nodded.

'And why do you feel wretched?'

'Because family comes first.'

'Why?'

Aster shrugged and raised her eyebrows. It was obvious. It didn't need saying, family always came first. That was the beginning and end of everything.

'Family comes first because we love each other,' said Ari, spelling it out. 'Like I love Seb, Will, Leo and Hector. Yes?'

Aster nodded.

'So a family can grow based on love. Yes?'

Aster nodded again. This made sense, but had nothing to do with Edward. As her sisters had brought new people into the family, Aster had taken to them slowly. Some more clearly than others. Seb and Hal were completely in. As was

Otto. Mary was as well, she supposed, but she wasn't convinced about Gabe. Aster had her own private grading system that she wasn't prepared to share or explain, but so long as one of her sisters loved them, they were part of the circle.

Ari studied her sister as she took another cup of coffee, apparently waiting for her to speak. Aster remained silent, so she carried on.

'Okay. Why did you say no?'

'Because he isn't a threat.'

'How do you know? Nick is concerned.'

'Because he isn't.'

'But you thought I'd asked for you to do this.'

'I know.'

'And you still said no. Why?'

'Because it's wrong.'

'Why? Lots of what you do is "wrong". Why is this any different?'

Aster shrugged again. In all honesty, she had no idea why she felt this so strongly. Why on earth was she taking the side of a stranger over her own sisters?

'Oh Aster,' said Ari with a soft smile. 'This is different because you've fallen in love with him. And why wouldn't you?' She began to tick off her fingers. 'He saved you at the nightclub. He stepped in and helped the family business and then he included you in his plans to bring down Anthony Jones and make a load of money for the nuns.' As she tapped her third finger, she stared hard at her sister. 'He's just like you.'

Aster snorted. 'Hardly. He's the life and soul of everywhere he goes. He's always talking to people. Laughing, chatting. Ugh, he even goes out of his way to talk to strangers. We are nothing alike.'

'Rubbish. You are both brilliant. You are both driven by a burning sense of right and wrong and you both agree on what those rights and wrongs are. And, of course, he is also madly in love with you.'

The silence returned and Aster wondered if she was going to faint or throw up. The pounding in her ears was a roar that wouldn't be hushed.

'He is not.'

'And what would you know? You don't even know that you love him! I had lunch with him the other day.'

'What? Why?'

'Because I wanted to know him better. I had a hunch he had feelings for you ever since he tore a strip off me and Nick. He was furious.'

Aster glared. 'He had no right.'

'We've gone over this,' said Ari, waving her hand dismissively. 'We screwed up. End of. But I was intrigued by his reaction and all his subsequent behaviour, so I thought I would invite him out to lunch, see how the land lay and I was impressed. He strikes me as a good person, an interesting one certainly, but most important was how he spoke about you.'

'This is ridiculous.' Aster pushed back her chair and got to her feet. 'I came here to apologise to you and now you're trying to tell me that I am betraying you because I'm in love. It's a joke.'

Ari stood up wearily. 'You're acting like Clem. Think about it. This is nothing like you. What new variable could cause you to act in unexpected ways?'

'Well, it's certainly not that I'm in love and I'm going to prove it.'

Chapter Forty-Two

Aster's little Mini raced along the winding country roads, eating up the miles. Behind the wheel, Aster gripped the steering wheel with one hand, the other occupied with a bacon butty that Seb had thrust into her hands as she'd left Hiverton. The rich, salty taste of the bacon mingled with the sweet, tangy brown sauce, providing a much-needed burst of energy after her sleepless night.

Ari's words still echoed in her ears, a persistent whisper that refused to be silenced. Love? Her? It was preposterous. Aster Byrne didn't do love. She did logic, reason, and cold, hard facts. Emotions were messy, unpredictable things that clouded judgement and led to poor decision-making. And yet she couldn't deny the flutter in her stomach every time she thought of Edward. The way her heart seemed to skip a beat when he smiled at her. The sense of calm that washed over her in his presence, even in the midst of chaos. It was... unsettling.

The landscape gradually changed from rolling farmland to more rugged terrain. Ancient forests gave way to craggy hills, and Aster found herself winding up a narrow road that seemed to lead straight into the clouds. Just when she thought she must have taken a wrong turn, a break in the trees revealed her destination.

Edward's home was, frankly, ridiculous. A sprawling manor house that looked more like a castle than a private residence, it perched atop a hill like some medieval lord's stronghold. Aster couldn't help but roll her eyes. Men and their need to compensate.

As she pulled up the long, gravel driveway, Aster's practical mind kicked in. She glanced at her phone, pleased to see that she still had a signal despite her concerns. She could also see he had acknowledged her earlier text and was at home waiting for her.

The gravel crunched under Aster's feet as she got out of the car. Her jaw was set, a mixture of anger and confusion, but she couldn't help but snort as she saw him waiting for her. His tall frame leaning casually against the stonework of the massive oak front door. He seemed to fit perfectly into this setting, like some dashing hero from a period drama. The thought irritated her more than it should have.

'Aster,' Edward greeted her, his eyes crinkling in delight. 'To what do I owe the pleasure of this unexpected visit?'

Aster didn't bother with pleasantries as she slammed her car door shut. 'My sister seems to think you're in love with me,' she blurted out. 'Which is, of course, ludicrous.'

She waited for Edward to deny it, to laugh it off as some absurd misunderstanding. Instead, he simply raised an eyebrow, that infuriating smile still playing at the corners of his mouth.

'Is it?' he asked, his voice maddeningly calm.

Aster felt wrong-footed, her carefully prepared arguments crumbling in the face of his composure. 'Well, of course it is,' she insisted. 'I mean, it's not as if… that is to say…'

Edward's smile widened. 'Not a chance, eh?'

Aster felt a surge of relief at his words, followed immediately by a strange sense of… disappointment? She pushed the feeling aside, focusing on the matter at hand. 'Exactly,' she said, nodding emphatically. 'It's completely-'

'Although,' Edward interrupted, taking a step closer, 'that's not quite right, is it?'

Aster frowned, confused. 'What do you mean?'

'Well,' Edward said, his voice dropping to a low, intimate tone that sent shivers down Aster's spine, 'it's not that there isn't a chance. It's simply that there isn't a chance that *I'm* not in love with *you*.'

Aster's mind reeled, trying to process his words. 'But… but that's not right,' she stammered, 'because I don't love you.'

Edward's eyes sparkled with amusement and something else, something warmer and deeper that made Aster's breath catch in her throat. 'I don't need you to love me, for me to love you,' he murmured. 'But are you sure about that?'

Aster felt her anger rising again, this time mixed with confusion and a hint of fear. 'Oh, for heaven's sake. Stop being ridiculous,' she said, her voice rising. 'Of course you don't love me…' Her mind was freewheeling at his sudden declaration, delivered with such a ridiculous smile. She needed to find another angle of attack. 'And what about when you shouted at my sisters? You had no right to do that!'

Edward's expression softened slightly. 'Ah, I was wondering when we'd get to that. I admit, I may have overstepped. But Aster, they put you in danger. Can you blame me for being concerned?'

'That's not your place!' Aster retorted, her emotions in turmoil. 'They're my family, Edward. You can't just go around berating them because you think—'

'Because I think what?' Edward pressed, taking another step closer. 'Because I care about you? Because the thought of you in danger terrifies me?'

Aster took a step back, feeling overwhelmed. 'This isn't… I didn't come here for this,' she said, her voice trembling slightly.

'Then why did you come, Aster?' Edward asked. 'What are you really here for?'

Aster hesitated, then reached into her pocket and pulled out a small USB drive. 'My sisters… they asked me to dig up dirt on you. To find something they could use against you if needed.'

Edward's eyebrows raised slightly, but he remained silent, waiting for her to continue.

'I'd already done the research,' Aster admitted, holding up the drive. 'Everything's on here. Your past, your connections, your… less than legal activities.' She took a deep breath. 'But I couldn't give it to them. I don't understand why, but I couldn't betray you like that.'

Edward's expression was unreadable. 'And this confuses you?'

'Of course it does!' Aster exclaimed, her frustration bubbling up again. 'I always put my family first. Always. So why couldn't I do it this time? Why does the thought of betraying you make me feel sick?'

Edward took a step closer, his eyes never leaving hers. 'I think you know why, Aster.'

Aster shook her head vehemently. 'No, I don't. This doesn't make any sense. None of this does!'

'Doesn't it?' Edward asked softly. 'Think about it, Aster. Apply that brilliant mind of yours. Why would you protect me over your own family?'

'I don't know!' Aster cried, running a hand through her hair in exasperation. 'That's what I'm trying to figure out!'

Edward's voice was calm, almost maddeningly so. 'I think you do know. You're just afraid to admit it.'

Aster glared at him. 'Admit what?'

'That you have feelings for me,' Edward said simply. 'That maybe, just maybe, you are in love with me.'

Aster's eyes widened in shock. 'That's... that's ridiculous,' she spluttered. 'I don't... I can't...'

'Can't you?' Edward challenged gently. 'Think about it, Aster. Think about everything we've been through together. The way you feel when we're together. The way you couldn't betray me, even for your sisters.'

Aster felt a surge of déjà vu, remembering her similar protestation to Ari just hours ago.

'Just for a second,' he said gently, as a sweet smile lit up his face 'pretend you love me. Add that factor into all your equations and hypotheses. Does this make the situation make sense, if you accept that you love me and I love you?'

Aster took a step back, bumping into her car as her analytical mind kicked into overdrive. She thought back over the past weeks, over every interaction with Edward, every flutter of her heart, every moment of inexplicable joy in his presence. She thought of how she'd been willing to defy her sisters for him, how the mere thought of betraying his trust had felt like a physical pain.

'I…' she began, then stopped, her voice failing her.

Edward's eyes twinkled with mischief. 'Perhaps I can add another variable to your dataset. May I?'

Chapter Forty-Three

Edward tipped his head towards her and Aster looked up at him, a mix of fear and excitement in her eyes. For once in her life, she stopped thinking and started feeling. She stepped forwards, wrapped her arms around his neck, and kissed him.

As their lips met, Aster felt an explosion flood through her. Like a thousand champagne bottles all exploding at once. It was like nothing she'd ever experienced before – a perfect melding of emotion and logic, passion and reason. In that moment, everything fell into place. The confusion, the fear, the denial – it all melted away, replaced by a certainty Aster had never known before.

When they finally parted, Aster panted softly. 'Ah,' she said, wonder in her voice. 'So that's what all the fuss is about. When physical desire hits emotional desire. Wow.'

Edward chuckled, pulling her close. 'Welcome to the world of emotions, Lady Aster.'

Aster swatted his arm. 'Don't get cocky. I'm still processing all of this.'

'Take all the time you need,' Edward said, his voice warm with affection. 'We have the rest of our lives to figure it out together.'

Aster looked up at him, her eyes wide and vulnerable. 'I'm still not convinced I love you, though.'

'Take your time,' Edward replied, smiling down at her.

Aster tried to create some space between them whilst she tried to get a grip on her emotions. 'So, are you going to invite me in, or are we going to stand out here all day?'

Edward's eyes lit up. 'I thought you'd never ask,' he said, taking her hand and leading her towards the door. 'Come on, I can't wait to show you my IT setup. I think you'll be quite impressed.'

As they stepped into the grand entrance hall, Aster looked at her hand enclosed in his and marvelled. Was he right? Was her sister right? Did she love him? She was still reeling from how overwhelming his kiss was just now and now she was just following him willingly into his enormous home. Looking around, she found herself pleasantly surprised. Despite the building's imposing exterior, the interior was warm and welcoming, a perfect blend of modern technology and classic elegance. Edward led her through a series of rooms, each more impressive than the last, before finally arriving at what could only be described as a tech lover's paradise.

Banks of monitors lined the walls, displaying real-time data from what looked like a dozen different systems. A sleek, custom-built computer setup dominated one corner of the room, its processing power almost palpable in the air.

'This,' Edward said, gesturing to the room with a flourish, 'is where the magic happens.'

Aster's eyes widened as she took in the sophisticated setup. 'This is… impressive,' she admitted, running her fingers along the edge of one of the desks.

Edward laughed, pulling her close. 'I'll take that as a compliment, coming from you,' he said. Then, his voice growing softer, he added, 'You know, I think you could be quite at home here.'

Aster raised an eyebrow. 'Oh, really?'

Edward nodded, his expression growing more serious. 'Really. Aster, I... I don't want to spend another day without you in my life. I know it might seem sudden, but I've never been more certain of anything.'

Aster felt her heart skip a beat. 'What are you saying?'

'Aster Byrne,' he said, his voice filled with emotion, 'I have a proposal.'

She flinched and took a step back. This was too fast. She needed to think. It hadn't even occurred to her that this was an option. The silence lengthened and then Edward laughed.

'Relax. I'm not going to ask you to marry me. At least not today. I happen to think you'd make a fine duchess, but that's for another day.'

As he chatted on, Aster continued to stare at him in shock. Why did he want to marry her? And if he had made his mind up, why was he waiting? He made no sense. If she knew what she wanted to do, she would just get on and do it. He was decidedly odd.

'Are you listening?' he said. 'Whilst I don't need a wife right now, I do need a partner.'

'A partner?'

'In crime!' Edward gave her a wolfish grin. 'I think you'll like this.' He delved into the box and handed Aster a small packet. 'This is an anti-spike kit. Each kit contains a pill that you drop into your drink which will change the colour of your drink if certain chemicals are introduced. For coloured drinks, we have a coated paper strip that you can dunk into your drink. If that changes colour, you also know your drink has been spiked. Finally, there an elasticated cap and metal straw to slip over your glass.'

Aster turned the packet over in her hand and nodded in approval. Her mind instantly focused on the new topic and leaving his troubling mentions of marriage to one side.

'And what do these cost?'

'Free to everyone in the first month.' He opened another box full of pill containers. 'It's a condition of licence that any premises I rent to that serve drinks will give these tests free to every client, male or female, with every drink. They can brand the straw and caps with their logo and sell them if they wish.'

'And what happens if they find their drink has been spiked?' asked Aster. She had a few suggestions, but wanted to see what Edward had in mind.

'Then they take their drink to the bar for a new one and the servers immediately notify management. A public announcement will be made via screens and sound system that someone in the venue is dosing drinks.'

'Smart. What about CCTV?'

'That will immediately be accessed and the potential culprit identified if possible.'

'And then you put his image up on screen.'

Edward laughed. 'Absolutely not. We are not into vigilante justice. Are we?'

Aster grumbled as Edward continued.

'We then hand the evidence over to the police for them to determine if it is conclusive.'

'Fat lot of good they'll be.'

'Now, now. With all my venues doing the same thing, other venues will quickly replicate these actions. It will become a selling point for the venues that show they care about their patrons. Plus, following your impressive campaign, the police are not likely to make the same mistake twice.'

'And if they do?'

'Well then, I'm sure we can think of ways of getting certain faces out into social media. Plus anyone my tenants suspect will be instantly banned.'

Aster looked at all the boxes and then back at Edward.

'It's going to cost a lot to you.'

'Initially, yes, but after the first month the venues will pick up the bill.'

'So, why not make them pay straightaway?'

'Because I want this to work and I can afford it. I never want another person to go through what you did.'

He pulled her back towards him and stared down at her intently.

'This is the right thing to do.'

Aster's mind raced with possibilities. 'You know,' she said thoughtfully, 'we could do a lot of good from here.'

Edward nodded encouragingly. 'I'm listening.'

'Well, with your connections and my... let's call them "skills",' she said with a wry smile, 'we could really make a difference. Root out corruption, protect the vulnerable, maybe even change some laws that need changing.'

Edward's eyes sparkled with excitement. 'I wouldn't expect anything less from you.'

Aster nodded enthusiastically. 'Exactly! And with the resources at our disposal, there's no limit to what we could achieve.'

Edward pressed a kiss to her temple. 'I can't think of anyone I'd rather save the world with.'

She looked at him suspiciously again.

'You know your own mind, don't you?'

'I think that's a given.'

'And when you want to do something, you act on it?'

'Absolutely.'

'So why do you want to marry me in the future but not now? Do you need to run background checks on me or something?'

He laughed loudly and shook his head.

'If I ran a background check on you, I suspect you would come up squeaky clean.'

'I would.' She grinned slightly and then laughed as well. 'But just to let you know, I do have skeletons.'

'I assumed as much. Incidentally, I love your laugh. You should do that more often.'

'Wally. I laugh all the time.'

'I've only seen you laugh around your sisters.'

'Well, yes. I'm not a hyena. I laugh when I'm happy, relaxed and in good company.'

'Hmm.' He tilted his head. 'I think there's another factor.'

'Really, oh wise one. What's that then?'

'I think you laugh when you feel safe, when you can really let your guard down.'

Aster raised her eyebrows and scoffed. 'Oh, and you think I feel safe around you, do you?'

'I do.'

She paused, deciding to file that one away and process later on.

'You're avoiding my question. Why not ask me to marry you today?'

'My turn to call you Wally. I'm not going to ask you to marry me because it hasn't occurred to you and I don't want you to say no before thinking things through.'

'I might say yes.'

'But you might say no. And whilst this is what I want, I won't ask again until I feel comfortable that this is also what you want.'

Aster tilted her head.

'Even though you think this is the right thing?'

'Indeed. The law frowns on forcing people into wedlock. So, I'm going to wait.'

'Very well. I need to think this through.'

'There's no hurry, Aster. I'm not going anywhere and we have lots of projects to be getting on with.'

As the last rays of sunlight disappeared beyond the horizon, Aster felt a sense of anticipation building within her. The kiss had been wonderful and the laugh had been better. He was right, she was guarded, but since knowing him she had felt that sense of reserve melting. This was the start of something new, something exciting. Why wait? She had processed all the variables, everything equated.

'Yes,' she said, a grin twisting around her lips.

Edward looked at her, his face creased in confusion.

'Yes, what?'

'Yes, you'll do.'

Edward stared at her, his blue eyes open wide as he tried not to hold his breath. As she looked up into his face, she watched his pupils dilate, she was aware of every eyelash and knew she would spend a lifetime studying his face, and engaging with the razor-sharp mind behind those eyes.

'I'll do? Aster Byrne, is that your way of saying you love me? That you'll marry me?'

She laughed, grinning up at him and shrugged.

'I guess.'

Swinging her up into his arms, he showered her in kisses, laughing as he held her aloft. She looked down at him, smiling so hard that she thought her face would crack as she returned his kisses before he gently lowered her back to the ground, but not letting go of her.

'We should probably call my sisters,' she said reluctantly, not wanting to break the spell of the moment but knowing it was necessary. 'They'll want to know what's happened.'

Edward nodded, a mischievous glint in his eye. 'Shall we give them a video call? I'd love to see their faces when we tell them the news.'

Aster laughed, already imagining the range of reactions they were likely to get. 'Ari will be smug, of course. Nick will probably want to run a background check on you... again. Paddy will cry, and Clem... well, Clem will likely start planning the wedding before we've even finished telling her.'

Edward chuckled, leading her back inside. 'I always wanted siblings, but I think this might be more than I can handle.'

'They're a handful,' Aster admitted. 'But they're my handful. And now, I suppose, they're your handful too.'

As they settled into the plush sofa in Edward's study, Aster pulled out her phone and began setting up the video call. Just before she hit the connect button, she paused, looking up at Edward with a mixture of love and mischief in her eyes.

'Ready to face the family? But no telling them off this time.'

Edward took her hand, bringing it to his lips for a gentle kiss. 'With you by my side? I'm ready for anything.'

Aster smiled, feeling a rush of affection for this man who had so thoroughly upended her life and her heart.

The screen lit up, revealing the faces of her sisters, and Aster took a deep breath. 'Hello, everyone,' she said, unable to keep the smile from her voice. 'We have some news.'

Author's Note

Well, it's been a few years and I thank you all for your patience. Aster's story has been a long time coming. Because I wanted to take her in quite a different direction from her sisters, my lovely publishers felt that the change would be too much of a departure and didn't want to publish her. This was completely reasonable and probably sound commercial sense, but I just felt that Aster was going to have to be a different sort of story. Initially, she was going to be a serial killer, and I may yet write that story, a female vigilante who dispatches abusive and violent men, but I did still need to stay close to the Hiverton vibe. I hope I got the balance right.

I want to thank my lovely and very talented editor, Julian Barr who has worked fabulously, helping me shape the story and tackling the grammar. I would also like to thank my readers who gave it a final polish. They are Rosamond Carling, Diana Cravey, Nimita Graves, Sue Hyde, Ehsan Roudiani, Heather Sharp. As ever, all errors are mine and mine alone.

I would also like to thank my friends and family who have all been asking when Aster will be ready. Their support and that of my readers has really kept me going as the months turned into years and I'm thrilled to have finally been able to tell her story.

Liz Hurley
December 2024

Printed in Great Britain
by Amazon

55863303R00199